The ⌐

# of Mo

by

Peter Black

Cover design by Daz Smith of nethed.com

ISBN: 9781093198140
Imprint: Independently published

About the Author

Peter Black is a graduate of Swansea University, a former member of the Welsh Assembly, Deputy Minister for Local Government in Wales from 2000 to 2003, and has been a Swansea Councillor since 1984. Awarded the CBE for service to public life, he is due to take up post in May 2019 as Lord Mayor of Swansea for the civic year 2019-20.

The Assassination of Morgan Sheckler is his first novel. He blogs regularly on political matters at **www.peterblack.blogspot.com** and writes the occasional article for the South Wales Evening Post. These can be read at **www.peterblack.wales**.

Peter can be found on Twitter @peterblackwales and on Facebook at peterblack.wales. He is also on Instagram, where you will be able to find many pictures of his cats.

Acknowledgements

My fond and loving thanks are due to my wife Angela, who has had to put up with my sudden obsession with writing once I lost my Welsh Assembly seat in 2016, and who has always been patient and supportive in all my endeavours, even when it seemed that I had lost the plot completely.

Thanks too are due to my editor, David Lawlor, who helped me knock this story into shape, showed infinite patience with my inability to punctuate properly and used his invaluable experience to help a first-time novelist get past first base.

I also owe profound thanks to Christoph Fischer, Melinda Moore, Rhian Vaughan, Joanne Foster, Helen Ceri Clarke and many others for their support, feedback, suggestions and assistance in putting this manuscript together and getting it published.

Finally, my thanks to the City of Cardiff, which forms the backdrop to the counterfactual world in which this story is set. Please don't take any part of this work of fiction the wrong way. I love you really, though not necessarily your football team.

All the good things in this novel are there because of the assistance of those named above, any mistakes, inaccuracies, curiosities, or inconsistencies are entirely my own.

Chapter One

It's still difficult to come to terms with what has happened. I feel as if I have lived a lifetime in just a few days. My world has been turned upside down. I have been used, abused and assaulted, intimidated and maligned, and yet I am still standing.

One violent act still hangs over me. Everywhere I turn the memory is there, accusing me, questioning me. And yet, as I look back, I find myself asking whether it happened at all. Can I still distinguish reality from delusion? Am I living a false memory?

Of course not. I know that it happened because days later, it's there on the internet, visible on pirated CCTV footage and recorded for posterity on mobile phones, just like every other event in our lives. It's there on the radio and the television. It's there on that footage, in a confusion of blue lights, sirens and helicopter rotors, a cacophonous backdrop to the nightmare that engulfed me and my city.

I recall that like every other day that week, it had been a hot, cloudless August afternoon. The pictures show that the sun had reached its zenith a few minutes earlier and was continuing to burn strongly as Morgan Sheckler, the Cardiff region's newly elected executive mayor, stepped out from beneath the ornate Portland stone portico of City Hall. The blue Cardiff City scarf that is draped around his tieless neck stands out against his white linen suit, which seems to flare against the summer sun.

The Bluebirds were playing their first game of the season after being promoted back to top-flight Premiership football. It was the third time they had secured promotion. Hopes were high that this time they would last more than one season.

Sheckler had told anybody who would listen how excited he was at attending the match. He had a place of honour in the Directors' Box alongside the First Minister of Wales and other dignitaries. But it wasn't just the perks of his new job that drew him, he was a lifelong season ticket holder, and his grandfather had once played for Cardiff City.

I watch the video on my phone as Sheckler pauses for a moment to take in the columns of water hanging in the air from the fountain opposite, and looks towards his car, which is waiting at the far end of the concourse. He starts forward and then hesitates, apparently startled by a noise on his left.

He turns towards a motorbike speeding in his direction. Sheckler jumps to avoid a collision. As he regains his balance, he is faced with a figure dressed from head to toe in black biker leathers, boots and leather gloves. The rider has come to a stop a few feet away, face hidden by a black helmet.

The motorcyclist raises the visor. It's obvious to me from the video that the mayor knew his assailant. And then the moment of recognition turns to shock and surprise. Sheckler jumps as an outstretched arm points a gun in his direction. There is a loud bang and our recently enthroned regional mayor crumples onto the floor, blood pouring from what remains of his head.

As Sheckler falls, the assassin revs the bike and speeds off past the National Museum of Wales, turning left into Park Place and up towards the University. News media say that the City's CCTV cameras lost sight of the bike as it turned into one of the side roads off Cathays Terrace.

The mayor's chauffeur, his aide, senior staff, a few journalists and some passers-by stand, staring in mutual incomprehension, too numbed and terrified to do anything else.

And then they all move at once. I'm still astonished at how quickly.

A few pull out their mobile phones to record the scene, others to phone the police. The aide and chauffeur check on Sheckler. A passer-by vomits at the sight of the mutilated corpse. A small crowd begins to gather.

The place is in chaos. Barriers are being erected to keep people away from the City Hall car park. The crowd of onlookers grows by the minute, straining to see events they had just read about on their smartphones, gathering outside the museum building, which adjoins City Hall.

Twitter, Facebook and other social media buzz with pictures, so-called eyewitness accounts, speculation on motives and the identity of the killer and, of course, some sick jokes about Sheckler and his record.

Within minutes, several TV news crews have set up at the edge of the cordon and are looking for people to interview. Who in their right mind would want to re-live such a traumatic moment on national television? But there are always a few diehard attention seekers, keen to give their two-pennyworth for a few minutes of notoriety.

The video coverage is still shocking. A tent has been erected over the body. Investigators in white forensic suits are busy photographing the area, others are conducting an inch-by-inch search for clues.

I spoke to my boss, Tim Finch, on the phone the next day. He had recently taken over as acting chief executive, responsible for running Sheckler's office, and was present to witness the shooting.

A 55-year old balding redhead with thick round glasses and a prominent paunch, friends say that he looked even paler than usual, if that was possible. He was in a right state, choking back tears as we spoke, asking what would bring somebody to blow Sheckler's brains out?

He had been in his post for just a few months at that time, but was hanging onto his job by a thread under Sheckler's nascent reign as regional mayor. If anything, he should have been relieved that his late boss was no longer a threat to his career. But Tim is a fundamentally decent man, and I doubt if any of that self-interest stuff would even have entered his mind,

I pick up my tablet and scroll until I discover a

9

contemporary TV news report from the location, and the other focus of my attention on that day. Standing out in all the coverage, dominating the early media interviews with her shiny, blonde hair and her sexless police forensic suit. I recognise her as soon as she comes into view. It is Detective Inspector Jennifer Thorne.

I watch over-and-over again as Jenny finishes her appeal for witnesses, the camera following her as she starts to walk back towards the crime scene. Somebody must have called out her name, she turns and looks towards the speaker. It is as if she was staring right at me through my computer screen.

I freeze and enlarge the picture to get a better look at her. In spite of the overalls I can still make out the outline of her slim body and firm breasts beneath. In her mid-thirties and a natural blonde, she turns heads wherever she goes. Her skin is smooth and translucent, her eyes a piercing blue.

I watch for a few minutes more that the camera follows her as she works, discussing the evidence with her colleagues, liaising with various officials and interviewing witnesses, as the journalists switch their attention elsewhere. The crowd has grown considerably.

The camera pans, giving us the full picture; reporters speaking into microphones; police officers holding back the crowd; consulting with forensic experts; scouring the tarmac for evidence; members of the public straining to see what is happening; and the hulking mass of City Hall dominating it all.

And then the cameras show yet more police cars approaching along the dual carriageway in front of the Hilton Hotel, their blue lights flashing. They were in a hurry. Surely, they had missed all the action. It was my mother.

My reaction, the first time I saw this dramatic entrance was that irrespective of her job, Mother was chasing the cameras. How could she resist? Jenny had chided me for my cynicism.

'She *is* the elected Police Commissioner,' she had said, 'and our regional mayor had just been shot. Don't you think people would have expected her to be there?'

Jenny added that the Police Superintendent had been worried that the killer might still be at large and targeting public figures. He had doubled Mother's security detail and assigned armed officers to her. I told her to stop trying to cheer me up.

Mother had texted me as she arrived that day, but I had not been aware of it at the time. I had my hands full and had no wish to speak to her. Nor had I been able to look at Twitter, although reviewing the feeds later I could see that it had exploded at the news.

It was as if the whole world had refocused its virtual self to stare at Cardiff and our drama. Tweet after tweet, reporting and retweeting the news - #shecklerassassinated. No wonder so many people had gone down there to see for themselves. And Cardiff lost three-nil. Sheckler would have been so pissed.

I found more footage and watched as bit by bit, the crowd parted, like a slow-motion Red Sea, to allow Mother's mini-convoy to pass. If they had known that her vehicle contained just another politician, I wonder if they would have bothered to move out of the way at all?

The cameras captured the barriers being moved to allow the lead vehicle through the cordon. A uniformed officer opened the door, two officers with standard issue semi-automatic carbines stood guard as Mother heaved herself out of the car. She was wearing a mauve skirt and jacket over a white blouse, and looked as imperious and self-important as ever as she was ushered into City Hall.

I don't live that far from City Hall. A ten-minute walk through the terraced streets of Roath, at best. Under normal circumstances, it would not have taken much effort to go there myself and watch events unfold, but I'd had other problems that day, which prevented me from joining the crowds.

My life had just come apart at the seams. Sheckler's death lay at the bottom of a long spiral of corruption, violence and deceit. My own future seemed about as promising as our late mayor's. Was it inevitable that we would both end up at this point? Could things have worked out differently?

Either one of us could have made other decisions, taken another turn that would have put us onto an alternative path. I have still not made sense of it all or understood at what point this outcome became inevitable.

Chapter Two

It was the week after the Mayday bank holiday, just over three months ago. A few days previously, Morgan Sheckler had come from nowhere as an Independent to defeat the Labour incumbent and become only the second directly elected mayor of the Cardiff Capital Region.

I was sitting in a room in City Hall with other senior staff to meet our new political boss and here him outline his agenda. It was to be a traumatic meeting for all of us.

The first thing I noticed was that Ted Jones, the chief executive was missing. I assumed that he was briefing the new mayor and that he would appear with him. I was wrong. When Sheckler appeared, he was accompanied only by his personal assistant.

It was some years since I'd last met Sheckler - more than fifteen in fact when I'd been a young planning officer at East Gwent Council where Sheckler had been a councillor. Because of the rural nature of his ward he'd taken a strong interest in planning matters, and in me.

He was a well-known businessman in the area, independently wealthy, with his finger in many pies. Essentially though he specialised in public relations, with a sideline as a landlord. He owned large tracts of land, much of which he let out to tenant farmers, as well as several properties he rented out to businesses.

The intervening years had been kind to him. Like many men he had grown more handsome and rugged with age. Now in his early fifties, he was slim and well-built. He obviously worked out, though I had never seen him at my gym. The suit looked new. The usual pin-stripe had been discarded for a trendy dark grey two-piece, white shirt and plain blue tie. He looked like he'd been dressed by a spin doctor for a TV appearance.

His full head of dark brown hair was parted on the left and he wore expensive designer glasses. Sheckler had certainly cleaned up his act over the last decade and a half. It was amazing how a little power enhances a person's desirability.

We were invited to sit down whilst Sheckler composed himself, as if he was waiting for somebody else to join us. Sure enough, Tim Finch, our director of human resources, rushed in, looking flustered and panic-stricken. He sat down next to our new regional mayor.

'Now that we're all here, we can start' Sheckler began, 'I want you to think of me as a new broom, an outsider who has overthrown the old order and I've inherited you as my officials.'

This was not a good start.

'My intention is to spend the next few weeks talking to you, reviewing your files and assessing what it is you can bring to my mayoralty. As you know, I have a clear agenda and some popular policies. I'm in a hurry to deliver what I promised, so I need a strong focussed team behind me. If your face doesn't fit, then I'm going to replace you.'

Several of the section heads went visibly pale at this statement, even though they knew that they had employment law on their side. Like me, they had been close to the previous regional mayor, Byron Harris. These were not political appointments. They had not expected to find their position under threat because of a change of regime.

Frank Tyler had come with Byron from his previous local authority to take up the post of director of finance for the region. They had been at school together, had worked their way up the ranks of the Labour Party (and the Masons) and still played a round of golf every Saturday morning. I couldn't see Sheckler tolerating Frank on his staff for long. He had made it clear during the campaign the contempt he felt towards Freemasonry.

Ted Jones was another close buddy of the defeated

regional mayor. As chief executive, he had wielded huge influence both within the region and with the Welsh Government. He didn't play golf, but I was aware both men and their wives had holidayed together, and that Ted and Byron were long-standing drinking companions.

Their business trips were legendary among the staff, albeit everything was kept on a need-to-know basis. 'What happens on tour, stays on tour' was the motto the tight-knit group around them lived by. Rugby internationals were another source of gossip and intrigue where Frank, Ted and Byron were concerned.

From my experience of Sheckler, I knew him as a bit of a loner. He had never been one for getting involved in any sort of lad-culture and he wouldn't tolerate it now within his organisation, even if those pursuing it were mature men in their late fifties and early sixties. And he was as sure as hell, not going to allow Byron to maintain a presence within his office through his mates and drinking companions.

My father, Stephen Highcliffe, had been part of this group too. His late-night drinking, his frequent absences and the all-male trips abroad were some of the reasons why my mother had divorced him. That and the fact that he had met somebody else, after her own affair with Byron.

Dad had met Byron through his work and been drawn into the former mayor's circle. He was a building contractor who had done a lot of work for Byron's former council. Their friendship had done me no harm whatsoever in securing my present job, though their association had also got me into trouble later on.

Sheckler paused to allow his words to sink in, scanning everybody's faces intently to see who was the most panicked. Then he dropped his next bombshell.

'Before I came in here, I had a long conversation with Ted Jones. We agreed that my agenda was incompatible with the work he had been carrying out on behalf of my predecessor and that he was too closely associated with the former regime to be able to serve me effectively. As a result, Ted has resigned with immediate effect.'

You could have heard a pin drop in that room. Everybody was waiting to hear what the next announcement would be. Frank looked across at me. He seemed shocked and angry. I shrugged my shoulders. Why hadn't we all expected this? It was not as if Sheckler had been coy about his intentions on the campaign trail.

Someone once said that politicians use poetry on the campaign trail but govern in prose. Here was one who had campaigned with brimstone and fire and was now intending to govern in the same way. Sheckler waited until everybody had taken in the news properly.

'I've asked Tim Finch to act as chief executive for the time being. As a human resources' specialist, he will be assisting me in reviewing the staffing structure so that it's fit for purpose and to help me deliver my priorities. He will also assist me in finding a replacement for Ted Jones.'

He leant forward on the table in front of him, so that we could almost smell his breath. He wanted us to know he was serious, as if that was really necessary.

'And let me be clear, this is just the start. I said during the campaign that this office was over-staffed and too cosy. I meant it. You're all fighting for your jobs, so you need to impress me. I want to see you working your butts off, day and night because I'm going to hit the ground running and there is no room for passengers.'

He paused to allow this latest pronouncement sink in. We all knew what was coming next.

'My predecessor was very keen on this new so-called revolutionary power station,' he continued. 'It lost him the election. He not only invited the developers in, he bent over backwards to find them a site, gave them a preferential price for it and has lobbied the Welsh Government to give it planning permission. As of today, all of that is going to change.

'I pledged during my campaign that I would do everything in my power to cancel this project and that's what I am going to do.'

He looked directly at me. Sheckler knew that I'd spent nearly a year working to bring this power plant to fruition, from identifying the site, overseeing the tender process for the land, getting the option agreements in place so that the purchase would go through the moment they got the go-ahead, and talking the developers through the planning process and what they needed to do to find favour with the Welsh Government.

He knew how much effort I'd invested in it. I guess he was hoping that I would kick back against his new policy direction. I didn't. I kept my views to myself. My face was expressionless, as if I was hanging on his every word.

'Ms. Highcliffe,' he said addressing me, 'could you please outline what we need to do to stop this power plant going ahead?'

'I think that's a complex matter, Mister Mayor. As you know we have contractual obligations and an on-going planning application, which we have initiated alongside the developer. I'm going to have to sit down with lawyers to establish what elements we can disentangle and backtrack on immediately and what parts of the deal are going to be more difficult to get out of.'

I could feel everyone's eyes on me as I spoke, but pushed on, 'If we renege on the option we have contractually offered Maga Power Holdings Limited for them to buy the land without proper cause, then it could cost us a lot of money.'

He looked at me impatiently. I could tell that this was not the answer he wanted to hear. Sheckler had been a councillor for a long time, but never in any sort of executive position. He specialised in stirring things up and wrecking projects, not in running things. He was certainly no lawyer, and most probably had no idea how these big deals were put together.

He pursed his lips. His arms were crossed across his chest and his eyes had narrowed.

'I don't want to know the problems, Dawn, I want solutions. I want a full briefing paper by the end of the week, together with a clear course of action as to how we can kill this thing.'

I did my best to remain expressionless, but I think he could see my irritation. Indeed, his manner had been designed to elicit such a response.

In truth, I was furious, not just at this upstart who had stormed to victory on the back of a populist revolt against a project that I'd owned from the start, but at myself for not anticipating the outcome of the election and preparing for it.

There was though more at stake than just wasted time and lost work. There were stakeholders, of which I was one, who would not allow this power station to be abandoned without a fight. And there were commitments that could not easily be jettisoned that would be used as weapons in a savage rear-guard action.

The question was, which side would I be on in that action, and could I survive playing both sides off against the other long enough to find myself a more tolerable berth?

If the development goes ahead then Sheckler's reputation would be massively diminished, but his revenge on those he perceived as letting him down could be terrible to behold.

I smiled. Some might have said it was a sly smile, but it was the best I could muster.

'Of course, Mister Mayor, I will get straight onto it.'

He seemed happy with that answer and turned to other matters. I continued to seethe in a corner of the room, almost oblivious to the rest of the business. As the meeting came to an end, a full two hours after it had started, I fell into conversation with Tim Finch.

The acting chief executive seemed to be in a state of shock. His sudden promotion had been a brutal one as far as he was concerned. Tim had always been an honourable man, one who stood by his friends and who couldn't do enough for them. He was not designed for the cut and thrust of workplace politics, never mind the vicious dog-eat-dog world of electoral politics.

Although Tim went through the motions of attending staff socials and tried to be one of the boys on business trips, he was fundamentally a shy, retiring family man who much preferred to be at home with his wife and kids, or ensconced in the City Stadium with his two sons cheering on the Bluebirds. He would make Clark Kent look like Genghis Khan.

Ironically, he had risen to his job as director of human resources after his predecessor had been jettisoned in a workplace coup. But he had got the job on merit and because nobody else perceived him as a threat to their own position. I quite liked him.

'This is a rum do,' he said to me. 'Poor Ted didn't have a chance. One minute he is putting together briefing papers for the new mayor, the next he's being escorted from the building. My first task is to empty his desk and send his personal possessions on to him.'

'I take it that this is going to cost us?' I asked, to move the conversation on.

'Oh, yes, the compensation will be humungous. Mr Sheckler is impossible. Doesn't he realise that people have mortgages and families to support? You can't just go around interfering with their livelihoods for no good reason. We may serve at the whim of the people, but the buck stops with the politicians not their officials.'

'I suppose that's a consequence of being an independent,' I ventured.

'How do you mean?'

'They have no roots, no party to give them a sense of belonging, no values. It's always them against the system and when they get on top, then they feel that they own us and can do with us what they want.'

Tim looked a bit confused at this analysis. He was completely apolitical. I suspect he might even vote for an independent if the candidate's manifesto was attractive enough. Good grief, he might even have voted for Morgan Sheckler. Now that was a vote he must be regretting.

We had reached the chief executive's office, so Tim took his leave. I steeled myself for the task of briefing my own development department staff on the morning's events. They were not going to be happy. They, too, had a lot invested in this project.

The rest of the day was a whirlwind of meetings, of which the stickiest was with the lawyers. To say that our best legal minds were flabbergasted at the task I'd been charged with was an understatement.

By five o'clock I was exhausted, angry and demoralised. I felt like smashing up the place. There was only one thing for it... I headed for the gym.

It had been a while since I'd exercised so vigorously. I pedalled myself to near-exhaustion on the exercise bike and then worked out on the power rack. I collapsed onto a nearby bench, a mess of sweat, my face bright red, my hair plastered to it. It was then that I realised I was being watched.

The woman looked familiar. She was in her mid-thirties, with long blonde hair tied up in a bun and bright blue eyes. Her gym clothes clung to her firm, slim body. I tried to smile but could only manage a half-hearted grimace. Her beauty intimidated me. She stood up and walked over to where I was slumped.

'I'm told that you benefit more if you pace yourself,' she said. 'I was starting to fear for the equipment.'

The west country accent caught my attention immediately. I'd always been attracted to the Devonian twang. And there was something about this woman, I couldn't quite put my finger on. She radiated sexiness. I felt myself drawn to her. It was obvious that she'd noticed that the attraction was mutual.

I tried to respond but could hardly speak. She smiled and extended her hand.

'Jennifer Thorne,' she said by way of introduction. I took it. Her skin felt warm and soothing.

'Dawn Highcliffe,' I responded. 'You look familiar, have we met before?'

'Well, I've seen you here a few times. Maybe you've seen me. Or perhaps through work. You're connected to the regional mayor's office, aren't you?'

I sat up straight.

'Have you been spying on me?'

'Absolutely. I find it pays to know as much as possible about the attractive women who I see before I formally meet them.'

I was suddenly conscious of my appearance. I took a swig of water and tried to smooth my hair back into place. She laughed.

'You look beautiful as you are,' she said placing a strand of my hair behind my ear. I felt my face burning red again, this time from embarrassment. I pushed her hand away.

'Don't you think you're getting ahead of yourself? All I know about you is your name.'

'Maybe we should get a drink and get to know each other better.'

'Now you're coming on a bit strong. I'm beat. I just need to go home and crash.'

'Another time then?'

'Perhaps.'

She gave me a card. It had the South Wales Police logo on it.

'Detective Inspector Jennifer Thorne,' I read out loud. 'What did you do, look me up on the Police National Database?'

She laughed... an alluring, magical laugh, like fairy bells

pulling me into a half-hidden glade.

'Of course not. I've done some security work at the mayor's office. I saw you there. You are the director of development or something, responsible for getting this new power plant built.'

I clapped my hands together a couple of times.

'Very good. Now I'm afraid I have to go and shower.' I stood up. She followed suit.

'Good idea.'

'Alone,' I said. She nodded and positioned herself in front of me. She placed her hand on my elbow. I flinched as what seemed like a spark of electricity passed between us. She winked.

'We'll bump into each other again,' she said. 'Maybe then we can take that shower together.'

I stood there open-mouthed. I'd never known anybody so self-confident, so full of themselves, so forward and yet so irresistible. I watched as she walked away, my eyes firmly fixed on her shapely arse. I surprised myself realising that I couldn't wait until our paths crossed again.

I wandered into the showers and stood for what seemed like ten minutes beneath the hot water, letting it wash over my face and my naked body. Not moving, just soaking up the warmth of the water.

I'd worked off the anger. Now I was washing it away, watching it pour down the drain. It was some time since I had been with a woman. I couldn't think about the power station anymore, instead I was concentrating on Jenny, imagining her naked body next to mine, touching me, kissing me. In the few short minutes we had conversed, she had succeeded in captivating me, totally.

As I drove home, I looked out for her, on the off-chance. I knew I wouldn't see her, that she had most probably already gone home herself, or into work, and was otherwise engaged, but hope is a funny thing. I was infatuated and not thinking straight.

I opened my front door and Myrddin, my black and white cat, came running towards me. He rubbed himself against my legs. He was hungry. I opened a cupboard and spooned some food out of a tin onto a saucer. He dug in straight away.

I looked in the fridge for something to eat for myself, pulled out a salad, emptied a tin of tuna on top, taking care to share it with the cat, and consumed the lot.

I collapsed into bed and fell asleep straight away. Myrddin settled beside me, my hand on his soft, warm fur as he cwtched into my body. My sleep was a just one, without a thought to power stations or regional mayors, but eased by the warm glow left behind by my encounter with a certain Cardiff police officer and her shapely behind.

Chapter Three

Just how complicated the power plant saga had become became evident the next day.

I arrived for work early. Despite all of Monday's tribulations I'd slept well. I put that down to my mammoth exercise session and to Jenny.

I remained intrigued by her. Should I ring her, or could I leave it to fate. Her presence lingered in my memory. The thought of her standing naked in the shower with me, of us touching and caressing each other, was a welcome distraction from the knotted web I'd been told to untangle.

The parent company of Maga Power Holdings Limited, which wanted to build the power plant, was based in America, but they were using Chinese money and they were negotiating a subsidised price from the UK Government for the electricity they would generate. There was also the Welsh Government planning division to accommodate.

Wales had acquired strategic planning powers over energy shortly after the creation of the Cardiff Capital Region and the formation of a regional, mayor's office. Ministers of course, knew about Sheckler and his mission to stop the plant going ahead. I was sure that they would resist him, but I also knew that they had restless backbenchers in the Assembly who agreed with what he had in mind.

The Americans were due in City Hall that morning. My on-off partner, Alec Croxley worked for them. I never had a preference for a particular gender. Sex was sex, and I had always taken a casual approach to the whole business. Looking at my parents, I had seen how much damage a committed relationship could do, it was not something I ever wanted for myself.

Alec was the latest in a long line of flings, and although I refused to admit it at the time, he was more significant than most, if only for the impact he had had on my life. He had also stayed around longer than most, when he was in Cardiff that was. Whether the attraction was me or the power plant deal, I was never sure. It didn't matter to me.

He was currently away on business, but I knew from him that these Americans took no prisoners. He had also hinted at an organised crime connection, but Alec sometimes tended to exaggerate and it was not something I took seriously.

I settled down behind my desk and started to work through the many emails that had been building up in my inbox. Just then my secretary entered. The Americans had arrived and were waiting for me in the conference room. They were early.

I asked her to give them some coffee while I gathered my papers and my thoughts. I would have been happier if the mayor was prepared to do his own dirty work, but then there was no knowing what damage he would do if unleashed in a tricky legal situation. I picked up my files and headed for the conference room.

The three Americans were standing together sipping their coffee. They were all male, of course, dressed in expensive plain dark suits. I was wary of them. They had already caused me some discomfort.

Pat Marshall was the most senior and the eldest. He was in his late fifties with white thinning hair and rimless glasses. His plain tie was held in place with a gold pin that matched his gold cufflinks. He was the epitome of corporate America, smooth, focussed, and used to getting his way.

With him was Rob McCoy, a thirty-year-old whizz kid with swept back brown hair, a neatly trimmed beard and immaculately polished shoes. His one concession to non-conformity was a gold stud through his left ear.

This was a man in a hurry, poised to sweep away all before him as he assumed his rightful place in the board room. You could tell he was snapping at Pat's heels, waiting for the older man to move on so he could succeed him.

The third executive was Don Watkins, the company lawyer, representing their interests in the UK. In his early forties, Don's sharp mind was matched by good instincts and an ability to quickly size up an opponent. His head was clean shaven. He, too, was wearing rimless glasses.

I'd spent hours with these three in meeting after meeting, thrashing out the details of the land acquisition for this power plant, putting together the bid to the UK Government for them to subsidise the electricity, and commissioning the various studies needed to support the planning application, which would be decided by the Welsh Government.

Now I had to tell them that there had been a change of policy and that all that work had been in vain. The mayor was going to cancel their option to purchase the land for the power plant if he could legally do so, and withdraw his support for the planning application.

I greeted each of them in turn. As far as they were concerned this was a routine meeting to review progress on the various elements of the scheme. They must have been aware of the new regime though. No doubt they suspected that something was wrong.

Perhaps they thought it was academic, that the rhetoric of the campaign would not translate into action once in office. I looked at their faces. Yes, that was exactly what they thought. They really did believe that everything was on track.

'Dawn, it's good to see you again,' Marshall formed his expensively reconstructed molars into a dazzling smile and opened the dialogue. 'I see that there have been some changes around here, a new boss, a new regime. And he doesn't like us very much. I hope that's not going to be a problem.'

I invited them to sit down.

'The truth is Pat, that the mayor has instructed us to pull the plug on this scheme.'

You could have heard a pin drop. They looked flabbergasted, but quickly recovered their composure. Watkins spoke first.

'I appreciate that the mayor has an agenda and a constituency he needs to satisfy, Ms Highcliffe, but surely he realises that it's not possible to abandon this project now. From his perspective, the contract we have, giving our company an option to buy the land, is watertight.'

His soft American drawl became terser with each word spoken.

I looked at each of them in turn. I wasn't sure that they fully understood the situation.

'Look,' I said, 'up until now we have all been singing from the same song sheet. The fact that the regional mayor has different policies has changed all that, but not irreconcilably. This is where we stand:

'The regional mayor is the land owner with responsibility for economic development, and under the previous administration, as you know, his office initiated and supported this development.

'The scheme is too big for us to do ourselves, so we are looking to Maga Power Holdings to do it for us.'

Marshall was starting to look impatient.

'So here is the thing, as this is a large scheme of strategic importance the Welsh Government will determine the planning application, which has been lodged with them. You are already aware that you need to submit detailed impact studies around the environment, transport and community before the scheme is even ready to be assessed, and before it goes out to public consultation proper, and we have been helping you with that. The regional mayor is likely to instruct me to stop co-operating on those reports.

'One last point, regional mayors in the UK do have substantial executive powers, but they are nowhere near as powerful as mayors in the states. That means that Mayor Sheckler can influence, but he cannot put a complete stop to your project.'

Marshall at least seemed more at ease with that explanation, but his companions still felt that they needed to place all their cards on the table, Don Watkins, in particular.

'Thank you for that, Dawn, but you do understand that if there is an attempt to renege on our deal then we will sue for full cost recovery plus substantial compensation.'

So far, so expected. I knew he was right, but I needed to go through the motions.

'Thank you, Don. I fully understand your point of view. As you know I am a servant of the mayor and I am obliged to follow his instructions. I will, of course be passing on your comments to him and, with my colleagues, advising him on the implications of the course of action he has chosen.

'You must understand though that Mayor Sheckler is a very determined man. He will do what he can legally and politically to stop this power station from going ahead. There is a substantial body of public opinion who back him on this. That was evident from the fact that he was elected.

'I'm taking legal advice on the contract with Maga Power Holdings Limited and I will respond to you on that issue in due course. You should know, however, that without the political cover provided by the mayor's office, the Welsh Government may well find it more difficult to give the plant planning permission.'

Marshall finished his coffee and placed the cup back on the saucer. He leaned across the table towards me, speaking slowly and softly.

'I hope that we're on the same wavelength, Dawn. We all have a lot invested in this power plant, in our case millions of dollars. I sense that you're not supportive of Mayor Sheckler's position. I am asking you, in the privacy of this room, to do what you can to help us frustrate him.'

This was difficult. Marshall was right. He knew where I stood. He also knew how I'd worked with Alec to ensure Maga had preferential treatment. They had leverage over me. In their parlance, they had me over a barrel. I was a natural, although reluctant ally. I smiled.

'You know I will do what I can, Pat.' He flashed that smile again.

'Good. Now tell me, how is that fella of yours? I haven't seen him for some time.'

'He's away on business, talking to some of your financiers, I believe. Doesn't he answer to you?' Marshall shook his head.

'I'm afraid not. He's a go-between for us with some of the people putting up the money for this plant. He works for them.'

'I thought that most of the finance was coming from the Chinese?'

'It is. But there are other parties involved too... people who have taken a substantial stake in this plant and who will not be amused if that money is lost. Trust me Dawn, you do *not* want to cross these people.'

I could sense McCoy's eyes bore into me; his jaw muscles flexing above the collar of his crisp white shirt. All three of them were leaning forward now, as if willing me to understand what was really at stake here.

I nodded my appreciation. This was all news to me. I determined that whenever Alec re-appeared, I was going to get him to tell me everything. We should have no secrets on this, not because of our relationship, whatever that actually was, but because of our mutual stake in the power station.

The whole situation was starting to get over my head. I was beginning to drown in the swamp that now surrounded this project. Somehow, I had to get back on top of it.

I needed some time to think, and yet everybody was crowding in on me, demanding more. I turned to Watkins.

'Don, I need to sit you down with our lawyers, so we can establish exactly what the legal situation is. If we're going to stop Sheckler, we need to work together.'

'I'm happy to do that Ms. Highcliffe. I hope that we can sort this out.'

'We'll do our best, but you know I am putting my neck on the line here. I need to work surreptitiously. I can't be seen to be openly working against the mayor.'

'Of course.'

The meeting was over, and the three men stood to leave. As I escorted them from the building, Marshall steered me to one side.

'We recognise that this is a critical time in the gestation of this project so we're staying in the country for a few weeks. We'll be meeting officials in the Department of Energy in London and keeping in touch with the Welsh Government.

'Our people will continue to deal with queries from the planners and to identify contractors who will build this plant.

'Dawn, I need you to keep us in the loop on anything else Sheckler tries to throw at us. We must marginalise him.' Marshall's voice was pure steel, the time for schmoozing was clearly over.

'There are still a lot of hurdles to overcome. That's hard enough, and I can do without the project being sabotaged from within.

'I want you to work through Alec. You already have a connection there, so it won't be too difficult. I'll arrange for him to be briefed once he gets back into the UK. Remember, while we continue to hold evidence of your father's financial indiscretions, you work for us, not the Mayor. Is that clear?'

I nodded. It was an order, not a request. I was well aware that Marshall had documents proving that my father had been involved in corrupt dealings in South Wales. Alec had told me he'd been trying to get them destroyed, but so far, he'd been unsuccessful.

Marshall didn't have to even hint at the consequences if I failed to comply. My career would be ruined, and God knows what else might happen with regards to my family.

He was right about what needed to be done, but it pained me to do it, when all my instincts were to act as an impartial civil servant. I had ceased to be their contact some time ago and had become their indentured mole. I was now a reluctant agent provocateur inciting my own colleagues to revolt against Morgan Sheckler's regime. I told Marshall that I would do what I could.

I watched them walk off in the direction of the Welsh Government's Cathays Park headquarters. It was starting to rain.

Back at my office I discovered there was a message to say that a senior civil servant from London was on his way and wanted to meet with the mayor. I checked, Sheckler wasn't available. It looked like the civil servant would have to deal with me instead.

I went out to get some lunch… a liquid lunch preferably but I knew that was too risky, so I settled for a salad from a nearby supermarket and sat at my desk eating, reflecting on the morning's events.

I'd never wanted to get involved in this. I was content doing my job, however, Byron was insistent. This power plant was his baby and he wanted this company to build and run it. Who was I to argue with a mayor who had done so much for me?

He was clear that Maga Power Holdings Limited should win the tender for the land and the project. That's how I'd met Alec. Byron paid the price at the ballot box. Now we were all living on the edge, waiting to see if our part in this arrangement would sweep us away, too.

But I'm getting ahead of myself. If I'm going to tell this story, then it needs to be in the right order.

As the time for me to meet the civil servant approached, I developed a headache. It was not a metaphorical one but a very real throbbing pain that caused my vision to become blurred, which was unusual. The stress was getting to me.

I reached into my top drawer and helped myself to some

painkillers. I looked at the packet, they were out-of-date. I shrugged. It would be fine. All I needed to do was get through this meeting and then, maybe, I could sneak off early and have a hot bath.

Myrddin would be pleased to see me. He had a habit of sitting on the edge of the bath and watching. Why was it that of all the cats in the world I had to have adopted a perverted one?

I smiled. Perhaps I could tempt that cute police inspector into having a bath with me. I'm sure Alec wouldn't mind. What he didn't know wouldn't upset him, and besides it was hardly as if we were engaged or anything. He was aware of my preferences.

My thoughts were interrupted by my secretary. She had come to tell me that the civil servant from London had arrived. I asked her to send him in.

He turned out to be a she, a middle-aged bureaucrat in a tailored charcoal skirt and jacket over a plain white blouse and a silk scarf. Her brown hair was cut into a neat bob, her make-up looked expensive, Clarins most probably. The shoes weren't cheap either. She was carrying a black leather briefcase. The whole outfit was off-set by gold chains around her neck and wrist of a traditional Indian design, together with matching ear-rings.

Despite her aura of affluence and influence I thought she might benefit from a few sessions down the gym. I noted the expensive wedding band sitting next to a substantial diamond engagement ring. This was not a woman familiar with the sort of deprived communities the mayor's office had traditionally tried to assist.

We shook hands.

'Ms Highcliffe, it's good to meet you. I'm Patricia Cassell, from the Treasury. I've been asked to come down here at the very last minute to try and bottom out what is going on with this power plant.'

I invited her to sit down and waited while my secretary

served her with black coffee, no sugar. I suspected that she could do with the caffeine hit after the journey. The train from London to Cardiff was quicker and smoother since they had electrified the main line, but it was still tiring, especially the journey either end, to Paddington and the taxi ride in Cardiff.

She continued: 'I'm very sorry that Mr Sheckler was not able to meet me. It would have been good to have heard his point of view first hand. I understand that he's a busy man and that this is very short notice.

'We haven't met before, but you will have dealt with my staff on this project, David Weir and Harry Shepherd. My minister felt however, that this err…crisis, needed a more senior intervention.'

'Crisis?' I decided to play dumb. We may both have wanted this project to go ahead but I was not going to have some Home Counties bureaucrat dictate to me what I could and could not do.

'This is a very important project, Ms. Highcliffe. My Government cannot sit back and allow the newly elected mayor to unravel all our work. It's in all of our interest for this power plant to be built, not least because we don't want to alienate the Chinese, who are providing a large part of the funding.'

Everything suddenly became clear.

'You're worried that if our mayor pulls the plug then it will sour our relationship with the Chinese?'

'In a nutshell, yes. You are very astute, Ms Highcliffe.'

'It's a Welsh trait, Ms Cassell. You will forgive me if I'm blunt. I'm the regional mayor's servant, in the same way that you're the servant of your minister. Mr Sheckler has been elected with a mandate to stop this power plant. It's my job to facilitate his wishes.

'You cannot override the will of the people by catching a train down from Westminster and issuing decrees from on high. We finished with that when we voted to have devolution and our own government back in 1997.

'I'm sure that I speak for the mayor when I say that our primary concern is to do what is in the best interests of the larger Cardiff Capital Region. Perhaps you can convey that message to your minister.'

Had I gone too far? It doesn't do to upset the UK Government. There are consequences. And it was clear that Patricia Cassell was going to spell those out.

'Your bluntness has been noted, Ms Highcliffe. The minister and I respect the democratic mandate you are working to. However, as I outlined there are wider interests at work here, and there are contractual obligations which Mr Sheckler will have to respect. I hope you understand that it's my duty to continue to promote this project.'

She hesitated as if trying not to make her next sentence sound like a threat.

'You may also wish to tell the mayor that there will be enormous benefits for him and this region if he works with us rather than against us.'

How diplomatic…but the implication was that if we didn't play ball then they would cut us off without a penny. That was certainly a message I would pass onto Sheckler, but I wasn't going to let this smug bitch think that she could cross the border and slap us around. I stood up.

'I think, Ms Cassell, that this meeting is over. Naturally, I'll pass on your message to the regional mayor, but I believe you'll find that we are more independently minded this side of the Bristol Channel than you give us credit for.

'We don't take kindly to threats, no matter how nicely phrased they are. Perhaps you can tell your minister that.'

I opened the door and ushered her out, leaving it to my secretary to ensure that she left the building. For some reason, my act of defiance had cleared my head.

Chapter Four

As planned, I got home early and had a long soak in the bath. Rather sulkily, Myrddin refused to play ball and settled down to sleep on a sunny windowsill as soon as he had scoffed his food. As a result, I was bathing alone.

I settled back with a flannel over my face and allowed the hot water and suds to soak into my pores. It was bliss. There was soft jazz music playing in the background and half a dozen scented candles provided a cosy, secure cocoon from the world beyond. There is no better way to wash away the cares and stresses of a day.

I must have lain there for an hour, my thoughts lingering more and more on Jenny, before reluctantly dragging myself out. I wandered into the kitchen wearing just a towelling robe and a towel wrapped around my head, and started to prepare a meal of pasta, crème fraiche and ham, sipping on a large glass of red wine as I cooked.

The cat had woken up and was demanding a share of the ham. Typical male, only paying attention when he wanted something.

I heard the front door open and sighed as Alec entered the kitchen in his black leather one-piece biker gear. He was holding a helmet, his brown hair was brushed back and his face illuminated by a boyish smile. It was one of the features that had endeared him to me.

I appreciated the fact that he didn't tower over me like other man, he was of slim build, well-toned and, at five foot eight inches, about the same height as me. He also took the time each day to shave properly. I am not a fan of hirsute men.

Alec had parked his motorbike on the street outside my end-terrace house. I don't really know much about bikes, but I knew this one was a Harley Davidson, that it was fast and that it wasn't cheap. The thrill of being able to ride with him through the countryside on the back of this monster was another reason I was with him.

I could be quite shallow when it suited me, but I also liked to live on the edge. Taking risks by speeding through country lanes at 80mph was one of the ways I relaxed nowadays. That or playing around with handsome young men like Alec or sexy young women like Jenny.

I'm not sure what it was that attracted me to people so different from myself? Was it their self-confidence, their bravado, the buzz it gave me just to be with them? Or was it my rebellious streak, which some put down as 'anything to upset your mother'?

Alec was about ten years younger than me. We had met in the early stages of planning the new power station when he had accompanied Pat Marshall and Don Watkins to a meeting. He took me out to dinner afterwards. One thing had led to another and we had ended up back at his hotel.

The sex was hot. We had kept at it most of the night and continued into the morning after a bite of breakfast to keep our strength up. Afterwards, we exchanged numbers and whenever Alec was in town, he stayed with me.

When it suited us, the relationship could be more than sex, but essentially it remained a practical arrangement. We would take his bike out and enjoy lunch in a country pub in the Vale of Glamorgan or Monmouthshire. We even had a picnic once amongst the bluebells in the Cwmcarn Forest.

Neither of us pried too closely into the other's affairs. We worked on the basis that we were each free to do our own thing when it suited us. And until the meeting with Marshall and his colleagues earlier that day I'd treated Alec's business affairs as need-to-know. Now I had a plethora of questions that I wanted answers to.

I studied his green eyes, as if they were a freak of nature, a puzzled look on my face. He wrinkled his nose and winked at me.

'What's wrong, aren't you pleased to see me?'

I was, but having a quiet time alone was becoming increasingly valuable to me. I told him he should move his bike into the back yard, where it would be safe.

'Are you hungry? I have some food on the go and, as usual, I've cooked too much pasta for one. If you don't share it with me, I'll have to compost it.'

'Sure. I'm starved, thanks.'

He went to move his bike, while I returned to the kitchen and put some more pasta into the boiling water. I spooned extra crème fraiche into the pan and added the last piece of ham and more mushrooms. Myrddin had rather limited my scope in terms of bulking up the meat.

Alec came through the back door. He had unzipped his one-piece suit, so that it was folded down below his waist, revealing a white T-shirt that clung to his fit body. He walked up to me, undid the cord of my dressing gown and slipped his hands inside, allowing them to linger on my naked back. We kissed, then I disentangled myself from the embrace and tied the robe back together.

'If you have designs on my body then you will have to let me eat first. It's been a very trying day,' I said softly.

He nodded and helped himself to a glass of wine, then sat at the kitchen table and watched me work. I continued to cook in silence, aware he was monitoring my every move.

'Would you like something to read?' I asked eventually. 'You're starting to freak me out.'

'No, I'm good.' He pulled his phone out of his pocket and started to scroll through his emails. I found that just as disconcerting, so I turned my back on him and continued with the cooking. I served it up at the table and sat opposite him. We ate in silence.

Later, I left the plates in the sink and we took our wine into the living room. Alec sat on the sofa, I crouched on the floor, propped up between his legs, the cat snuggled next to me. I unzipped his biker boots. He pulled them off and stretched his feet.

'That's much better,' he said. 'So, what have you been up to while I was away?'

I hesitated. Thinking what I could and couldn't tell him. I closed my eyes and saw Jenny. I opened them quickly, startled. This was not good timing on Alec's part.

He put his hands on my shoulders and rubbed hard. I leaned into him and sighed. He stopped.

'What's wrong, have you lost the strength in your hands?'

He laughed and resumed the massage.

'So, are you going to tell me?'

'I'm thinking about it. But you need to tell me first? Where have you been for the past week?'

'You know full well, where I've been,' he protested. 'Are you accusing me of having an affair?'

Now it was my turn to protest.

'Don't be absurd. If you want to go off and fuck other women that's your business. You know I'm not the jealous type. No, I'm talking about business.

'I had a meeting with Pat Marshall and his cronies today. He was asking after you.'

'Good, glad to know he has my best interests at heart.'

The massage was working. I could feel some of the tension ease away.

'Do you think so? He told me you didn't work for his company but for some unspecified financiers. How did he put it? Ah, yes, he said "you don't want to cross these people." What are you into, Alec?'

He had stopped kneading my shoulders. I turned to face him, propping myself up on his knee, staring at him expectantly.

'I've been in Chicago, meeting some of the people financing this project. They wanted an update. They have a big stake in this power plant and they want to ensure everything is going to plan.'

'And…?'

'And yes, I work for them not for Marshall.'

'So, I'm having difficulty putting all this together. Who's really driving forward this power plant project?'

'Ultimately, it's the Chinese, but there's a lot of preparation work to be done before any spade breaks ground. We've spent millions just getting to this stage. Consultants, planning, environmental studies, options, none of them come cheaply. Somebody had to put up the cash and someone needs to keep an eye on that investment. That's me.'

'And who exactly are these financiers? Should I cross them?'

'Now, why would you want to do a stupid thing like that?' There was a hint of irritation in his voice that he couldn't quite disguise.

'I don't, I just want to know the sort of people I'm getting into bed with.'

He smiled and ran his hand through my hair., then leaned down to kiss me. I responded briefly and then pulled away. He wasn't getting anything off me until I had some answers.

'The only person you're getting into bed with tonight is me,' he said.

'We'll see about that. I'm still waiting for answers.'

'Alright then, yes, you don't mess with these people. They don't take risks with their money. They invest in sure things and this is a sure thing. Not only do they expect to get a good return on their cash, but they'll also gain a sure-fire way to launder money into the UK. The value of this power plant is greater than the return on their investment.'

I sat there taking all this in. What had I got myself into? Who was this man I was seeing but who I apparently knew so little about? I was aware that he operated on the edge, but this was several steps beyond.

Alec watched me, trying to gauge my reaction. Had he

told me too much? He looked uncertain.

'And what exactly do you do for these mobsters?' I asked eventually.

'Now, that's not a term I would use and certainly not one I would like repeated in front of any of them, even the likes of Pat, Don and Rob.'

I waited for an answer.

'I'm their front man in the UK. I arrange things for them, ease the way for their deal, grease a few palms and remove any obstacles that might prove to be a problem.'

'Okay, full disclosure. How exactly do you remove those obstacles?'

He looked horrified.

'I hope that you're not implying that I'm some glorified hitman. I use persuasion, legitimate persuasion.'

'That might sometimes skirt the edge of what is legal?' I asked.

'Surely Dawn, that's a matter of perspective'

'Yes, it is. This is a lot to take in Alec.' Perhaps I had been in denial all this time and just refused to see what was blatantly standing in front of me. Maybe, I had ignored the signs, had wrongly accepted his explanation that he was the innocent party, when pressure was put on me to do Maga Power Holdings' bidding. Had I been better off not having the details spelt out to me?

He tried to reassure me by squeezing my shoulders, but I stood up and sat on the chair opposite. The cat stirred, rolled over onto his back and went back to sleep. Alec did his best to adopt a more innocent expression, but he was fooling nobody.

'Look, I'm not going to pretend that what we have has not been useful, but that was never the intention. My attraction to you, what we have, was a bonus. It enabled us both to mix business and pleasure.'

'Yes, and gave you additional leverage to assist your mob

bosses!'

'Perhaps, but the only difference is that it was a different group of people who benefitted than those you had expected.'

I had to concede that point to him, but it wasn't a revelation I was comfortable with. Alec concentrated on my reaction. He knew that if he didn't get this right then months of work would start to unravel.

It was like my emotions had been placed into a blender without the lid being fixed on properly. They were splattered all over a metaphorical kitchen. I'd been fine bending the rules a bit for Alec and the company that I thought he worked for but now I knew that the ultimate beneficiary was organised crime, I wasn't so comfortable with it.

'Does the UK Government know who they are working with?' I asked eventually.

'Good grief, no. Well they've never given any hint. Civil servants are not the most worldly of people. It's fairly easy to pull the wool over their eyes.' I let that remark slide, not wanting to get into a fully-fledged row.

'Well, it seems that Sheckler may be a different sort of challenge for you.'

He looked puzzled. And a little bit put out.

'Don't tell me that mad bastard is trying to make good on his promise. Doesn't he know that he's too late? It's a done deal. There's nothing he can do to stop this plant now.'

'Don't be so sure,' I cautioned. 'He's instructed me to prepare a report on how he can scupper the plant. And he has public opinion on his side. If he can harness that correctly, it will make it very difficult for the Welsh Government to approve the planning application.

'At least when Byron Harris was in that chair, he gave ministers some political cover. They no longer have that comfort blanket.'

Alec pulled a tissue from a box on the coffee table, sat back and wiped his brow. He emptied his wine glass, filled it up again and drank a further measure.

'For fuck's sake, this is a billion-pound project,' he said finally. 'Doesn't he have any comprehension of what he's dealing with? We need to stop him.'

'Well, you're the mover and shaker around here. You tell me how.'

'Seriously, Dawn, what can he do? The option agreement is water tight, the planning is out of his hands, he has no say on the price that will be paid for the electricity, and the UK Government doesn't want to upset the Chinese.'

'Don't underestimate this man, Alec. He became Mayor against all the odds. He will blunder his way around the system until he gets his way, as outsiders tend to do.'

'Well, I'll just have to take some advice then. Pat's still in Cardiff. We'll need to meet to compare notes.'

'I'm not your keeper, Alec. Isn't managing these hoodlums your job?'

He gave me one of those disapproving looks, he adopts when I take a joke too far. I laughed, partly because I found it funny but also because I knew it would wind him up further. His brow furrowed deeply like an old-fashioned squeeze box, and his eyes narrowed.

'Please don't joke about these things,' he said.

I stood up and turned to face him.

'You can't do anything tonight. Deal with it in the morning.'

I pulled his T-shirt loose, rolled it upwards and ran my hands over his naked chest.

His body was as firm and tanned as I remembered it. He relaxed a bit as I moved my hands towards his shoulders. I leaned in to kiss him. He undid the cord on my bath robe and opened it. My breasts swung freely as he sucked on my nipples.

I flung my head back, allowing him to unfurl the robe from my shoulders and down to my waist so he could explore my upper body better. He paused to take his T-shirt off, while I pulled the rest of his biker suit down over his hips. But before I could remove it altogether, he was on top of me once more, kissing my neck and my lips.

We had sex there and then, and again on the stairs as we made our way to the bedroom. These were acts of passion, roughly taken with very little tenderness, but that suited us both. We were living for the moment, for the pleasure and to hell with the cares of the last week or the uncertainties that lay ahead.

Later, we lay naked in each other's arms on the bed covers. We were both too overheated to climb beneath the sheets. My head rested on his hairless chest. His hand was on my arse, ready to arouse me again at the slightest invitation.

I looked up at him. He was wide awake, deep in contemplation. I kissed him on the chin. He stirred and pulled himself up, propping a couple of pillows behind his back for support. I sat up next to him, admiring the walnut colour of his tan. My fingers traced a path across his stomach, ready to seize the moment if it were required. He didn't get the hint. Instead, he had returned to the earlier preoccupations.

'You're right, Dawn,' he said, speaking slowly and deliberatively. 'There's no need for panic. All of this can be resolved in time. I just need you to delay Sheckler while I consult with Pat, Rob and Don. If we act quickly then we can avert a crisis.'

'Of course,' I replied, barely paying attention to what he was saying. 'You do what you think is best.'

'Are you taking this seriously,' he laughed, now awake to my interest.

'Absolutely not.' I replied, climbing over his body and pulling him inside me for one more fuck before we slept.

Chapter Five

I often think that we live our life in fear…, fear of commitment, fear of intimacy, fear of being found out for the shallow, doubt-racked beings we really are beneath the hard shell we present to the world.

We fill up the little time we have in this world with work, with play, with any activity that will stop us from confronting our own demons. We label the thrill of sex, the routine of family, the presence of companionship as love without once questioning its value or its meaning.

I have lived my life without thinking too deeply about the effect I have had on others. I have been selfish, self-centred and uncritical. I have judged people harshly when it has been unwarranted and allowed others to use me when I should have challenged them. I have spent too long getting by on my wits, taking pleasure when I could and to hell with the repercussions.

The events of the last few months have challenged all that. They caused me to realise that this approach was what got me into trouble in the first place, caused me to question my actions, doubt my motives, search inside myself. I have grown up, but my new-found insights have come at a heavy price – one I had never thought I'd have to pay as I finished my report for Sheckler and prepared to face his wrath.

I'd arrived in the office early. The past few days had been a flurry of meetings, with lawyers, planners, Welsh Government officials and with the acting chief executive. There was a consensus that we were contractually tied into honouring the option for Maga Power Holdings to buy the land to develop their power plant, but that did not preclude us changing our policy and opposing the planning application.

Such a U-turn would be an act of bad faith on our part,

but that decision was above my pay grade as they say in the movies. I have to act in accordance with the wishes of my political master.

In many ways, I was not sure why Alec and his mob bosses were so skittish. They held all the cards. I suppose that the level of investment and risk was so huge that they couldn't afford any hiccups, least of all an obstructive campaign by the region's mayor.

At the appointed time, I was shown into Sheckler's office. He had reverted to wearing the pin-striped double-breasted suits of old, which did not suit him. Was it a sign of poor dress sense or was he just rebelling against the strictures of his spin doctor? The smart suit he wore when he first greeted us after his election had presumably been put aside for special occasions.

He was at his desk reading my report. I'd expected Tim Finch to be there, too, along with Mike Kirk, who oversaw the legal department, but Sheckler was on his own. I stood and waited for him to acknowledge my presence. He continued to scan the report, furiously writing notes in the margin.

Eventually, he looked up and signalled me to sit on a chair in front of his substantial desk. He put down the report and fixed me with a determined look.

'I'm not happy, Dawn,' he said eventually. I tried to divert his ire.

'Will we be joined by Tim and Mike, Mister Mayor?'

'No, I don't see any need for that. They have given their opinion in contributing to this report, what we need to do now is to agree a course of action.'

'Nevertheless, Mister Mayor I would strongly advise that we take legal advice before agreeing anything.'

'Your views are noted, Dawn. Now, shall we get down to business?'

I placed my copy of the report on the desk and took him through it, section by section, answering his questions as I went. It soon became obvious that he did not accept the legal advice that he could not arbitrarily cancel the option on the land. I warned him that to do so would leave his office open to a massive compensation suit.

'I understand that you hosted a visit from a senior civil servant when I was away earlier this week, and that you sent her away with a flea in her ear,' Sheckler said at this point.

He looked pleased. At least this was one action of mine that we could agree on.

'I don't like officials from across the border coming down here and throwing their weight around,' I said. 'Whether they have a case or not, we have a devolved government in Wales and they have no right to push us around. I hope that I didn't take too much of a liberty.'

'On the contrary, Dawn. You did absolutely the right thing. If she had made it as far as my office, I would have had her thrown out. I can't abide being told what to do by Home Counties apparatchiks who think they're morally superior.'

At least we had bonded on something. Sheckler took the opportunity to order some tea and coffee, though to be frank I would have preferred something stronger, even at that time in the morning.

As we sipped our coffee, Sheckler speculated on the fallout if he refused to co-operate further on the planning application. My office was working quite closely with the developers on key environmental, transport and community-impact studies in support of their bid to the Welsh Government. He wanted to know if we were contractually obliged to continue with this work. I confirmed that we weren't.

'Good,' he said. 'That is one course of action we will consider, but I really want to cancel this option agreement. That will kill off the plant for good.'

'As you have been advised, Mister Mayor, that is not possible without a serious risk that we will be sued for breach of contract.'

'Yes, so I have been told. I will be taking further advice on that. Now, what about lobbying Welsh Government ministers? Can we put together an objection to the planning application? If so, how long will that take?'

'I'm sure we can do that Mister Mayor - it should only take a week or two to pull together all the threads. The Local Development Plan will be of some help as it is silent on a use for this land. However, we need to wait for the application to be advertised formally before submitting our views, and that won't happen until it's complete with all the studies.'

He indicated that he wanted me to proceed with that. I started to gather my papers together ready to leave but Sheckler was not ready to be left alone just yet. He came around and sat in the chair next to me.

What was he playing at? Was he going to coach me, take me into his confidence over some terrible secret, or was he just trying to put me at ease? I adopted a defensive posture, shifting my body ever so slightly on the chair away from him. This was beginning to look like the first move in some power-play seduction routine.

'You know, I didn't want this job,' he started.

You could have fooled me, I thought. Ever since I'd known him Sheckler had been playing the crowds, working the angles, promoting himself through his adoption of populist issues. There was no doubt he was a worker, but his motives had always been his own self-advancement, not the common good.

His campaign for the office of regional mayor had been classic-Sheckler. He had grabbed hold of the power plant issue (and many others as well), painted himself as the anti-establishment candidate, fighting the uncaring, unheeding City Hall bosses, thrown in a few accusations of corruption and of self-serving politicians and then ridden into City Hall on the back of a virtual white charger.

I'd never understood how he'd funded it. I knew he was wealthy in his own right and had crowd-sourced a lot of the money, but there were one or two donations on his expenses return that didn't quite fit in with the image he'd built for himself. He was still speaking, *at* me rather than *to* me.

'You might know that I was opposed to the creation of a Regional Mayor. I fought against the Welsh Assembly, too. I don't like this trend of taking power away from local people. But I suppose that once the councils in the Cardiff Capital region had been given over a billion pounds to sort out their infrastructure, it was inevitable that the Government would force this office on us.

'My job is to make it work, to show that a single person can govern ten council areas while listening to what people want and responding to them. My predecessor wasn't very good at that sort of thing.'

I was beginning to wonder where this monologue was taking us. Was Sheckler feeling so misunderstood that he felt he had to justify his existence to his own officers?

'I know that you have a big personal investment in this power plant Dawn, but I wanted you to understand where my opposition stems from. It's the wrong choice for our region. People recognise that, and I'm here to do their will. I made promises which I must keep. I will fight until my last breath to stop it.'

There was nothing new in what he was telling me. I'd been around long enough in local government to know what made politicians tick, after all, my own mother was a politician. I'd been immersed in her campaigns from an early age.

But I also know the difference between a principled politician who is prepared to stand up for what they know to be right and one who is bending with the wind.

'I'm a professional officer, Mister Mayor,' I replied eventually, 'I take my instructions from you and I will act accordingly. I don't need to know your motives.'

It was obvious that he had detected a certain distance in my response. I just wanted to get out of there. He was starting to creep me out. But there was no escape, not yet at least. Instead, Sheckler tried to turn on the charm.

He placed his hand on mine. It was marble-cold. This was a level of intimacy I'd not reckoned for.

'Please, call me Morgan,' he said. 'At least when we're not in a formal meeting.'

'You know I can't do that Mister Mayor. I need to keep our relationship professional.'

'I'm sure you can maintain your professionalism while using Christian names, Dawn. After all we've known each other a long time.'

Now he was starting to get under my skin, and it wasn't pleasant. I wondered how I might extract my hand from beneath his. He seemed intent on leaving it there for a long time.

'We were close once, Dawn.'

This revelation hit me like a gunshot. He was making a pass at me. It was unmistakeable. His hand moved to my shoulder, he shuffled along his chair in my direction. I was lost for words.

'That was a long time ago, Mister Mayor. I was young, just out of university, in my first job as a planning assistant. A lot of water has gone under the bridge since then.'

It was true, we'd had a relationship of sorts. It was more like a series of one-night stands. He was a member of the planning committee, in his early thirties, quite fit and attractive, confident and rich. For an ambitious officer like me, still trying to establish myself and physically attracted to this unconventional politician, it was an opportunity rather than a love match.

I've always been relaxed about my choice of lovers, never felt constrained by conventional morals. I consider myself a modern woman, capable of making my own mind up irrespective of what others think. If a man can sleep around,

49

then so can I. And besides I enjoy sex.

With Sheckler, I bit off more than I could chew. He was obsessive, and was still pursuing me long after I'd moved on from our little tryst. In the end, I'd had to go to my boss who, despite disapproving of my behaviour, got the council leader to tell him to back off.

Surely, he couldn't still be holding a torch for me all these years later. If that was the case, then it would be a problem. I was older and wiser. I'd learnt that there's no point in revisiting the past as far as relationships are concerned. Once it's over, then that was it, a little break-up sex maybe and then move-on.

He was also my boss, a politician who had humiliated the previous mayor - a man who was a close family friend. Just for a minute, I contemplated whether I could use him. He was still very attractive. It would not be a hardship on my part. If I slept with him again would it enable me to temper his opposition to the power plant? Could I help Alec by taking him into my bed?

I dismissed the thought immediately. Sheckler had never been prone to that sort of influence. He would certainly give me favourable treatment as an employee, but his agenda was sacrosanct. I understood that. Besides, once the relationship came to an end (and it would) life would be intolerable, as it had been all those years ago.

Allowing him to resurrect our long-finished affair was a non-starter. But how was I going to let him down gently? How should I tell him that I wasn't interested without causing him to dismiss me on the spot? There were no witnesses. It was my word against his. A sexual harassment case would not stand up. Now I understood why Tim and Mike had not been invited to this meeting. This had been planned from the start.

'Come now, Dawn. We had a good time all those years ago, didn't we?'

He was not going to relent easily. I had to think quickly.

He had moved closer and was looking to make his pitch.

'I haven't been able to stop thinking about you since that first meeting after my election. You're as beautiful and alluring as ever. Are you in a relationship with somebody?'

I mumbled something about not wanting to get tied down by anybody. I wasn't going to give up any details about my personal life to him. Unfortunately, my answer encouraged him further. He was almost in my lap. His hand had moved from my shoulder to my back. His other hand was on my knee. I was frozen by indecision. I had no idea how to extract myself from this situation with any grace.

'I can be a huge help to you,' he said. 'If you play your cards right with me, you could be the new chief executive.'

His hand had moved from my back to stroke my hair. At least he remembered which buttons to press to turn me on. I felt his other hand fondling my breast and was aware of his head moving towards mine.

He kissed me on the lips. I froze. He kissed me again and I responded. My hand was now on his back. But this was not what I wanted. I was no longer a young graduate out to make my mark in a new career, I was a full-grown woman with a well-paid and responsible job.

I pulled back from his embrace and gently eased him away from me. I stood up, brushed down my skirt and adjusted my blouse.

'I'm sorry,' I said, 'I can't do this. I need to focus on my work. I can't be romantically involved with my boss. It just wouldn't work.'

He looked disappointed and confused then stood and placed himself directly in front of me.

'But what about our history, what we had previously? Surely you don't want to let that slip away. We have the chance of a fresh start?'

Considering he was a politician; he could be remarkably unperceptive. It was difficult to understand how somebody who had been so expert in manipulating public opinion to come from nowhere and become regional mayor could fail to understand basic human interaction.

Was it that he felt that having attained high office he could do anything he wished? Was he really blinded by passion, lust, call it what you wish, that he could not see that things had moved on and that I wasn't interested?

Had he so completely failed to get the message fifteen or sixteen years ago that I wanted nothing more to do with him? For fuck's sake, I'd even threatened him with an injunction at one point.

I started to feel sorry for him, sorry that he was so emotionally crippled by our previous relationship that he had been unable to put it behind him. But I was angry, too. I was angry at being put in such a compromising position, and angry at myself for not having foreseen it.

Sheckler's confusion was slowly turning to anger as well. He was embarrassed at being rejected and felt the need to strike out to avoid looking foolish. If he could blame me rather than his own cackhandedness, then he retained the upper hand.

'I think I'd better go,' I said retreating towards the door.

His face was flushed a deep red and he could barely speak. I thought he might be on the verge of a stroke as he grabbed a water bottle off his desk and gulped half of it down.

'You're going to regret this,' he shouted as I closed the door behind me. I knew that he was right. We were now officially at war over the power plant and over my future.

Sheckler was a man who did not forget slights easily. He was remarkably thin-skinned and insecure. He hid it well in public, but the private person was a different sort of animal. Just as he had carried a torch for me for a decade and a half, so he would now take this rejection and turn it into a vendetta. There was no turning back.

Chapter Six

I had been summoned. The text message was short but explicit – 'lunch, my office, Monday.' When it came to communicate with me, my mother was a woman of few words, she saved all her energy for the public.

Spending a lunch break with my mother is no easy feat. Her office is at the South Wales Police Headquarters in Bridgend, mine at City Hall, Cardiff, a distance of over 20 miles. The journey can take 40 minutes, or longer in heavy traffic.

The only way to manage this on a working day is to take time off. That is how I found myself wandering around the shops on Queen Street first thing in the morning, looking for a new outfit for my birthday party.

The search for new clothes is not really a priority and nor is my birthday in the normal course of events. However, the day happened to coincide with a staff social, so I'd decided to take advantage of the free time I had to fill in a glaring gap in my wardrobe before heading off to Bridgend

I hadn't bought a little black dress in years and, having thrown the last one out after a particularly heavy night during which it had become stained with several substances and mysteriously torn after a drunken trek through some bushes, I considered it was time to get a new one.

I walked from shop to shop. Who knew that buying a simple item of clothing would be so difficult? Why hadn't I done what I usually do and bought one online? It would have arrived in time. Those who argue that shopping is a genuine leisure activity are kidding themselves, it is one of the most frustrating pursuits I have ever committed myself to.

Eventually, I found a dress in a small shop hidden away in one of Cardiff's arcades. The assistant was helpful and expert at gauging the right style and fit for me. I swung around in the dressing room admiring the outfit in a full-length mirror. I promised myself I'd not ruin this one.

Afterwards I sat in a café drinking coffee, scrolling through my phone, steeling myself for the journey west. I found myself wishing that I had something stronger than an espresso, but it wouldn't be wise to drive into police headquarters under the influence.

The journey was uneventful. The A48 was virtually empty at that time of day and because there are no cameras I could open-up the throttle in between roundabouts and traffic lights.

I was surprised how much had changed at police headquarters. The collection of ugly red brick buildings that defined the site had always been ensconced behind fencing, in a sort of makeshift compound but modern threats had seen the introduction of increased security.

A couple of observation towers had been added and there were officers with automatic weapons at the entrance. The barrier itself had been replaced with rising bollards designed to stop a suicide bomber driving onto the site, and more security cameras had been added to the surrounding area.

At the entrance, I showed a police officer my driver's license so that he could confirm my identity and check that I was expected. I was directed to park in a nearby visitor space. It was a sunny day and I had the roof down on my BMW convertible. I decided to leave it like that even though South Wales is notorious for unexpected showers.

I walked into the main building, where I had to be vetted by one of those airport-style scanners. The receptionist was expecting me and signed me in, before summoning a civilian to take me up to my mother's office.

As was befitting the office of Police Commissioner, my mother had secured a large room with a view of the supermarket on the other side of Cowbridge Road. It was sparsely furnished with a large desk and a conference table, surrounded by a dozen or so chairs and a television.

There was a laptop open on her desk next to a photograph of her receiving her OBE from the King. There were very few photographs adorning the walls, but I noticed that of those that were there, none were of me. It was much as I expected.

I'd been here before a couple of times, of course, but not for a few years. My mother was now in her third elected term as Police Commissioner and the novelty had worn off. She only invited me when she wanted something, and so I was not inclined to go out of my way to interrupt her busy schedule.

I am an only child and since she had ascertained that I would not be producing any grandchildren for her, the social visits had dried up, too. I was certainly not interested in spending my Sundays being lectured about my private life, so I found other things to do, such as actually having a private life.

After the divorce, Mother had reverted to her maiden name of Aileen Jenkins, an amalgam of her Irish and Welsh roots. I'd chosen to keep my father's name, partly to defy her, but also because I enjoyed having a distinctive identity in a country where those called Jenkins, Jones, Williams, Davies and Evans form the bulk of the population.

My mother's decision to revert to Jenkins had electoral advantages as it underlined her Welshness. It had nothing to do with principle, or a desire to assert her own individual identity. After all, she had taken my father's name when she had married him, and if he had been called Anthony or Aardvark, she would have left things alone on the grounds it would have placed her at the top of the ballot paper.

When Mother had gone into politics, she had tried to model herself on her political heroes, people like Hillary Clinton, Michelle Obama and Glenys Kinnock, but she was South Wales' answer to Mayor Daley from 1960s Chicago, a machine politician who knew how to get her own way.

Our relationship would have been so much easier if she had still been with my father, but his womanising, drinking and gambling problems had driven her to seek solace in the arms of Byron Harris, something I only found out much later, after my father had left her. He had relocated to the West Midlands and taken up with a new woman.

I was still young. Not knowing the circumstances of the break-up, but being aware of his issues, I blamed him. My father tried to keep in touch, but I resisted, and by the time I came around, it was too late. He had moved on and I couldn't find him.

I was so angry when I learnt what had really happened in my parents' marriage. I suppose it accounts for the frostiness between Mother and me. She had never been a natural nurturer anyway, she was far more comfortable in meetings than entertaining her only child, so I suppose the distance between us suited her.

Our rows had been terrible, the tears and the pain still scarring, but we had learnt to get along in our own way, even if it was best done at arms-length.

Mother had changed her hair since I last saw her, it was red now and she'd put on weight, her red trouser suit and white blouse were straining a bit at the seams. She either needed to have it taken out or buy some new clothes. I supposed that she was too busy. I wasn't going to offer to assist.

She looked up at me, her brown eyes peering brightly over her glasses. As I approached the desk she stood up and walked towards me. I thought she was going to shake my hand but instead she embraced me, adopting her best politician's demeanour.

'Dawn, it's good to see you. How have you been keeping?'

She guided me to the conference table and sat me down. I suddenly realised that I didn't have anything to say to her, so I resorted to small talk.

'I'm keeping well thank you, mother. How are things in law enforcement?'

'They're going very well dear. Shall we get some lunch and then we can talk properly?'

She walked over to her desk and pulled out two packets of sandwiches, some crisps and a bottle of reduced-sugar cola. She gathered up two glasses and brought them over to me.

'I hope you're not going through one of your vegetarian phases,' she said. 'I only have a choice of ham and tomato or chicken and coriander.'

'I was rather expecting something more extravagant,' I responded. 'Don't you have a canteen here or something? We could even go over the road and have one of those all-day breakfasts in the supermarket café.'

I was starving. She sat down and handed me the ham and tomato sandwiches.

'Of course, we could dear, but we wouldn't get any privacy there. Here, have some salt and vinegar crisps.'

She threw the packet over to me. I took them and pulled the cellophane cover open. I unwrapped the sandwiches. At least she had chosen brown bread. It was becoming clear that this was not a social invitation.

'So, what can I do for you, mother?' I asked between mouthfuls of ham and tomato.

'Why Dawn, can't a mother arrange a little lunch with her only child when she feels like it?'

'Yes, you can, but we both know that you have something you want to say or ask me. You always have an agenda.'

She smiled, a wry, knowing smile, and used her cola to wash down the remains of her sandwich.

'You know me too well, Dawn.'

I braced myself for some startling revelation or impossible ask. She had a habit of doing this, dragging me back into her life when she wanted something. I suppose I should have expected it, but she fooled me every time.

On this occasion, I'd allowed myself to be seduced into thinking she was trying to bond, only to be disappointed once more. It was the same old story. Why did she always do this? Why did I always fall for it?

'I wanted to talk to you about this power plant,' she announced eventually.

I pretended ignorance.

'I'm sure that the security details are all in hand, mother. I believe that the police are involved at every stage of the planning.'

She gave me that look she used to throw at me when I was naughty as a child. She knew I was just trying to wind her up. Nevertheless, she played along.

'You know full well that I wasn't referring to the security of the plant.'

'Oh?'

'Yes, believe it or not I have political interests beyond the police. My concern is this loose cannon, Sheckler. I've been hearing some disturbing things.'

Now I was really interested. Who had been briefing my mother on the goings on at my place of work? It had better not be Alec. I could just about cope with him working for a bunch of mobsters, but I wouldn't tolerate a collusion of any kind with my mother.

I was unaware, too, of any connection between the Police Commissioner's Office and the three amigos, Marshall, Watkins and McCoy. And then it hit me. She'd been having a little tête-à-tête with Ted Jones.

'What has Ted been telling you?' I asked.

She looked shocked.

'How do you know I've been talking to Ted?'

'Oh, come on mam, I'm not stupid. Tell me what you've heard, and I'll confirm or deny it.'

'He told me that the bastard who is now your boss sacked him as his first act in the job. He also tells me that Sheckler's doing all he can to stop this power plant going ahead.'

'Well that was in his manifesto. What did you expect him to do?'

'Good grief child, how long have you worked in local government? Nobody expects politicians to keep their promises, especially impossible big ones like stopping a power plant that is already sealed and delivered. You go through the motions and then plead that you were foiled by special interests.'

'That, mother, may be how you and Byron practise your politics, but Morgan Sheckler is a whole different animal. He wants to deliver on this promise and nobody is going to stop him.'

She looked shocked at this revelation. I don't know why as she had clearly been expecting it. Maybe she thought I would tell her that Ted had been mistaken or misinformed, that Byron's legacy was secure. I wish I could have. I felt I had to reassure her.

'Look mam, I know that you and Byron are close, that you have history, but he lost the election. Nevertheless, I will do what I can to obstruct Sheckler. The odds are in favour of the development going ahead, so there is no need to panic yet.'

'I hope so, Dawn. I don't think you appreciate how much is at stake with this development.'

On the contrary I thought, there were things I knew that she could only guess at, and which would severely compromise her position as the political head of the police in South Wales. The cosy little cabal she and Byron had formed over the years to their mutual benefit could well pale in comparison.

And that was the problem. There were too many vested interests who would benefit from this power plant - powerful interests all ranged against the mayor, with me in the middle. Who knew what they would do to get their way?

'There is a lot more at stake than you realise, mother. I've had all sorts to see me this week ranging from the UK Government to the big wigs with the development company. There's a lot of money being invested in this plant and apparently the future of our relationship with the Chinese is under threat as well, if you can believe that.

'I'm sure that Ted, Byron and you have a lot tied up in this as well but trust me on this mother, you need to back off. Let me deal with it. Not all of these people are legit. There may well be a conflict between their business and your position.'

She seemed shocked. I wasn't sure whether it was at my revelation about the nature of the investors in the power plant or at the fact that I'd warned her off.

'It's nice of you to think of me, Dawn but I can look after myself.'

'Fine,' I said standing up to go. She watched as I walked towards the door. As I reached it, I stopped and turned back to face her.

'Tell me,' I said, 'what's your interest in this project. Do you have a financial stake, are you acting for somebody else, maybe Byron or Ted, or is it just curiosity?'

She sat contemplating her answer for what seemed like an eternity but was most probably just a couple of minutes. For the first time, today I could see that she was uncertain how to respond. Eventually, she spoke, choosing her words carefully.

'My interest is in my friend's reputation and that of the party. Byron staked a lot on this power plant. It was his legacy, the final piece in the Cardiff Capital Deal jigsaw, that will guarantee self-sufficiency for the region and encourage industry to relocate here. I can't just stand back and let that investment in the future be swept away out of political spite.'

So, this lunch had been a fishing expedition on behalf of her pals. I couldn't blame her I suppose. I might have done the same. I moderated my tone.

'Listen mam, you really can't get involved in this. You know that don't you? That's why we're having this private lunch, though to be frank I think you could have sprung for a bowl of soup from the canteen or something.

'I've a lot invested in this power plant as well. I'll do my best to protect Byron's legacy. You can count on me.'

Her face softened as she stood up and walked towards me. She embraced me. It was awkward but also far more convincing than when she had greeted me in the first place. She had never been the most tactile of people. I placed my hands on her shoulders, unsure whether to return the gesture. By the time I'd made up my mind she had disengaged.

'Thank you for that, Dawn. I appreciate it. I know I can rely on you to do your best for our friends.'

I didn't like to disabuse her by stating my own reasons for getting the plant up-and-running. She would have been both shocked and outraged. Whatever people said about my mother, no matter how much of a politician she was, she had always been up-front, honest and above reproach.

Sure, she had done a few favours here and there for her mates, but then that was how she and I had been brought up. In my experience, in the political world I was raised in, you look after your own. If you can help your family or friends, then you bend over backwards to do so. It's how many of the politicians I have worked with and for in Government have always worked.

The key was to keep it on the straight and narrow. Once you broke that tenet then it was a slippery slope, a downward spiral of corruption that could only end in ruination. I knew that the nature of my association with Alec and his colleagues had placed me on that slope, irrespective of the reasons for getting involved in the first place.

I opened the door and started to make my escape. Mother came out after me. She was in a conciliatory mood.

'We don't see each other often enough, Dawn. Why don't you come around for Sunday lunch sometime? Bring a friend. Are you seeing somebody? I would love to meet him or her if you are?'

Somehow, I doubted whether she would be so keen on meeting Alec, though he could be charm personified when he tried. I said that I would think about it.

'Good,' she said. 'I'll get my diary secretary to send you some dates.' Only my mother could ruin the mood with a throwaway line like that.

Chapter Seven

That night I had a terrifying nightmare, that I was trapped in an upright metal box at the bottom of the ocean. I was naked and shivering. Water was rushing in. It was surprisingly warm and soapy, as if I were in the bath.

The water level climbed up my body until it covered my head. My lungs were filling with water. I was drowning, and awoke sweating, gasping and terrified.

It was early morning and the cat was snoring on the pillow next to me. I tried to go back to sleep, but something or someone troubled me. I couldn't quite put my finger on it.

My mind was racing, and it took an hour or so to get back to sleep. When the alarm went at 6am I was exhausted. Nevertheless, I forced myself out of bed and into my tracksuit and trainers for an early morning run that would, hopefully, clear my head.

This pattern continued night after night. It was not always the same dream, sometimes I was drowning, at other times I was buried alive and suffocating under an avalanche of snow. I was always naked, and each time I awoke struggling for air.

My early morning runs were becoming a regular feature. I felt I needed the exercise to settle myself after such a disturbed sleep. Unfortunately, the runs did not stop the nightmares, which were rooted in my anxiety and the pressure I was under to satisfy competing parties.

Alec had disappeared again. Presumably he was off keeping his mob bosses happy. My mother's PA had been in touch and we even agreed a date for me to go to her for Sunday lunch, only for it to be cancelled a few days later. I'd not heard anything more regarding a rearranged date. All of this was par for the course.

My trips to the gym had also been severely curtailed due to the amount of work I had to get through. There was no skiving off early at present. The only exercise I was getting were those runs, though they seemed to be keeping me in good shape for the time being.

And as for Sheckler, I'd not spoken to him nor he to me since the meeting and the attempted pass, some would class it as harassment, inappropriate behaviour, even assault. He was obviously keeping his distance. The odds that he was avoiding me from embarrassment were very short. He was using Tim Finch as a go-between while he plotted his revenge for the slight, I had supposedly delivered to him.

It was a relief then when my birthday came around. There was an opportunity to celebrate at a pre-planned office party. The cast of this party was my development department together with anybody else in City Hall who might wish to join in. We had a mutual determination to get shit-faced, to relieve the unending grind of working for the new mayor and his impossible demands.

We were gathering in an exclusive cocktail bar in Cardiff City centre before going onto the Brewery Quarter for a bite to eat and more drinks. No doubt we would end up dancing the night away in some club into the early hours of the morning.

I was looking forward to it. I'd not been able to let my hair down since Sheckler's election. I was raring to go.

It was a Friday night and I'd managed to get out of work early. I got home just in time to shower, put on my new black dress, apply make-up and catch a taxi into town. Some of the girls from my department were there already. They had changed in work and had a head start on me.

I bought a round of cocktails and settled down with a margarita. Others joined us, so that by the time we were ready to go on to a nearby tapas bar there were twenty-five of us, men and women.

At this point, I'd drunk a few margaritas and developed a

warm feeling towards my colleagues and anybody else who might want to join in. We ordered lots of wine to wash down our food and chatted about everything apart from work.

Later in a nearby bar I watched as a few of my co-workers danced to the very loud music. I was drinking strong cider and trying to conduct a conversation at the top of my voice with two staff members from finance about the state of the country.

It was then that a familiar face caught my eye. Jenny was at the other end of the large room dancing with two women. All three looked as tipsy as I felt as they attempted a rather vigorous twist. She looked up and our eyes met. She smiled and continued to throw her lithe body around the dance floor.

She was wearing a thin white cotton dress that showed off all the best parts of her body, highlighting her perfect breasts and flat stomach. The dress was so short that her bare legs were on display right up to the tops of her thighs. I imagined my hands pressing on that soft skin, lifting her skirt and moulding themselves to the contours of her tight arse.

Suddenly opinions on Britain's economic and political crisis seemed less important. I'd become detached from the conversation as they continued it over me. I picked up my drink and left them to it, wandering nonchalantly over to the edge of the dance floor.

I looked for her again among the mass of writhing bodies but couldn't see her. Where had she gone? Had I imagined her? Just how drunk was I? And then I felt a tap on my shoulder. She was standing beside me, drink in hand, radiating happiness and joy.

'I thought it was you,' I said. She pointed at her ears and shook her head. The music was too loud, and she couldn't make out what I was saying. It takes a special sort of person to be able to communicate effectively in a club atmosphere. We were both at least 10 years too old to qualify for that status.

She grabbed my hand and led me to a quiet area downstairs. There was nowhere to sit so we stood in a corner, talking, just inches apart. I couldn't stop peering into her blue eyes, they were hypnotic, pulling me closer to her as we talked, so that there was just two tongues' length between my mouth and her full, soft lips.

She had one hand on my arm, the other on my waist. Her drink was resting on a nearby shelf. I wanted to kiss her then and there, to run my hands over every inch of her body. I'd never felt like this about anybody before, least of all somebody I'd just met. I listened intently as she interrogated me.

'You were the last person I expected to see here.'

'Why?' I asked. 'Do I look like the stay-at-home spinster type?'

She laughed.

'Far from it. I'm just glad to see you. I've been looking out for you at the gym. I was beginning to think you were avoiding me.'

'I'm sorry, I've just been really busy. It's been murder at work.'

'Really? Anything the police can do? Murder is our specialty.'

She seemed to be enjoying our proximity as much as I was. Her hand had come to rest on the small of my back. It felt good.

'I'm sure I can cope with it on my own.' She looked disappointed. 'However, if I do need to relax a bit. Maybe you could assist me with that.'

Now she looked interested. Jenny leaned forward and kissed me. I responded. She tasted good as she pulled my body against hers. I could feel my heart beat faster, my whole-body tingle. This felt like the real deal.

She broke off the kiss but kept me close to her. I just wanted to grab her and whisk her back to my flat. I was losing control of my emotions. I might not even be able to wait that long.

'What's the big occasion? What is it that brings you to this den of iniquity?' she asked.

'It's my birthday. I won't tell you my age.' I was slurring my words slightly.

'I could always pull your record and find out.'

'Isn't that forbidden? And I don't have a record. Do I?'

'I've no idea,' she grinned, 'would you like me to check? Chances are that there's something on you. A person in your position is always of interest, for your connections if nothing else.'

I must have looked horrified. She laughed, a long joyous laugh that sounded like music to my ears.

'I'm thirty-seven,' I confessed, lying to her. I was really thirty-eight but then what does a year matter? It mattered a lot. She kissed me.

'You don't look a day over twenty-four,' she said.

'For a police officer, you don't lie very well.' She decided to change the subject.

'Should we get another drink?' she asked. 'That might help you relax.'

'It wasn't quite the sort of relaxation I had in mind,' I responded, kissing her again, my hands inside her dress, pulling at her knickers.

She grabbed my arms and placed them on her waist and smiled broadly.

'If it's that you're after then we had better find somewhere a bit more private. I could give you your birthday present.'

She took my hand and led me out of the bar towards a taxi rank. Ten minutes later we were at my home, it was closer than her flat. I opened the door and Myrddin came to greet us. Jenny scooped him up in her arms and rubbed the top of his head. Getting over his initial surprise the cat relaxed in her arms and purred loudly.

She was a cat person. This might be love, the real thing. I didn't dare say it out loud in case it scared her away.

'It seems that you have the magic touch whoever or whatever you're with,' I told her.

She put the cat down and followed me into the kitchen. I picked up a half-full bottle of red wine, pulled out the bottle stop and poured us a glass each. We sat together on the sofa. The cat sat at our feet.

She put her arm around me and placed her head on my shoulder. I drank from my wine glass, put it down on the coffee table and turned towards her. She placed the palm of her hand on my cheek and kissed me. I responded, sliding the zip down on the back of her dress and placing my hand on her bare back. She wasn't wearing a bra.

She felt so good, so warm. My nerve ends were tingling just touching her. She unzipped my dress and unhooked my bra. Her hands cupped my breasts as she tongued my nipples.

I slipped my hand inside her knickers and caressed the cheeks of her arse. Her fingers were inside me. I yanked her knickers down and reciprocated. We shed what was left of our clothing and fucked each other to a standstill.

Afterwards, we lay silently in each other's arms, enjoying the feel and the smell of each other. Her head was rested against my shoulder, her arm stretched across my body. I stroked her hair gently. It felt so good, so soothing just to be with each other. I closed my eyes and imagined that we were closeted on some Caribbean island, soaking up the sun, the crash of waves and the cry of birds the only sound to define our idyll.

She looked up at me and kissed my neck. Her hand had slipped down to my waist.

'You're not falling asleep on me, are you?' she asked. Her West Country accent caused my heart to beat just a little bit faster.

'No, I'm just enjoying the moment, trying to picture us

secreted away on a desert island somewhere, away from all the cares and woes of this city.' She smiled.

'A dreamer, eh? Just give it time. I'm sure we can find our own exclusive paradise here. Or failing that we'll go in search of it together.'

I turned and kissed her forehead. I wanted to know about this incredible woman who had just entered my life.

'Tell me something about yourself, Jenny. How did you end up in Cardiff?'

'How do you mean?'

'You didn't get that sexy Devon accent being brought up in Grangetown or Splott, did you?'

'No, that's a fair point. I'm originally from deepest, darkest Devon, but I've been here almost fifteen years. I went to University in Plymouth and joined the local police straight after I graduated. After a few years in rural Devon, and after some local difficulties, I decided that I needed something bigger, so I transferred here. But the accent won't go away. I still get comments about it.'

'It is rather strong.'

'Do you think so?' she asked, sounding thoughtful. 'It does set me apart from the rest of the team. And that's not a good thing. It's bad enough being a woman in the police force without also being the token Devon yokel.'

My fingers traced a path across the silky tresses of her hair as I held her close.

'Surely, women get better treatment in the police nowadays?'

'Yes, they do, but there are still those who think they can take liberties and we still have to contend with the funny handshake brigade.'

'Is that what your difficulties in Devon had to do with?'

'Yeah, but I don't want to ruin our evening talking about that…some other time.' I let it go, she would tell me when she was good and ready.

'Well, she may be a complete numpty when it comes to parenthood, but the one thing my mother won't stand for is sexism. She's very committed to equal opportunities.'

Jenny looked taken aback at this statement.

'Whoa, back pedal a bit there, Tonto. Who's your mother?' Now it was my time to be surprised.

'Oh. I thought you knew. Didn't you do one of those profiles of me before you spoke to me at the gym?' She drummed her fingers on my body impatiently. 'My mother is Aileen Jenkins.'

'Fuck off!' She almost shouted the words, jumping back and nearly falling off the sofa. Our chatty cwtch appeared to have ended as Jenny sought to process that piece of information.

'Your mother is the Police Commissioner?' she asked incredulously. 'How does that work?'

I gave her my version of my mother's cynical reversion to her maiden name. She laughed at the 'aardvark' reference.

'This is fucking unreal. I've never shagged my boss's daughter before.'

I could see that she was coming around to the idea. She turned back towards me and kissed me on the mouth. It was a long, passionate kiss. I responded in kind, my hands fondling her breasts. Her hand was already on my crotch, her fingers sliding inside me. She broke off briefly.

'This is such a turn-on,' she said as she kissed my neck, my nipples, my stomach, my thighs. And then she had both hands on my inner thighs, pushing them up and apart, her head between my legs. I arched my back in pleasure. And then I came, long and hard…. screamingly hard.

We held each other tightly. I felt a bit over-whelmed. She gave me a quizzical look.

'Are you okay?' she asked. It was the first hint she had given of possessing any self-doubt.

'I'm fine,' I said smiling. 'I haven't felt this safe and

secure for a long time.' She seemed pleased.

'Good. I was beginning to worry that you had become a bit distant. It was almost as if you had sidled off to another place.'

'I was just thinking how perfect this is,' I said, and then regretted saying it. What if I scared her off by coming on too strong? What if she thought me too intense?

She grinned, a broad toothy grin that put me at ease. She didn't need to say anything. That one gesture was enough to reassure me. She kissed me on the lips.

'It's getting cold,' she whispered. 'Can I impose on you to stay the night? Could we get under some covers?'

I didn't believe for one moment that a tough police inspector might be feeling the cold, even with the amount of booze we had both consumed. It was a clever manoeuvre, cheeky and calculating. It was as if she had read my mind.

'Just don't expect to get much sleep.' I retorted.

Later, I slept the sleep of the innocent. There were no disturbing dreams, no waking up struggling to breathe. When I finally awoke it was late on Saturday morning. Jenny was still fast asleep, her naked body curled around me.

I stroked her back to convince myself that she was real and then drifted back into unconsciousness.

Chapter Eight

It had been nearly three weeks of being persona non-grata with Sheckler. Somehow, I had to break the deadlock, get ahead of him before he could take revenge for the perceived slight of me throwing his advances back in his face.

If he decided to kick me out, as he had done with Ted, because he thought I was too close to the previous regime, then there was nothing I could do except take my compensation and walk.

The fact I was still in a job I put down to him needing my expertise. Maybe he hadn't realised that there were others in the department who could advise him just as well. Perhaps he still had a use for me, or maybe he had still not worked out where my loyalties lay?

I needed some leverage, an insurance policy to protect myself and that meant carrying out some research of my own on Sheckler. What had he been up to since I'd worked with him all those years ago? What skeletons did he have in his closet?

I arranged to meet up with some old colleagues from East Gwent Council to catch up on what had been happening since we had last met a few years previously. We ended up in a restaurant in Cardiff Bay.

Maria Pathakis is a short dumpy woman in her mid-thirties with black curly hair and olive skin. Apart from one significant incident in her life, her family history is more interesting than she is.

Her great grandfather had been a merchant seaman from Crete, who had met a girl from Cardiff and settled down amongst the small Greek community in the Butetown area. Her great grandmother was a Macedonian Greek whose family had been established in Cardiff for some generations before she met her sailor husband. The two of them founded a small Greek restaurant, which they later uprooted and moved to north Cardiff.

Maria herself, had bucked the trend amongst her family and gone to university, where she studied to be a town planner. She was not a natural restaurateur and was reputed to be an awful cook. She had ended up working with me in East Gwent and had so far failed to progress past that career high point.

She had entered a conventional but childless marriage with a family friend until, just a few years ago she announced that she could take it no longer, moved out of her comfy two-bedroom terraced home in Chepstow and straight into the arms of Gwilym Barratt, one of her co-workers.

Gwilym was a no-nonsense, larger-than-life Welsh baritone, who sang in one of the local male voice choirs. At six-feet-four and close on eighteen stone, he looked every inch the rugby player he had once been.

He was also a town planner and former colleague, whose full black beard and loud, distinctive voice seemed to precede him into every room he entered.

As a couple, they had become inseparable. As former colleagues, their love of gossip and their bitchy manner offered an asset that I was keen to exploit.

The restaurant where we met was not a Greek one, but Italian, albeit with a macabre taste in music. An iPod played a mix of music over the PA system throughout our meal, featuring third-rate covers of songs by Radiohead, Leonard Cohen, The Smiths, Coldplay and others. If they had wanted to drive customers away, they could have at least played the original artists.

When I arrived at the restaurant, Maria and Gwilym were already seated at the table and halfway through a bottle of red. As I approached, they both stood to greet me. We exchanged hugs and kisses. I sat down and immediately noticed that Gwilym had eaten all the bread sticks.

I apologised if I had kept them waiting but they would have none of it. They had arrived early and had settled down to sample the local vino. Throughout this conversation they were quietly pawing at each other. It had been three years and they still couldn't keep their hands to themselves.

I poured myself a glass of wine and perused the menu. I was getting a bit bored with pasta, but this restaurant was their choice, so I buckled down anyway. After we had ordered we got to business.

'How are you two keeping?' I asked. 'It's so lovely to see you.'

Maria and Gwilym were two of the most genuine people you could hope to meet. Neither of them would dream of asking me why, if today's rendezvous really was such a pleasure, then how had it been so long since our last meeting? As ever, I'd contacted them because I wanted something, having rebutted Maria's overtures with excuses over the previous two years.

I should have felt guilty at my neglect, but I couldn't summon up any, maybe I was turning into my mother. Nevertheless, I was here and if I was going to get what I wanted out of this meal then I needed to be sociable.

Maria was gushing about all the 'couplie' things they had been up to, their holidays abroad, the little cottage they were renting in Penarth, a recent visit to centre court at Wimbledon, even an international rugby game. She had never been interested in sport before.

It was as if she had a new lease of life. Gwilym sat there smiling broadly, chipping in occasionally, holding Maria's hand throughout her monologue. I was half expecting her to get photos out, and sure enough she pulled out her phone to show me a picture of their dog. And then there was the opening I was waiting for.

'How have you been doing?' she asked between mouthfuls of pasta. 'How are you getting on with Morgan?' I was about to answer when Gwilym jumped in.

'It was such a shock him winning that election. We all voted for him of course, but the odds were so much against him.'

'I know,' I replied. 'It helped of course that the election was fought using proportional representation but you're right, it was an extraordinary achievement.

'To be honest, Maria, it's been a bit of a rollercoaster. He's got us running around like blue-arsed flies. You remember how impossible he could be.'

'Oh, yes. If he didn't get his way, he could be a nightmare,' Gwilym interjected. Maria nodded in agreement.

'Didn't you have some trouble with him,' Maria asked me, half-remembering.

'Yes, he was hassling me. I had to get the council leader to tell him to back off.'

Gwilym looked shocked. This was the first time he had heard this. He topped up our glasses from the second bottle of wine.

'In what way was he hassling you?' he asked.

'Sexually,' I said matter-of-factly. He whistled. I didn't see the need to give him the sordid details.

"I'd heard that things are not good between you and Morgan,' he responded. 'You need to hang on in there. I'm sure it will work itself out. That could explain though, why he went off the rails, got himself a drink problem.' I sat up straight. Now this was interesting.

'I hadn't realised that,' I said. In fact, I hadn't seen him take a drink since he had become regional mayor. At reception after reception all I'd seen him drink was orange juice. I probed a little further.

'What happened? I don't recall him having a drink problem at East Gwent Council.'

'Yeah, well, you were doing your best to keep as far away from him as possible,' Maria said. 'We felt it best that you didn't learn the consequences of rebuffing his advances.'

'So, what happened?' I asked, anxious to gather as much information as possible. They looked at each other. I'd been rumbled. I tried to throw up some smoke to make my little fishing expedition look less obvious.

'It's just that I didn't know any of this, so I'm curious.'

'Of course,' Gwilym chipped in. 'It was the usual really, he drank himself into a stupor a few times, and then he got some help. I'm told he's been dry for years now.' I feigned a laugh in a further attempt to throw them off the scent.

'It's none of my business anyway, I'm just glad that he found his way through his problem. It must have been awful for him.'

I refused to accept any responsibility for Sheckler's alcoholism. He was an adult, who had taken advantage of his position to prey on a naïve young employee, barely out of college. He had made his own choices. He needed to take responsibility for them. What I was not clear about was whose side Gwilym and Maria were on in the blame-game stakes.

I'd not reckoned on them having any sense of allegiance to Sheckler, least of all having voted for him. I suppose he could turn on the charm when he needed to. I'd seen that when he had seduced me.

But I'd also seen the other side of him, the ruthlessness, and the single-minded pursuit of his own interests at the expense of everybody around him. He was a maverick, pitched against the ruling order and that was part of the attraction. But at the end of the day, it was what he believed was best for him that was his main motivation for everything he did.

I topped up everybody's wine glasses and ordered another bottle. Gwilym looked like he needed a pudding. Maria struck me as somebody who wouldn't turn down a tiramisu either. They met all my expectations. I decided that I could do without.

'Did you get involved in Morgan's campaign?' I asked,

forgetting my earlier attempt not to look too obvious in my search for information, though by this time we had consumed the best part of three bottles of wine, most of it going down the Odd-Couple's throat. It was unlikely that they would notice my lack of subtlety.

'I guess that it must have been one big adventure?' I added,

'Oh yes, we loved every minute. Gwilym and Morgan are members of the same rugby club, so it seemed natural to give him a hand.' Maria was positively beaming. 'It was a real buzz.'

'It was the power plant that did it' Gwilym added. 'Nobody wants that monstrosity where we live, backing Sheckler was the only chance we had to stop it.'

I nodded in agreement. That much was obvious. What I really needed though was a smoking gun, something I could use to keep him in check. I was certain that these two didn't have access to anything of the sort. I decided to probe deeper.

'Yes, I was impressed with how he managed to rally so much support behind him given there were others fighting the power plant as well. And not just the usual suspects but some big names in the Labour and Tory parties plus one or two local millionaires.'

Gwilym took another swig of wine and grinned. I could see that he knew something.

'Sheckler's been around a long time. He'd built up a lot of contacts, done favours for people, helped them get things done. You know, the usual. He just called in everything he was owed. It was a real people's campaign.'

Maria jumped in.

'Oh God, yes. Do you remember that man, what's his name? Chaffont I think, who was spearheading that big development, I can't remember where now. Sheckler really stuck his neck out for him, got the planning committee to overturn our recommendation. Well, he was well up for the fight. Donated quite a bit of cash, introduced Sheckler to some of his friends.'

'It was a lot like that,' Gwilym confirmed. 'That's what politics is like, I suppose. You scratch my back, I'll scratch yours. The big parties have been doing it for years. Sheckler just played them at their own game.

'And he had the big issues on his side, the power plant outside Chepstow, fighting an opencast in the Vale, standing up for green spaces in North Cardiff, exposing all those years of neglect in the Cynon Valley. Quite remarkable really. No wonder those in charge are squirming.'

I'd been aware of the narrative that Sheckler had constructed of course, but not the level of patronage he had exploited. It was depressing really.

The discussion had come to a natural conclusion. We were all a bit tipsy, Gwilym and Maria more than me. We ordered coffee to wash down our meal, cappuccino for Maria and me, a latte for Gwilym. I insisted on paying for the three of us. After all, I had initiated the meal, it was the least I could do.

The restaurant ordered a taxi to take them back to Penarth. We embraced as we parted. Gwilym pecked me on each cheek.

'You take care of yourself,' he said. 'Morgan's a good person with good intentions. He can make a real difference around here, if he's given the chance.'

I thanked him for his concern whilst trying to hide my contempt for his naivety. Sheckler had them all eating out of the palm of his hand, but then that was to be expected. He was still in his honeymoon period - the promises he had made to get elected had not yet been tested. People still believed in him. How much longer could that go on?

I was beginning to despair of ever getting the information I needed to use against him. But Gwilym and Maria had given me some useful stuff to work with. It was worth knowing about Sheckler's alcoholism, but I wasn't sure what

I could do with that knowledge. If he was functional, people would give him the benefit of the doubt.

More interesting was the link to Chaffont. He was known to me as a bit of a chancer but a very rich one, somebody who was used to getting his own way. I could well imagine him working on Sheckler to get a planning application passed. However, none of that could be proved.

It was all circumstantial, a grateful multi-millionaire funds the campaign of a politician who had once backed one of his projects. I'm sure that there were others like him, too. It didn't mean anything. Even my mother couldn't make that stick, no matter how much she loathed the new mayor for ousting her friend from his cosy position.

I stepped out onto the quay. A light drizzle was falling so I pulled my jacket close around my body, turned the collar up and raised my head skywards. I let the rain wash over my face to clear my mind. I was still a bit fuzzy from the alcohol and from all the issues running through my mind.

I started walking towards Lloyd George Avenue. Jenny's flat was nearby, she was expecting me. Our nights there were becoming a regular feature. It was best that way, while Alec still had a key to my place.

Jenny had been very good. She hadn't even mentioned Alec's stuff strewn all around my house. I thought it best not to raise it, at least until I'd resolved the situation, if that were possible.

He was still away on business, no doubt with his mob friends in America. His absences were becoming more and more frequent, even so, it was not going to be easy to close that chapter in my life.

I could kick him out, of course, but that wouldn't be enough. We had too many other ties, both business and personal. What's more, Alec knew too much about my involvement with the power plant. He wasn't going to let me walk away easily.

I was caught up in a no-man's land, between Jenny who I

wanted to be with and Alec, who I wanted to dump but couldn't. Thank God Jenny was not pressing me to commit exclusively to her. But surely it was only a matter of time. I sure-as-hell wanted her to commit to me.

I reached her apartment complex and buzzed her number. She answered almost immediately and let me into the block. I walked up the stairs rather than use the lift. She was waiting for me at her open door, wearing a rather sheer silk gown. She looked like an angel. It was as if I'd come home.

Chapter Nine

The next day I arrived in work early. Jenny had the first shift, so she had been up at the crack of dawn. She'd invited me to stay in bed a bit longer, but I thought it best to get home and feed Myrddin. As I sat down at my desk, Tim Finch appeared in the doorway, looking unusually pale.

'Do you have a minute, Dawn?'

I followed him into his office. Sheckler was sitting at Tim's desk. He was bright red with fury, his fists clenched a piece of paper, knuckles white with the effort. He looked up and his expression softened as he saw me.

Tim invited me to sit down, then pulled up a chair next to me. He looked across at Sheckler who, uncharacteristically speechless, waved the paper at Tim who took it and handed it to me.

It was a carefully typed note full of bile and abuse of the worst kind. Packed with spelling and grammatical mistakes, it essentially berated Sheckler's manhood, his parentage, his honesty and integrity and his right to exist. It concluded by warning him that if he continued to oppose the power plant then he would be shot.

I looked first to Tim, and then Sheckler, and then back to Tim again. Why were they showing this to me? Surely this was a police matter. Tim seemed to read my mind.

'Yes, we've involved the police,' he said. 'This is not the first letter of this kind. There've been many more, as well as untraceable emails from dummy accounts and some Twitter messages, which have also proved impossible to pin down. However, this is the first time that the power plant has been mentioned.'

Sheckler had returned to a more natural colour and was now sitting upright in the chair.

'Politics can be a difficult game,' he started. 'I'm sure that your mother will tell you the same thing, Dawn. You come to expect this sort of abuse, no matter how unacceptable it is. I've had letters like this before and, no doubt I'll get them again.'

For the first time, I was starting to feel sorry for him. Nobody deserved this treatment, no matter what they did.

What was it that Byron Harris had confided in me once? 'Politics is not a matter of life or death' he'd said. 'You shouldn't confuse it with rugby.' Somebody had failed to educate the author of these letters of that fact.

I don't recall my mother ever having abuse of this sort. She'd certainly never told me about it if she had. Maybe she was not a controversial enough politician, much more likely she'd just decided to protect me from the hate.

I was beginning to become as angry as Sheckler. How dare this individual, whoever he or she was, assume that they knew him, how dare they try to assert some form of power over him. What right did they have to act in this way? This was no part of the democratic process, this was a crime.

And what did they hope to achieve by these actions? Did they really think they would get him to back down on the power plant with these tactics, or were they just trying to project their own hateful nature onto him?

'The reason we showed you this letter was because we were concerned that you might get caught up in this.' Sheckler was talking. I tried to focus. Tim put his hand on my arm as if to reassure me. He could see that I was disconcerted.

'The police are trying to establish where this threat came from,' he continued. 'I seriously doubt that they will get anywhere. Nevertheless, we have a duty of care. If somebody is going to commit a violent act to try and get this power plant back on track, then it's possible that you might become a target.'

'We just need you and your staff to be careful,' Tim added. 'Keep an eye out for anything suspicious and report it to us and to the police if necessary.'

I nodded. What if these trolls weren't a threat at all? What if the letters and the emails were a form of masturbation for them? I couldn't believe that I was even thinking such a thing. I mean it could be that these nutters are harmless, but Tim and Sheckler were right, it wasn't worth taking the risk. Then I had a revelation.

'Do we have any idea who might be behind these threats?' I asked. 'I mean, it makes no sense. All the insurgency, the popular sentiment is against the power plant. I would expect this sort of abuse from some nutcase who wanted to stop it, but not the other way around.

'The supporters of this power plant are corporations, governments, politicians, not keyboard warriors with a thesaurus. Somebody is sending you a message alright and I think they're deadly serious.

'The person who wrote these isn't some random lunatic with nothing to lose, it's somebody who has invested their future in this plant, trying to warn you off.'

Sheckler was staring at me, his eyes wide. I could see that he'd already worked all of this out. Tim not so much.

'You're very perceptive, Dawn. I think we can all see that this campaign has a sinister ring to it. I hope that the police will be able to see it, too. The problem is knowing where to start.

'The corporations involved in this power plant are all above suspicion, apparently. But somebody is playing dirty, trying to intimidate me. What they need to know is that it won't work. I'm resolute on this issue. I *will* stop this power plant.'

By now he was standing up, his hands pressed firmly on the table, supporting the full weight of his body. I thought that he seemed a bit unhinged. I stood up and made my excuses.

'I'll ensure that my staff are all aware that they need to be vigilant', I said.

'Thank you,' Tim responded. 'I've spoken to the police and they are stepping up security at City Hall for the time being. I hope that will make us feel much safer.'

When I got back to my office, I gathered my staff together to brief them.

'Some fucker has threatened the mayor that they will kill him if he stops the power plant going ahead. So, that means we have two warring factions prepared to do anything to get their own way and we're stuck in the middle.'

That's what I wanted to say anyway. What I actually told them was that the police were concerned about security and they needed to watch their backs and report anything suspicious.

There was a message on my desk from Jack Chaffont. It was an extraordinary coincidence. I rang him back. He wanted a meeting, urgently. I asked what it was about, but he wouldn't say. We agreed to meet at a nearby pub for lunch.

It was warm and sunny outside. I don't get out enough to enjoy it. Feeling the sun on my back, I thought that maybe I needed a holiday, a getaway to somewhere hot, where I could enjoy good food and lots of wine, and lie half-naked on a beach with Jenny.

The pub was almost empty. I recognised Chaffont straight away. We'd met before, when I worked in East Gwent. He'd also been present at some of my mother's fundraisers, the ones she dragooned me into attending only for me to end up serving drinks.

Chaffont had never been fussy about which politicians he supported. It was never about ideology for him, more about promoting his own interests - whatever gets him what he wants, or whose policies will create the conditions he needs for his business to succeed.

He was sitting in a corner alone, nursing a pint of beer. There was a glass of white wine in front of him, presumably bought for me. I noted his long white hair, tanned leathery face and thin lips, which he had pulled into a sinister half smile.

He was wearing an expensive white shirt, unbuttoned low enough to allow a few strands of chest hair to peak out, and blue jeans that looked new. For a man of seventy, he was in good condition, thin and wiry like a marathon runner.

He beckoned me to sit and handed me a menu.

'I'm not hungry,' he said, 'but I figured you would want something, seeing as it's the middle of a work day an' all.'

He drawled his words in the manner of an American B-list actor. It was an act. My mother had told me once that he regularly binged on Clint Eastwood films and often tried to imitate him in certain business situations to throw his opponents off-guard. His mimicry skills left a lot to be desired, as did his consistency. He'd never been able to sustain it for long, slipping in and out of accent almost at random.

I ordered a salad and mineral water and returned to the table. He looked disdainfully at my choices.

'You'll waste away if you don't get some proper food down you.'

I nodded. I wasn't really in the mood to discuss dietary choices. I looked at him expectantly.

'Jeez, you don't mess around, do you? You're as bad as your mother. Okay, I'll get straight to the point. I need to know what's going on with this damn-fool power plant.'

That was the last thing I expected to hear. Why did he need me to tell him that? Couldn't he just phone up his marionette mayor and get what he wanted from him? I sat waiting for more. Nothing came. He just sat there expectantly, waiting for me to answer. Eventually, I cracked.

'You know I can't divulge confidential information to you, Mr. Chaffont.'

'Jack, please call me Jack. For Christ's sake, Dawn, I'm not asking for nuclear launch codes, just a briefing on the major project you're nursing into fruition.'

I hadn't given him permission to be so familiar, nor did I think it was good business for him to be so. After all, apart from meeting on a few occasions we hardly knew each other.

'I'd appreciate it if we could keep this on a more formal level, Mr. Chaffont. Yes, I'm the lead officer on the power plant, but surely, you'd have more success talking to the regional mayor.

'I understand that you helped to fund his campaign. Perhaps I'm not the best person to talk to with regards to your mutual aim of stopping the plant going ahead.'

He took a virtual step back, sitting up straight and stroking his chin.

'Well, well, I think we have a small communication problem here, Ms Highcliffe. I'm not trying to stop the power plant. I want it to go-ahead.'

This was a bombshell, and one I'd not foreseen. For a long, long minute I was lost for words.

'If you're in favour of the power plant, then why did you give so much money to Morgan Sheckler's campaign?' I asked eventually. 'You did know he was campaigning against it, didn't you?'

'Yes, yes, of course. Morgan and I go back a long way, as I'm sure you know. He'd done favours for me in the past, so naturally I was keen to get a more amenable occupant into the regional mayor's chair. And let's face it, who expected him to win?'

I wasn't satisfied with this explanation and he knew it. I pressed him further for a reason that made sense. In the end, he relented.

'Okay, you're right. I changed my mind. Or rather I had it changed for me. To be frank with you, I had another reason for wanting to stop the power plant. I've had my eye on that land for some time as a development opportunity but, let's say, that has ceased to be an option. Morgan was er... assisting me in that ambition.

'I've got a lot of fingers in a lot of pies in America and

some of my partners were getting jittery. They were unhappy with my association with Morgan. It was made clear to me that it was in my best interests to try and get him to do a U-turn on this power plant.'

'So why me? Why not go straight to him?'

'I've tried. He's as stubborn and as 'ornery as I remember. He sent me away with a flea in my ear, told me that he had a mandate, pointed out that we'd once been on the same side and that he was only doing what I'd once urged him to do in fighting this proposal.'

Chaffont gave an exasperated sigh in a futile attempt to garner some sympathy.

'Frankly, Dawn - sorry Ms Highcliffe - he had me bang to rights. I had no answer. And what's worse he was suspicious - downright paranoid in fact - accused me of having been got at, of siding with his enemies. I gave it up as a bad job and left him to his ranting and raving.'

'So why me?' I asked. 'I work for him. I can't be part of any campaign to undermine his key policies.'

He could tell I sensed a trap. Maybe Sheckler had sent him to test me. Or perhaps Alec's mobster friends were using him to see where my loyalties lay. I knew that I couldn't give an inch on either side. Much as I hate cricket analogies, I had to play this particular ball straight down the line.

'My business partners suggested that you could be trusted to do the right thing,' he said.

I dug into my salad, dispensed with the mineral water and took a large gulp of wine instead. When I'd agreed to this meeting, I hadn't expected it to be quite so difficult.

'Look, Dawn, I'm not expecting you to betray any State secrets, or even to put your job in jeopardy. I just need you to know which side I'm on in this affair. Sheckler's a good politician and he'll do a great deal for this region, especially with the money from the Cardiff Capital deal still working its way through, but from a businessman's perspective he needs to pull back a little.'

I still felt that I couldn't trust him, but it would have been remiss of me to let this opportunity go without trying to get something out of it in my best interests. And when it comes to Morgan Sheckler, Jack Chaffont knew where all the dirt was buried. If I wanted an insurance policy to protect my own job, then I could do no better than to get him to furnish it.

'Look Jack,' I said, allowing the conversation to assume a more informal air, 'don't get me wrong, I've been a champion of this project from the beginning. I helped Byron bring this plant to South Wales and I understand what it means in terms of regenerating our region.

'It will bring jobs here in its own right and it will guarantee power supplies for other high-energy companies to relocate here. This plant allows the country to be less dependent on others for its energy supplies and it brings security, prosperity and jobs to South Wales. It's a no-brainer.

'So, I'm torn, between what I know is the right thing to do, and my boss who has consistently played to the crowd and to those environmental campaigners who have whipped up opposition based on scare stories, half-facts and tales of corruption and dodgy dealings.

'Byron had the moral fortitude to stand up to them and fight for what is right, to stick with his principles against all the hysteria, and he paid for it by losing his job. I don't intend to suffer that fate.

'If, therefore, you want me to fight your corner, and those of your so-called business partners, then I'm going to need some insurance. I need you to give me leverage I can use against the regional mayor.'

It was the longest speech I'd given for some considerable time and it seemed to have an effect. Chaffont stroked his chin again, pondering on what he could tell me without incriminating himself. Eventually, he spoke up.

'Okay,' he said, 'I think we understand each other at last. You need security. I can accept that. However, I can't give you chapter and verse on my dealings with Sheckler because to do so would mean exposing commercially confidential information.

'What I can tell you is that some of the favours he has done for me have been well-remunerated through campaign donations and my personal support. I know that I'm not the only one to have worked with him in that way.'

I looked at him askance. This was hardly news to me, nor of much use. Chaffont continued:

'His genius, if you like, was to call in all those favours to pay for a campaign that pulled all the right levers with the public, matching the bigger parties for expenditure on propaganda and surpassing them. He had some good people helping him, some of whom I recruited on his behalf.

'Now that I know what I know, I'm beginning to regret backing him, but at the time it seemed that shaking up local government was good business.'

For the first time, I could see that Chaffont was afraid. It was as if he'd got in too deep with certain people and didn't know how to extract himself. He pondered for a bit on his next move.

'Look,' he added, 'You know I can't give you what you want, but I can guarantee you that if this goes tits-up, you'll be looked after. I don't give that promise lightly. If necessary, I'll honour it myself.

'I understand that you want this project to succeed, we all do, so whatever support I can provide, you just have to ask. In the meantime, I'll back off and let you get on with it.'

I was disappointed. I wanted more, but it was clear I wasn't going to get it. I wanted to bury Morgan Sheckler and his half-cock populism, I wanted to make him pay for the way he had treated me. I'd never felt such strong disdain, or hate for any individual before. This had become personal.

Chaffont finished his pint and started to gather himself to

leave.

'Just one more thing, Jack,' I asked, stopping him in his tracks. 'Just how far are your friends prepared to go to stop Sheckler?' He paused.

'Well, that depends, doesn't it? If he won't listen to reason, and if it seems that he really is a threat to this plant going ahead, then I can't speak to the consequences.'

'Seriously? This is Wales, not some third-rate gangster movie. Nobody does business like that here.'

'You're right, Dawn, of course, but there are some very jittery men out there who are worried for their own futures, and I've no idea what they'll do if things don't go their way.'

With that he picked up a huge Stetson, placed it on his head and strode out of the pub.

Chapter Ten

When I arrived home that evening, Alec was already there, sitting on the sofa in my living room wearing only a pair of shorts. As I came through the door, he turned to look at me. The muscles on his torso rippled.

I bit my lip to remind myself that I had decided to resist temptation. It was time we moved on, but I had no idea how that was going to work, what with everything going on with Maga Power Holdings.

Myrddin was sitting quietly by his feet on the rug. He stirred enough to acknowledge my presence, but no more. Alec had obviously fed him and there was, therefore, no reason for him to go out of his way to greet me further, the mercenary little monster.

I dropped my bag on the floor and flopped onto the chair opposite them. I was exhausted, both physically and emotionally. Alec picked up the open wine bottle in front of him and poured a huge quantity into an empty glass nearby, and gave it to me.

I nodded my appreciation and drank deeply from the glass. He topped it up and then went back to the sofa.

'I've ordered Chinese,' he said. 'It should be here soon.'

I smiled.

'Thank you, that's very thoughtful.' The cat was now looking directly at me. Either he'd heard talk of more food or he was about to make a bid for my lap. It turned out to be both.

'Do you think you could put some clothes on?' I asked, stroking the cat to settle him down. 'I'm sure the delivery boy won't want to see you in your pants.'

He didn't argue, just stood up, left the room and re-emerged a few minutes later wearing a baggy T-shirt. I wanted to send him back for some trousers but decided I couldn't be bothered. It was better than nothing.

The door-bell rang. Alec went to answer it. He emerged a few minutes later having emptied the takeaway cartons on to plates and handed me one, along with a fork.

'Would you prefer chopsticks?' he asked slyly. He knew that I couldn't handle them.

'No thank you,' I said, pushing the cat off my lap. Myrddin got a piece of chicken as compensation for the inconvenience - he gulped it down and started to agitate for more. I ignored him and started to eat my food.

'Tell me,' Alec asked between mouthfuls, 'why has my stuff been moved into the spare room?'

'I felt like we should have a bit of a break,' I said matter-of-factly. 'Obviously, our business arrangements will carry on as before, but I want to have some space.'

He shrugged, playing it cool. What did it matter to him? He liked the sex of course, as did I, but Alec knew where he stood with me, even if the no-sex rule was going to be inconvenient.

'You got somebody else then?'

I ignored his question and carried on eating. When I'd finished, I put my plate on the floor, inviting the cat to pick off any remains.

He tried again.

'So, what's brought about this change of heart? Who else are you fucking?'

His voice was calm, but his tone took me a bit by surprise. I had never put him down as the jealous type.

'I told you I needed a break. I can't cope with you treating me like your cheap whore all the time, coming here whenever you like, eating my food, using the place like a hotel. Did you never think that I might want more?'

I didn't actually feel all that strongly about these things, but I was tired, stressed out with the Maga business and needed to vent. Besides, my feelings towards Jenny had made me reassess this whole fuck-buddy arrangement with Alec.

Now it was his turn to look surprised. He turned up the volume a notch.

'Where the fuck is this coming from? I thought we were both happy with the arrangements? What do you want, a fucking ring on your finger?'

'Ooh, you old romantic,' I mocked, refusing to be drawn too deeply into an argument about our relationship, when I had other matters I wanted to discuss with him. I regretted the sarcasm instantly and took a more conciliatory approach.

'Seriously, Alec, this is not a bid for a church wedding, it isn't even a statement about you. The sex is good, but we are never going to move beyond that as a couple, it isn't something either of us want, nor are we suited to that sort of relationship. I just want to see what else is out there.'

He looked a bit hurt at this statement, maybe he had some feelings for me after-all, maybe he did want more. However, we both knew that he wasn't in a position to act on it. His job was too transitory.

He shrugged again.

'If that's what you want, we'll give it a go for a bit, two can play at that game.'

'Go for it,' I said, 'just don't bring anybody back here.' He grimaced.

'You've got no need to worry on that score, Dawn.'

'Right, I've got a question for you,' I said, changing the subject. 'What the fuck are you and your, mobster friends up to trying to intimidate Sheckler into dropping his opposition to the power plant?'

He looked blankly at me as if he didn't know what I was talking about.

'Don't give me that butter-wouldn't-melt-look, you bastard. Sending threatening letters, even to fucked-up-tossers like Morgan Sheckler is not big and it's not clever, especially when it draws in my department and my staff.'

'I really don't know what you are talking about,' he protested.

'Really? Well somebody has decided that they want to put the wind up our beloved regional mayor and has started an intimidation campaign.' I was now more furious at his denial than the acts themselves.

'Is that the real reason you've moved my stuff into the spare room? Because you're pissed at me for something, I know nothing about?' There was clear anger in his voice.

Typical. Suddenly it was all my fault. I felt like picking up the plate from the floor and launching it at his head. I decided to ignore the attempt at deflection and go back on the offensive.

'Weren't you listening just now? I *am* capable of separating my personal life from my job you know, so don't change the subject. Are you saying that you know nothing about the threatening letters that Sheckler's been getting recently?'

'How could I? You know what the great unwashed are like. Do you read social media? The world is full of keyboard warriors just itching to have a go from the safety of their bedroom, issuing threats to anybody and everybody, all while surrounded by dirty underwear, smelly socks and skid-marked bed sheets that haven't been changed for six months.

'So why focus this on me? Sure, I want the crazy bastard out of office but I'm a legitimate businessman. I don't get involved in that stuff.'

I sat open-mouthed at the audacity of this rant, not least the use of the term 'legitimate businessman'. Just getting my head around the contradictions between what I knew of Alec and what he now claimed, somehow calmed me down.

'I don't recall mentioning threats on social media,' I said quietly. 'I just told you about the letters.'

He laughed.

'Now you're just playing games.'

'Very well, I can see that you're not going to play ball, so let me put it like this. The great unwashed as you describe them have no reason to take your side on this power plant. They're standing against you.

'This campaign of hate and intimidation has come from those supporting the plant, and that means you and your pals.'

'Dawn…,' he was reaching for something to say

'No, don't speak. Let me finish. There's something else. Some of your business chums have been leaning on Sheckler's funders and supporters, to try and get him to back off. I had lunch with Jack Chaffont today. He's been told that his business interests in America will be threatened if the regional mayor goes ahead and stops this plant.

'Now Jack's a sensible man. He knows what's important in this world, and it sure as hell aint Morgan Sheckler. He's switched to your side. The problem is that Sheckler won't listen to him. So, are you going to tell me what's going on or not?'

Alec raised his palms skywards, as if in surrender.

'Okay, I'll do my best. But you've got to believe me, these threatening letters and stuff have nothing to do with me.'

He looked resigned, almost panicked. Alec didn't like people to know more than they needed. That was how he exercised power and influence, by playing one person off against another, allowing his colleagues and adversaries only enough knowledge to fulfil the role he had designated for them.

Now he was being forced to break that rule and take me into his confidence. I didn't expect to get the full story, only enough to satisfy me for now. I might have to push him further at some time in the future to discover more.

What I didn't count on was that having opened the door to this world's murky interior, I could be sucked in further until it consumed me altogether.

'You're right,' he said finally. 'Pressure is being applied where it can. Business contacts are being exploited to try and get your fucking regional mayor to back down. However, he's stubborn. He believes that he speaks for the people, that he has some divine duty to stop progress. Well, our sort of progress anyway.

'So, it's possible that some of our associates may have gone the extra mile and started to apply personal pressure. You know, threats and that. It isn't something I've been consulted about. I've been too busy talking to the likes of Jack Chaffont, if you know what I mean.'

'But why? He's just one person. Sheckler can't stop this plant. It's out of his hands now. And yet everybody is running around like headless chickens?'

'You've said it yourself, Dawn. He has influence. He has the public behind him and those making the next set of decisions are jittery. Even the UK Government is worried. They don't want to appear weak to their new Chinese friends and all that money they want to invest in UK PLC.

'The people I work for don't like to take chances. When the sums of money at stake are this big, they want certainty and they aint going to take no shit from no-one. But there's more...'

He hesitated, giving me a moment to take in what he was going to say. So far it seemed that it was just a bunch of hoodlums throwing a tantrum until they got their own way, was he going to change that perspective?

'You'll recall that we bent a few rules to get to this position.'

I nodded. He wasn't worried about what Sheckler could do to sabotage the planning process, he believed that our beloved regional mayor might be able to unravel the process from the inside.

'What if he starts digging in the files, finds out what we did? What *you* did? How well did you cover your tracks, Dawn?'

I felt my stomach muscles tighten and some shortness of breath. I didn't know the answer to that question. After all, I'd acted when Byron was mayor, and although he had no idea exactly what I was doing, I knew I had his tacit approval in getting the project off the ground with the right developers.

Well, I'd assumed he approved. He had certainly encouraged me to deliver the plant in a specific way. This had been his baby. Pat Marshall had gone to him with the idea and although the rules meant that we needed to put the land out to tender, it was clear that it would only go ahead if Marshall's company won that competition.

'I did my best, Alec, but I don't know if it will stand up to proper scrutiny.'

'Well then, now you know why we have to put in place other measures.'

'But threatening people, with this sort of abuse? Seriously? It isn't good and it certainly not clever. It's that sort of behaviour that puts people off from going into politics. What's worse is that there are individuals who see these things and take them seriously.

'MPs have been murdered in recent times by nutters who have read this sort of abuse and thought they should act on it. Other politicians have been assaulted and seriously hurt. I don't want anything to do with this sort of behaviour and neither should you.'

Alec looked chastened, but he was still not admitting any involvement in the trolling of Morgan Sheckler.

'I promise you, Dawn I had nothing to do with this campaign, I knew nothing about it, and I don't condone it.'

'Well, I've no doubt that it's down to some of your cronies, so if you could tell them to stop it would be appreciated.'

My plea was met with silence. I decided to take that as consent. I picked up the plates and took them into the kitchen. Myrddin dragged himself to his feet and followed me in hope of more food. I found a piece of ham in the fridge and fed it to him.

As I rinsed out the plates, I was aware that Alec was standing behind me. He placed his hands on my shoulders and kissed the nape of my neck. I turned around and allowed him to kiss me on the lips before pulling away.

'You're still in the spare room,' I said. He bowed his head and attempted some sort of lost puppy expression.

'Don't bother, it doesn't suit you.' I told him. 'And don't expect me to believe that you're completely innocent of the hate mail incidents either.'

He shook his head and gave me a muted look of astonishment, turned and went back into the living room. I followed him.

'I'm not having this discussion again,' he said. 'I've given you my assurances. If you don't believe me then that is your business.'

'Fair enough. Perhaps you can tell me what you've been up to then during this latest absence, apart from meeting Jack Chaffont that is?' He gestured towards the chair.

I sat down and poured myself another glass of wine. He followed suit. I sensed a reluctance to keep me in the loop. He looked uneasy at sharing any information. Perhaps he thought that he couldn't trust me. Maybe he was just pissed at being relegated to the spare room.

I wondered whether I should make an exception just this once and invite him back to my bed. After all, once more wouldn't hurt. That kiss had been sensational, and God he was fit. But then I thought about Jenny. I needed to move on and commit to her. I couldn't do that while I was fucking Alec at the same time, no matter how meaningless the act.

'I've been meeting a number of local businessmen,' he said. 'Trying to get them to put pressure on Sheckler to back the power plant. Some have been amenable, others not so much.

'There are a lot of lucrative contracts associated with this project, plenty to negotiate with, apply pressure with. Most of them saw sense. I think the few who refused to play ball are too closely tied into contracts with the regional mayor's office. We'll pick them off in time.'

'And yet Sheckler still resists. You must be losing your touch, Alec.'

'I told you, the mad bastard is obsessed. He's high on the buzz of an adoring public. It seems that no matter how many planks we pull from beneath him he carries on regardless. My associates need some certainty, and yet I still can't offer it to them.'

'Maybe you're placing too much store on turning him. There are other routes to getting this power plant built. You don't need him on-board, you have the land, the planning process is out of his hands, you'll get what you want.'

'We've had this conversation. You made it very clear that his influence could distort that process. We can't take that risk.'

I was getting bored with this conversation. Morgan Sheckler and the consequences of his election were starting to dominate my life, my relationships and my future. Maybe I'd shag Alec anyway, just for old times' sake, just to change the subject.

I stood up and walked to the sofa, leant over and kissed him. His hands came to rest on my arse as we embraced, me standing over him. And then I changed my mind again and pulled back. He looked up at me, puzzled.

'For fuck's sake woman, make up your mind.'

'Get your gear back on,' I said. 'I fancy a ride into the country to clear my head.'

He smiled and followed me upstairs. I went into my bedroom and allowed him to watch as I stripped down to my underwear and pulled on my own black leather one-piece outfit. I reached into the wardrobe, grabbed my helmet and then turned towards him expectantly. He took the hint.

A few minutes later he had emerged from the spare room dressed similarly. We were two black knights, ready to assume our rightful place on the road.

He wheeled his bike out from the back yard. I put my helmet on and I climbed on behind him, wrapping my arms around his waist. He revved the engine and then sped off up the street, heading north to Caerphilly Mountain.

As we left the outskirts of Cardiff, Alec opened-up the throttle and eased the bike through the narrow lanes. We climbed up towards the summit, nearly 900 feet above sea level, guided only by the headlight on his machine.

As we pulled up alongside the triangulation point, we could see the lights of the City below. We dismounted, removed our helmets and took in the scene. I put my arm around his waist and looked up at him.

'I need to move on, Alec. You understand that, don't you? This has been good, but it can't last. We can stay friends and you can stay over when you're in Cardiff, but I need some stability in my life and I'm not getting it through this arrangement.'

'I thought we were good together.'

'Don't get me wrong. The sex has been great, but this isn't some great love affair, it's a series of booty calls. You know that. We've never been exclusive nor does either of us want that.'

He kissed me on the forehead and then turned away to look at the scene below us. I waited for him to say something. He didn't appear to be in any hurry. Instead, he took my hand and stood there silently for what seemed like an eternity.

Below us I imagined that people were rushing around, heading out for the night after a long day's work, ready for the weekend. The streets of Cardiff would be buzzing by now with revellers letting down their hair, enjoying each other's company, maybe even eyeing up others for sex.

Despite myself I was enjoying his company. We didn't

need to speak to understand each other. In other circumstances, I would take it as a sign that we were made for each other. But it was familiarity and friendship, with a large dollop of intimacy. It wasn't love.

Eventually, he turned to me.

'Let's go back to your place,' he said, smirking. 'I'm looking forward to the spare room, without you pestering me for sex.'

I thumped him hard on the arm.

'You're such a fucking bastard,' I said, smiling. 'Just make sure you behave yourself tonight. No sneaking around and disturbing the cat.'

Chapter Eleven

I usually like to take it easy on a Saturday but there are occasions when that isn't possible. The day after my trip up to Caerphilly Mountain with Alec was one such time.

A rally against the power plant was planned to take place in Alexandra Gardens at the rear of City Hall. It was to be addressed by Sheckler and several local Assembly Members.

Momentum is important in any political campaign, especially if it keeps pressure on the decision makers. Sheckler and his campaign committee had decided that they needed to show ministers the strength of feeling around this issue.

I felt it was important to show my face, not because I wanted to be part of the demonstration but to keep an eye on the opposition. Alec already knew about it and had planned to be there for the same reason. It was a sunny day, so we walked into town together.

We headed through Gorsedd Gardens, past the circle of standing stones placed there some time after the 1899 National Eisteddfod, brightly-coloured flower beds, and a small kiosk serving coffee, and onto the tree-lined Museum Avenue.

We could hear the collective chatter of voices up ahead, but the chaotic scene that greeted us still took us by surprise. There were banners and placards, children dancing around their parents, hardened political activists selling left-wing newspapers, and a couple of TV news cameras.

It was more of a carnival than a political event. There was a band, and people serving cold drinks and snacks. I saw a couple of families having a picnic and there was even a tombola stall and a man lining up children to 'hit the rat' at the end of a piece of pipe.

As we walked amongst the crowd, I heard my name being

called out. It was Maria, arm-in-arm with Gwilym. They seemed pleased to see me. I reluctantly introduced them to Alec.

'Isn't this great,' Maria enthused. 'The Welsh Government have got to listen to us now.' I nodded. Alec looked on passively.

'It's really great to see you both again,' I lied. 'I think that Morgan is on his way to the lectern. You'd better make sure you get a good place at the front.'

They thanked me for the tip, shook both our hands and headed off towards the centre of the park.

I looked around, the anger and passion of previous meetings was missing, the sun had brought out the best in everybody. At least I hoped so. I couldn't take any more chanting, shouting or screaming. The crowd had their man in a position of power and influence. They believed they were winning and that was enough to transform the mood.

A lectern and microphone had been set up on a raised platform in front of the war memorial pillars at the centre of the park. Loudspeakers were dotted around the outer edges of the crowd. Sheckler was not going to settle for crackly half-understood messages shouted through a megaphone, he was using all the resources of his office to produce a professional-looking public meeting.

He was about to bask in the worship of his adoring fans and was determined that it would look and sound good on television and the local media. No doubt the other politicians joining him would benefit from the arrangements as well.

Alec and I lingered at the edge of the crowd, partially obscured by some bushes, though not intentionally. There was still fifteen minutes before proceedings were due to commence and already there were about five hundred people there, and more were arriving every minute.

There were some police officers present too, standing discreetly at the edge of proceedings. I doubted if they were expecting any trouble, but Sheckler had been threatened, so they couldn't take any chances. He certainly hadn't.

When he appeared, he was flanked by two burly bodyguards. Two Welsh Assembly Members, an MP and a couple of councillors trailed in his wake, anxious to benefit from the fruits of his victory.

Suddenly, I realised that they were heading straight for us. I looked around for an escape route. Alec was oblivious to the danger, I was too late, Sheckler had seen me. He strode over smiling, bodyguards trailing a few feet behind anxiously surveying the crowd.

'Dawn, I'm so glad you came. It's good to know that I have the support of my senior staff.'

The words shook Alec from his trance, he seemed only now to become aware he was face-to-face with his nemesis. He took my hand, more by way of reflex than anything else, it was a big mistake.

'Is this your boyfriend?' Sheckler crowed, stretching out his arm. Alec reluctantly shook the outstretched hand and grimaced. I could see that this was not a situation he was happy about.

'Oh, this is Alec Croxley, one of my oldest friends,' I lied. 'He's staying with me for a few days. We thought we'd take in the rally before heading off into town to do some shopping.'

'I'm delighted to meet you,' Sheckler said, with all the sincerity of Sylvester reassuring Tweety Pie that he was not about to devour her. 'It's a good turnout, don't you think Dawn? Hopefully, the powers-that-be in the Welsh Government will take note of the strength of feeling.'

I muttered something about how well organised the rally seemed to be. He took this as his cue to introduce me to the other politicians in his entourage. The MP and one of the Assembly Members I knew already through my mother. Just wait until she hears how her political allies were lining up against Byron's pet project.

We listened intently as one of the Assembly Members explained how ministers were starting to listen to opponents of the power plant. I could see that Alec was worried. Perhaps he didn't understand that under planning rules ministers would not be able to give any comfort to either side of the argument. This politician was deluding himself if he thought that he had been made privy to inside information.

The two councillors were also familiar to me. I'd come across them as part of my work in East Gwent. Both were longstanding allies of Sheckler – 'The Usual Suspects' as we came to know them. They, too, were captivated by the aura of invincibility that he had erected around his mayoralty.

I had never ceased to be astonished by how politicians always rally to popular causes like bees to a honey pot, only to move onto another topic when the public grow tired of the first. Their appetite for media exposure never receded, their need for the adoration of voters never wavered.

Alec pulled gently on my hand. He wanted to escape this torture as soon as possible. I squeezed his fingers in acknowledgement, but we needn't have worried, Sheckler's public were calling, and he was keen to move on.

'I have to address the crowd. Have a good weekend, I will see you on Monday. It's nice to meet you, Alec. You look after her now.' There was no fooling Morgan Sheckler. And with that he led his group towards the microphone.

As the rally got underway, I watched the reactions of those around us - Sheckler was first on the stage and the reception he got was prolonged and rapturous. He knew how to play a crowd, starting off with a denunciation of Byron and his policy of encouraging the building of a power plant in the first place.

By the time he had got onto all the arguments against the power plant I'd started to lose interest. I'd heard it all before. Alec, though, was transfixed. This was his first time to see Sheckler in action. I could see that he was mentally making notes. After a while he turned towards me looking appalled.

'It's almost messianic,' he said. 'The man is dangerous.'

I agreed with him and turned back just in time to catch the tub-thumping denouement. Was Sheckler really going to lead large numbers of protestors down to Cardiff Bay and storm the Welsh Assembly building? Some in the crowd thought he might.

As the cheering subsided the other politicians took turns to address the crowd. Sheckler stood at the side cheering them on. Today he was a puppet-master pulling string after string to deliver a show that would please his audience.

Alec and I started walking towards an exit to the gardens, situated to the right of the platform. We'd had enough and had decided to go for a drink. Suddenly there was a loud, indecipherable shout and a man rushed from the crowd heading straight for Sheckler. He was clutching an object in front of him.

The man must have been in his mid-fifties, with short cropped brown hair. He was close enough for us to see that he was wearing blue jeans and a check shirt though we couldn't make out what he was now brandishing above his head. It looked like a small bottle of liquid.

He must have been in his mid-fifties, with short-cropped black hair. He passed close enough to us to see that he was wearing blue jeans and a check shirt. He had a distinctive scar on one of his cheeks.

The man continued to shout as he advanced. I could just discern some expletives but that was all. The Assembly Member had stopped speaking and was staring directly at him. Sheckler had instinctively tensed up, his eyes focussed closely on the advancing form.

Suddenly, the man launched the bottle at Sheckler. It shattered at his feet. The regional mayor jumped back as the liquid splashed around his feet. He rubbed at his hand, there was a small cut where a piece of glass had pierced the skin.

I looked around; the man had disappeared into the crowd

with Sheckler's bodyguards in hot pursuit. I turned my gaze back to the mayor. Sheckler had recovered his composure and had grabbed the microphone.

'We must not be intimidated into giving up our opposition to this plant,' he said to loud cheering and clapping. 'There is no place in our democracy for violence, intimidation and threats. We will win this debate on the arguments and by showing the powers-that-be that we have the will of the people behind us.

'We will face down the corrupt establishment who seek to ruin our way of life. We will fight to protect our environment, to preserve our communities, and to secure the future of our children. We will stand up to whatever they throw against us and WE WILL PREVAIL.'

He punched the air as he shouted the final three words and the crowd erupted into a frenzied rapture. They could not get enough of him as he stood at the podium with both arms raised. He had turned an unprovoked attack by an apparently deranged individual into an assault on democracy. It was a triumph.

The rally was over. There was no point in any of the other politicians speaking. He had outclassed them with his rhetorical improvisation and monopolised the media coverage with the attack and his response to it.

His rallying cry would be repeated on every news channel, appear in every newspaper, dominate social media, be repeated in every debate on the power plant for some time to come. Morgan Sheckler had gone viral and he could not be happier about it.

As the crowd dispersed, Alec and I slunk away with them. We went to a pub in town to review what we had witnessed over a glass of wine and a pint of beer. Alec sat there looking worried and depressed. I was struggling to focus. I needed to know more about the attacker, his motives and his intentions.

'Did you know who that man was?' I asked him, 'or why

he might want to attack Sheckler in that way?'

'For fuck's sake, Dawn, what do you think I am? Of course, I didn't know him. If you're accusing me of organising that attack or having anything to do with it, then I'd better go now.'

He started to stand. ready to leave. I grabbed his hand and pulled him back.

'I'm not accusing you of anything, Alec. I just needed to ask the question for my own peace of mind. I don't think for one moment that you were involved with that nutter, but I am not so sure about some of your associates. I just needed the reassurance.'

He settled back down and drank from his glass. He knew that I had to ask. He also knew what answer he had to give me

Deep down though I was certain that this attempt on Sheckler's life was not the work of Alec's mobster friends or their associates. It smelt too much of a lone wolf. It was too unsophisticated, too desperate.

'So, what just happened?' he asked.

'From what I saw, Sheckler used an attack on him to promote his campaign to stop the power plant and is going to get a lot of media coverage from it.'

'To be honest, I was more worried by what those Assembly Members had to say. If they're right, the Welsh Government is on the verge of caving in over the planning permission. That's not good. Pat and Don won't be amused at all.'

'Come on now, you can't take that seriously. That AM was a backbencher, he has no idea what the minister is going to do.'

'He's a member of the ruling group. I would be failing in my duty to my employers if I didn't take this intelligence seriously. In my view, Sheckler poses a real threat to the success of this project. I need to take advice on how we deal with that.'

There was no point arguing with him. Alec was utterly focussed on getting this plant built and nothing was going to distract him from his mission, even me, though that sort of distraction was no longer on my radar.

I was concerned that he was reading too much into what he had been told today. He was from the other side of Offa's Dyke, and unfamiliar with the way that Welsh Government worked. Some things should not be taken literally, and this was one of them.

'So, you're leaving again?' I asked.

'Yes. Pat and Don are in London. I need to brief them on developments. Besides, it isn't as if you're desperate for me to stay. I don't want to cramp your style.'

I stared at him but didn't comment.

'When are you planning on leaving?'

'I'll get a train later today. That way I can brief them in time for the catch-up meeting first thing Monday morning.'

I finished my glass of wine and started to get my stuff together, but he stopped me. Instead he went to the bar and bought some more drinks. We sat there is silence for a bit, not needing to say anything. I took his hand.

'We're still friends, aren't we?'

'Of course, we are,' he said softly. 'Why do you ask?'

'I just don't like the way this Sheckler business is going. I feel it's driven a wedge between us, that we're being pulled into something beyond our control.'

He started to protest his innocence once more. I stopped him.

'I know, I know, I did believe you when you said you hadn't made those threats. But this is not just about you. It's your mobster workmates. I need you to rise above that and show me you are the man I thought you were.'

'Look, Dawn, I've got a job to do. You have to take me as I am or not at all.'

It wasn't the answer I wanted but I had learnt by now not

to press him when he considered the conversation over, there was no point. We had thrashed it out and he had moved on. I wasn't ready to do the same, not yet.

I finished our drinks and headed back to my house, enjoying the sunshine as we walked. We barely spoke.

As we rounded the corner into my street, I saw Jenny walk out my front gate, get into her car and drive away. I didn't think she had seen me. I must have missed her by a few minutes. Why hadn't she phoned ahead. I checked my mobile. There was a missed call from her. I hadn't heard it due to the noise of the rally.

I suppose it was just as well she had not caught me in. I wasn't ready for her to meet Alec. I just couldn't have coped with the questions. Worse, I wouldn't have been able to handle the two of them playing the sympathetic partner, trying their best to avoid intruding on my privacy for fear of alienating me.

I watched Alec pack a few things into a bag and then dropped him off at the railway station. He was totally committed to this job. My concern was that he was pulling me deeper into whatever mire he was creating for us. I was caught between his mobster bosses and a power-mad populist who was intent on bringing everything tumbling down around him.

As I watched him disappear into the bowels of Cardiff Central railway station, I set my mind to a different objective. If I had plans before then they had now changed. I pointed my car at Lloyd George Avenue and drove. When I got to her block of flats, Jenny buzzed me in.

She met me at the door, wearing sweatpants and a tight cropped T-shirt that exposed her toned midriff and highlighted her nipples. She was barefoot, and her tousled hair was loose around her shoulders. She wasn't wearing make-up – there was no need, she sparkled. It was almost as if she had been expecting me.

'I thought I saw you earlier,' she said, leaning into me in

the close confines of the hallway, the warmth of her breath on my ear. 'I hoped you'd follow me down here once you had got rid of your guest.'

'How could I stay away?' I asked, pulling her closer.

Chapter Twelve

When I arrived at work on Monday morning, Tim was waiting for me, looking agitated. He followed me into my office and closed the door.

'I hear you were at the rally on Saturday,' he said. 'Did you see the lunatic who tried to attack the mayor?' I confirmed that I had. 'Good. I mean, are you okay?'

'Yes, I'm fine Tim. Shouldn't you be asking Sheckler that question?'

'Oh, I have. He's more than fine. In fact, I'd say he's energised by the whole thing. Curious really, not a natural reaction at all. I do wonder about him sometimes.'

He paused and stared into space as though expecting the answer to that conundrum would be presented right there in my office. Finally, he shook himself out of his reverie.

'Anyway, there are a couple of police officers here who would like to talk to you. They just want witness statements, that's all. Nothing to worry about.'

'Oh, right. Well I'm not sure what I can add to the no-doubt hundreds of witness statements they already have, but I'm happy to give it a go.'

Tim opened the door and pointed me in the direction of his office. The door was ajar. Inside, sitting on his sofa was Jenny and a male detective. She was wearing a white blouse with black trousers. I wanted to joke that I didn't recognise her with her clothes on, but I stopped myself in time. She grinned when I entered and then composed her face in a more business-like arrangement.

'Ms. Highcliffe,' she said. 'It is good of you to lend us some of your time. I'm Detective Inspector Jennifer Thorne, this is Detective Sergeant Darren Pyke.'

The burly, six-foot-two, detective with short blond hair and an ill-fitting brown suit stood up and shook my hand.

Jenny followed suit. I sat down on a chair in front of them while the sergeant took out a pad and pencil.

'I understand that you were at the rally on Saturday,' Jenny started, 'and that you were close enough to the mayor to see the attempted attack on him.' I confirmed that was the case.

'Could you please outline your version of events?'

I told her everything I could about the attack, including a vague description of the attacker. The sergeant wrote it down. Jenny asked me if I recognised the man from any previous events or whether I'd seen him in or around City Hall. I hadn't. She wrapped up the interview.

'Thank you, you've been very helpful Ms. Highcliffe. I wonder, could we arrange for you to come down to the station to give us a formal statement?'

I was more than happy to do this and went to get my jacket. They drove me to the police station in Cardiff Bay. As I entered the station, I saw Sheckler leaving. He had a determined look on his face. I presumed he was there to give a statement as well.

'Ah, Dawn,' he said, stopping me in my tracks. 'Thank you for helping the police with this inquiry. We can't let violence interfere with the democratic process. Can you let my office know when you get back to work please? I would like to talk to you and your team.'

I promised I would and was ushered into a small interview room. Jenny left me with a police officer, who typed up my version of events. I signed the paperwork and got up to leave. Jenny was waiting outside for me.

'I'll give you a lift back to City Hall,' she offered. Her car was parked inside the complex. As we drove onto Dumballs Road, I put my hand onto hers.

'Thank you for looking after me in there,' I said. She smiled.

'It's my job. Why didn't you mention you'd witnessed the attack on the mayor when we were together yesterday?'

'Because we were both off-duty.' I replied stroking her leg. 'And besides I had other things on my mind. Do we know what the attack was about?'

'Not really. We think we know who the assailant was but unfortunately, we haven't been able to catch up with him yet. The mayor recognised the man. We've talked to some of his neighbours. He was upset because Sheckler got his wife sacked when he was at East Gwent Council. Sadly, his wife killed herself not long afterwards.

'His friends tell us that the poor bloke's been going through hell ever since, had a breakdown, been in and out of care, even tried to top himself once. We think that when he saw the mayor on TV, talking about this power plant, something snapped, and he decided to exact revenge. If that bottle of caustic soda had hit its target it would have caused some real damage.

'When we catch up with him, I suspect that he'll be sectioned for his own safety. I doubt you'll need to give evidence in court.'

I was quite relieved at this news. Testifying before a judge and jury was not my idea of fun, especially if it drew me deeper into Sheckler's circle. Still, at least the incident had given me a few hours extra with Jenny, and an insight into her working persona.

She pulled up at the side of City Hall, out of sight of the CCTV and too many prying eyes, leaned over and kissed me. A frisson of excitement rushed through me at the illicit nature of our tryst. I caressed her breast as we kissed.

'Call by tonight,' she said. 'I'll be home from the gym after 8pm.'

'Perhaps I'll meet you in the gym,' I offered. 'It's been a while since I was last there.'

She kissed me again. I watched as she drove away and went back to the office. My secretary was alert to Sheckler's earlier instructions and let his office know that I'd returned. He wanted to talk to the whole department at 2pm.

I sat at my desk and tried to do some work. I was meant to be reviewing the consultants' report on wildlife and ecology at the power plant site, but I couldn't concentrate. It was fortunate that I had a couple of meetings later that morning which helped me re-focus.

At 2pm precisely, Sheckler breezed into the meeting room where my staff and I had gathered. He was followed by Tim Finch and Mike Kirk. Tim was carrying a bundle of documents which he placed on the table. They both looked ill-at-ease.

'Thank you for coming here this afternoon,' he started. 'When I took on this role, I made it quite clear that the policy of this office had changed. We are now opposed to this power plant and will do everything we can to stop it going ahead. I also asked for a detailed objection to the planning permission to be prepared. I am still waiting.'

There was silence. It was entirely inappropriate for the mayor to be addressing junior staff in this way. This was my responsibility. If he had complaints, he needed to bring them up directly with me.

But that was not it. He was deliberately seeking to undermine my authority with my staff, to pull me back in line. I was furious, but I suppressed my anger and put on a professional face to respond to his demands.

'The objection has not yet been drafted, Mister Mayor, because the consultation period has not yet started. The planning application is with the Welsh Government and needs additional information before they start the clock.'

'Perhaps you can give me an update on what additional information is still outstanding, Dawn.'

'Of course. I am currently reviewing the consultant's report on wildlife and ecology before it's sent onto the Welsh Government planning department. We are awaiting further reports on pollution control, community impact, drainage and flood risk, geoscience, fire safety, a transport plan and the impact on archaeology and cultural heritage. I think that I had already included that information in the report I handed to you shortly after you took office.

'The main outstanding report, however, is the environmental impact study. It will incorporate many of the reports I've just mentioned but will provide a wider analysis and perspective on the overall impact of the plant.

'Once the Welsh Government has all that information then they will launch a formal public consultation on the proposal and then assess whether it's acceptable or not.'

Sheckler sat in silence for a few minutes processing everything he had just been told. My staff looked on bemused, waiting for some profound pronouncement from this extraordinary political figure. I expected them to be disappointed.

'And it is the developer who is producing these reports?' he asked eventually.

'Yes,' I replied. 'They commission them, and we're acting as agents for the Welsh Government in assessing them and then forwarding them on.'

'Well I want you to stop doing that.'

At this point Mike Kirk intervened. As the regional mayor's legal advisor, he had a duty to tell him when he was on the point of compromising the interests of his office. I was pleased as it saved me taking all the flak.

'With all due respect, Mister Mayor, if Dawn and her colleagues were to stop processing these reports then your office could be referred to the Ombudsman. We might also be subject to legal action and claims for significant compensation.'

'Thank you, Mike, that is noted', said Sheckler, not looking at all thankful for the interruption. 'Very well then, we can't just stop work on this planning application, but we can go slow while we investigate other options.'

'There are timescales attached to these things as well, Mister Mayor,' Mike added.

'Yes, yes, I know. I have been a local councillor, I'm

aware of the constraints we're operating under. Dawn, I'm giving you a direct instruction to delay dealing with these consultant reports for as long as possible. In the meantime, I want you to work on a formal objection to the planning application.'

Once more I was being asked to do the impossible, or at least the very difficult. My staff looked perplexed. They could see the dilemma we faced even if Sheckler couldn't. I followed him back to his office so as to make my point.

'Mister Mayor, although I fully understand and accept that you have the right to ask us to do this, I would be failing in my duty if I did not state that any objection needs to take account of the information in these studies.'

'Fine, fine, but you're still going to get the studies, just hold off passing them onto the Government. That way we can have the best of both worlds.'

I decided that silence was my best policy. There was little point in arguing with him when he was in this mood. A go-slow was tantamount to breaking faith with the developer and putting us on the verge of maladministration or perhaps an appeal on the grounds of us sitting on the application for too long. We were leaving ourselves open to challenge. More pertinently it would not get his objection drafted any faster.

I was frustrated that Sheckler had not gone through proper channels and held this discussion with senior officers and me in the privacy of his office. He was grandstanding in front of junior staff for effect, presumably hoping that his hard line would leak.

Whatever his reasons, his actions were wholly inappropriate. I made a note that I needed to lodge a protest with Tim. As acting chief executive, he needed to rein in Sheckler.

But Sheckler needed this stance to show his supporters that he meant business. He needed to follow-up his successful rally and all the publicity it generated with another victory to maintain his momentum. I worried that he would formally go public with this decision and draw attention to our potentially illegal behaviour.

On the way back to my office, I called in to see Mike Kirk. He looked as concerned as I was.

'Mike, we can only make this work if he doesn't go public himself with it, leaks are deniable, a statement by Sheckler is not. Once he's announced a go-slow, we would be effectively inviting the developer and anybody else with an interest to come and get us through the courts.'

'Yes, I'm aware of that, Dawn. What do you want me to do?'

'Well, you're the monitoring officer. You need to rein him in. Talk to the media team, make sure that any statement he makes is vague enough to give us deniability.'

He looked stressed, almost resigned to losing his job over this, even though his post was meant to be protected. In practice, as we both knew, that protection was meaningless. We had both seen monitoring officers leave the employ of their respective authority for one reason or another despite having done their job and making a stand.

The idea that any employee was truly protected from the whims of their political masters was nonsense, just as the idea that whistle-blowers were protected by legislation was also proven to be a fallacy. All of this was so much smoke thrown up by politicians who often found a way around their own rules as soon as they were inconvenienced by an officer.

And in many ways, Sheckler was right. He had the mandate, we didn't. But that did not put him above the law. He had to work within the same constraints as everybody else. If he didn't do so then he would eventually lose.

In many ways, the idea of allowing him to overstretch himself appealed to me. There were some opponents you could just watch as they self-destructed. The only downside was the collateral damage, especially when one's own career could be part of the wreckage they left behind.

Mike let out a long sigh. He knew what had to be done.

'I'll talk to Pete McClintock in the media team. We'll try and put together a statement that protects the regional mayor's office and keeps Sheckler happy, too. This man is going to be the death of me.'

I strolled back to my own office, shutting the door behind me and fishing my phone out of my handbag. I needed to text Alec to let him know the latest developments. I kept it short and sweet:

Mayor has ordered us to withdraw all cooperation with development company and concentrate on objection. Could cause significant delay to project.

I waited for a reply. Even by Alec's standards it came quickly. My phone rang, it was him.

'What the fuck, Dawn. I leave you alone in Cardiff for a day and already the situation has escalated. Can't I trust you to do anything?' He was shouting. I was taken aback by his tone.

'Calm down, Alec. This is not the end of the world. You need to let the process work itself out. Whatever he does now will have no effect in the long run. Let him have his moment in the sun.'

'I won't calm down. Don't you tell me to calm down!' He was still shouting. 'This is the final straw, Dawn. The bastard is toast.'

It was as if I was listening to a different person. Was this the real Alec Croxley? Had he been putting on an act for me all the time? I wasn't going to take this from anybody.

'Listen Alec, I'm not going to talk to you when you're like this. Have you been drinking? Ring me when you're in a better mood.'

'Fuck you!' he said and hung up.

I was furious…with him, with the way he behaved, with the way I had reacted and with Sheckler for putting us in this position in the first place. I fumed for the rest of the afternoon. The staff gave me a wide berth.

I got out of there as soon as possible and headed straight

to the gym. I needed to let off steam. I needed to see Jenny.
I needed the reassurance of her touch, her love.

When I got there, she was on the exercise bike. I got onto
the one beside her and cycled myself into exhaustion,
pouring all my anger and frustration into my legs as I
pumped the pedals. When it felt as if I couldn't move my
legs anymore, I switched to the rowing machine and
searched for a second wind.

After a few minutes of that, I collapsed next to her,
covered in sweat and hair, trying to get my breath. She lay on
the floor nearby, her knees up above her waist, her arms
stretched out in a cruciform style, breathing deeply. I looked
across to her and she smiled. Neither of us could talk for
now. Eventually, she felt able to strike up a conversation.

'I'm glad you came,' she said. 'Did you have a tough day?
At one point, I thought you were going to break that bike. I
had difficulty keeping up with you.' I laughed.

'I hadn't realised it was a contest, or I would have tried
harder.'

'What do you mean? I'm a police officer, I can't let a pen
pusher show me up in the gym. Of course, it was a contest.'

We were both laughing now, even though it hurt. Jenny
pulled herself up into a sitting position and then struggled to
her feet. She held out her arms and pulled me up next to her.
The gym was starting to fill up with people seeking to work
off the tensions of the day. We left them to it and headed for
the showers.

The changing rooms were deserted for now, so we shared
a shower, soaping each other's naked bodies, kissing and
cuddling under the hot stream of water. Afterwards we
towelled each other off and headed down to the bay and
Jenny's flat. As a deferred pleasure, it ranked among one of
the best.

Chapter Thirteen

I still can't work out at what stage in this saga I became the go-to-person for everybody who held a grudge against Morgan Sheckler, or even how they knew to come to me. At first, I blamed my mother. That's a natural reaction to anything unpleasant in my life. But I quickly ruled that out.

Maybe I radiated dissent. Sheckler could see it, so why shouldn't others? Or perhaps I was just in the wrong place at the right time. Whatever the cause and wherever I went, I kept tripping over people who wanted things from him or who were opposed to his agenda. There was Alec and his mobster friends of course - my mother, Byron, Jack Chaffont, the man who had tried to kill him at the rally... and now Debbie Redmond.

Debbie and I had both worked for East Gwent Council. She was a clerk in committee services whose job was to prepare agendas for planning meetings. I knew her, but we were not close. We used to meet regularly to prepare reports for councillors and had even been out on the town together as part of a larger team event.

She was about ten years younger than me, attractive, happily married with a son and living in Chepstow. She and I had often crossed paths in the gym. Debbie was an exercise freak, spending hours each weekend in the gym or walking in the Brecon Beacons, north of Cardiff. She was the only woman I'd ever met with a well-defined six-pack.

She always had a smile and a cheerful greeting for her work colleagues, often skipping around the office like a rabbit on speed. She was good fun on work-dos as well - her strict diet of healthy foods never seemed to exclude spirits such as vodka and gin, and she would be the first on the dance floor.

So, it was a shock to see how quickly she changed in the

last year of my employment in East Gwent. Debbie became depressed and seemed to lose interest in her work, going through the motions rather than embracing it as she had previously. Her marriage suffered, too, and then suddenly she was gone, disappeared from the workplace altogether.

Nobody seemed to know what had happened, not even her close friend Maria Pathakis. I got the job with the mayor's office and moved on and didn't give her another thought until one day, shortly after the attempted attack on Sheckler at the rally, I received a phone call at work. It was Debbie.

She had been speaking to Maria and knew that I was fishing around for information on Sheckler. We arranged to meet for lunch the following day.

I recognised her straight away as I entered the small café just off Queen Street. She was already seated, her long curly black hair and distinctive nose were unmistakeable. She looked older than I remembered, her face drawn and pale.

She stood as I approached and embraced me. Her sparkling green eyes had somehow become duller. We ordered coffee and a salad each. Nobody was going to judge my food choices at this lunchtime meeting. Debbie seemed extraordinarily grateful to me for agreeing to meet her.

'It's so lovely to see you again after all this time,' she said, recapturing briefly some of her old exuberance. 'When Maria said she had met you and that you were working for Morgan Sheckler I felt I needed to get in touch again. I hope you don't mind but she also told me a little of your history with him.'

I did mind as it happened. I minded a lot having others talk about it, but I smiled and offered some encouraging words.

'It's good to see you, too, Debbie. It's been so long. I'm afraid I lost touch when you left East Gwent. It was so sudden. One minute you were there, the next you weren't.'

'I know. I'm sorry about that. I wish I could have said

goodbye to you all, but I wasn't very well and couldn't face up to it.'

'What happened?'

'To be honest, Dawn, I had a breakdown. I couldn't take it anymore and felt I had to quit if I was going to save my marriage and my sanity.'

I put my hand on hers to reassure her. I had no idea that she had suffered in that way. Perhaps I was too self-absorbed when I worked in East Gwent to notice these things. Maybe I should have taken more of an interest in my work colleagues at the time.

'Do you want to talk about it,' I asked, trying to make up for my previous failure.

'Yes, that's why I asked to meet you. You know, I don't like speaking ill about anybody and I'm sure Maria doesn't believe me, but I hope you will. It was hearing about your experience that helped me come to terms with what happened. Knowing I was not the only one was a great comfort, it reassured me that I was not imagining the whole thing.'

Now I was really interested. Was this poor woman another victim of Sheckler - how many more victims did he have? And were they all going to take it lying down? Would some of them try and follow the example of the man in Alexandra Gardens? It made me feel better that other people had been subject to his abuse. It wasn't just me.

'Tell me what happened,' I requested as gently as I could

'It started on a committee day. He had come down into the committee clerk's room to collect a spare agenda for one of his constituents. I was the only one there. It was hot, so I was wearing a T-shirt and a medium-length skirt. The agenda was on a shelf above me.

'I was naïve, I suppose. I didn't even think twice about turning my back on him and stretching to get it. I thought my skirt covered everything. In fact, I know it did. Anyway, the hemline rode up a bit, just above the back of my knee and suddenly, before I could react, he was standing behind me, feeling my arse. I jumped, almost losing my balance and before I knew it, he had his arms around me on the pretext of catching my fall.

'I pulled away from him, trying to smooth my skirt down as far as it would go to cover my legs. I was speechless, and yet he carried on walking towards me. I was backed up against a wall and tried to push him away again, but he was stronger than me and before I knew it, he was kissing me on the lips.

'Somehow, I got away and put a desk and chairs between us. I threatened to report him to my line manager, but he told me that if I breathed a word of what had happened, he'd get me sacked. And then he left.'

Debbie was almost in tears. I could see that this was a tremendous effort for her.

'Was it just that one time?' I asked.

'No, whenever he caught me on my own after that, he tried it on again and again. It got so that I was always looking over my shoulder to make sure he wasn't there. I used to check the corridor before leaving my office, and I made sure that somebody was with me whenever we were likely to come across him.

'I was withdrawn and depressed at home. I didn't feel able to talk about it to Jim, my husband, in case he went off the deep-end and confronted him, or worse. And my marriage suffered. In the end, I had to quit for my own sanity, but not before I'd had a breakdown and months off work.

'I managed to salvage my marriage after that and now I help Jim with his publishing business, but it still dwells on my mind. It's such a relief to be able to talk about it to you and to know that you believe me.'

I ordered more coffee and watched as she sipped from the fresh cup. Eventually, I felt able to ask her the obvious question.

'Why didn't you report him?'

'I was afraid,' she replied. 'I didn't think anybody would believe me and I was worried that he would get me sacked. Of course, if I'd known that he'd done this before, by harassing you, then that would have been different. But I had no way of knowing.

'And I was so young. I had no experience of this sort of thing. I didn't know how to react, so I let the worry, the anxiety, the hurt build-up inside me, until I thought I would burst.'

I didn't know what else to say nor did I know what she expected of me. Her story helped to fill in some details about my time at East Gwent and about Sheckler's character, but it told me nothing I didn't already know about our beloved mayor.

Nor could I use this against him. Debbie's mental health was clearly too fragile to endure making these allegations public or even going to the police and coping with an investigation. I doubted whether any reputable news outlet would use it. It was her word against Sheckler's and of course the fact that she had had a breakdown left her so vulnerable it would not be fair to even suggest it.

Even in these enlightened times, people suffering with their mental health are treated poorly and are often not taken seriously. It was an appalling situation but one that Sheckler would exploit to his advantage.

The Brett Kavanaugh hearing in the States, and the way Christine Blasey had been ridiculed, was a good illustration of what can happen to accusers when subjected to ridicule by larger-than-life public figures. Nobody would want to put Debbie through that sort of scrutiny in her present state of mind, if ever at all.

'I'm sorry you had to go through all that. What do you need me to do to help, Debbie?' I asked as sympathetically as possible. She took my hand.

'You've helped just by being here and listening to me. I

know that I can't go and make him pay for what he's done to me. I'm past all that. I wouldn't want to go through it all again anyway. I just needed to be believed. Thank you for that.

'Maria thinks that Sheckler is some sort of paragon, but he's a monster. As good a friend as she is, I don't think she ever really believed me. It feels good to be taken seriously. Knowing that you know, is enough. Knowing that you have suffered something similar helps, somehow.'

She rose to go. She'd said her piece and in part exorcised a ghost. We hugged once more. I paid the bill and started walking back to City Hall. I was in no hurry. As I reached the Gorsedd Gardens, I sat down on one of the benches and reflected on what I'd been told.

It was a relief to me, too, to know that I wasn't the only victim of Sheckler's predatory behaviour. I'd suspected as much, of course, but it was good to have it confirmed. That poor woman had gone through so much and none of us were there to assist her. She was right, Sheckler was a monster and somehow, I needed to bring him down.

I drifted past the fountains and onto the car park, still thinking about Debbie's words as I passed underneath the portico, and up the steps into the impressive stone and marble reception area of City Hall. I ascended the main staircase and followed the corridor to my office. When I got there my PA immediately redirected me to see Tim Finch.

Tim was in a tizzy, there was no other word for it. Every time he reacted like this, I felt like slapping him and telling him to get some perspective. The urge was especially strong after hearing Debbie's story over lunch. He called me into his office and shut the door behind us.

'The man's lost his marbles,' he said eventually. 'He's suspended Mike Kirk and Howard Davies.'

Howard Davies was Director of Economy and Trade. He'd been responsible along with Byron and me for bringing the power plant project to South Wales in the first place. He was another one of Byron's drinking buddies and a key power behind the throne. In many ways, I was surprised Sheckler had taken so long to get rid of him.

Suspending both the monitoring officer and Director of Economy on the same day seemed excessive even by Sheckler's standards. If his actions backfired, then they could derail his whole agenda.

I gave Tim one of my best incredulous stares. The news had obviously come as a shock to him, a sign perhaps that although he was acting chief executive, he was not running the show in anyway whatsoever. I'd reached the stage where nothing surprised me about Sheckler anymore.

'Did he say why?' I asked innocently. Tim didn't pick up on the sarcasm.

'Not really. He had one of his fits and started blaming everybody and anybody he could for the fact that he hasn't been able to stop the power plant yet. He wanted to know the history of how plans for the plant had emerged in the first place, so I called Howard and Mike into the office to brief him.

'The next thing I knew he was telling them that they had acted inappropriately in their advice to Byron, that Mike was trying to stop him telling the press about his instructions to suspend work on the plant and that they were secretly working against his agenda. He gave them ten minutes to pack their personal belongings and leave the building.'

'But you're a HR specialist Tim, didn't you advise him that he was out of order? Doesn't he know that he's going to incur massive legal and compensation costs? And what's the situation regarding the dismissal of a monitoring officer anyway? Won't the Welsh Government intervene?'

Tim looked confused. He was clearly out of his depth in dealing with Sheckler. There was no way he could stand up to him, nor did he have any answers to my questions.

'I really don't know what to say, Dawn. I've got a family and a mortgage. I can't afford to lose this job, not now.'

I felt like telling him to grow a pair. He would walk into another job if he left here under his own steam. If he stayed though he would be tainted by the regional mayor's record, he would forever be the man who stood by while Morgan Sheckler wreaked havoc in City Hall.

And what about my own career, could I afford to hang around much longer. Unfortunately, I had no choice. My agreement with Alec, together with the stuff his colleagues had on my family and me, meant I had to see the power plant through to whatever conclusion it reached. And I wasn't prepared to allow that bastard to win just yet.

'I think we need to do what is in the best interests of the region,' I told him. 'You and I both know that that's to build this power plant. It will create employment and it will attract other jobs. We can't let the personal vendettas of Morgan Sheckler undermine that.'

'It's all very well you saying that Dawn, but he is the elected official, not us. He has a mandate. It isn't our place to frustrate his wishes.'

Again, I bit my tongue. I wanted to tell him that for a long time it had been the traditional role of civil servants to frustrate the wishes of their elected masters in the best interests of the country, that we needed to give strong and incontrovertible advice that could not be ignored, but Sheckler was a law unto himself.

When I got back to my office, I rang Mike. He was furious. I rather feared that he might blame me for insisting that he provide legal guidance to the media department, but he was more focussed on taking Sheckler to the cleaners for unfair dismissal.

He was also planning on involving the Welsh Government, getting them to issue stronger guidance on how monitoring officers should be treated. He had already sent an e-mail to one of his Assembly Members and was awaiting a response. I checked that he had not contacted one of Sheckler's Assembly allies in error. He hadn't, he had more sense.

None of this was going to make any difference in the short term of course. Sheckler was going to continue acting like a dictator, and would use the resources available to his office to fight any lawsuits.

I debated whether I should ring Howard as well but decided against it. I'd never been close to him. He was a good friend of my mother so no doubt he was already bringing her up to speed. I wondered whether she would ring me or if I would get another text summons.

I was past caring. I was heartily sick of being caught up in the middle of these machinations. If I could have walked away, I would have, but I was being pulled in all directions, by Sheckler, my mother, by Alec and by the fact that my future was so tied up with the power plant.

I struggled through the rest of the day's meetings on automatic mode. I didn't know what I should do next. Should I contact Alec again and add to his foul mood? Could I take another abusive conversation?

There was no excuse for Alec's behaviour. His lack of patience and that of his mob friends was putting this whole venture in jeopardy. The process was in train, it would work its way to a conclusion. If they just let it be then they would succeed regardless of anything Sheckler could do, at least that was my reasoning.

As I prepared to leave for the day, Sheckler appeared at my office door, looking pleased with himself. He believed that his little coup de-grace had made him stronger, that it had purged the rot from his little empire.

'Dawn, I'm glad I've caught you. I take it that you've been told I've had to suspend Mike Kirk and Howard Davies. I can't have members of my staff working against me and my mandate to stop this power plant.

'I've asked the deputies to step up and do their jobs for the time being, but this places a greater burden on you and your department to deliver for me.'

He paused to check that I'd understood the full importance of what he was asking me to do. His eyes were focussed intently on mine. They flashed with his obsession, his mission. His voice softened.

'I've known you a long time, Dawn. We've had our differences, but I know that you're a professional and that I can trust you to do the job you've been given. I'm relying on you. Please, don't let me down.'

I was taken aback by his audacity. And yet I could see that him reaching out to me in this way was a sign of weakness. He was feeling alone and unloved within his own citadel. He was a general without an army, with only the baying of the crowd for sustenance and comfort.

I gave him the answer he wanted. I couldn't do anything else. But in my heart, I knew that there was still hope and that he was not invincible after all. He left satisfied, content that he was still on track to stop the power plant.

I didn't have the energy to go to the gym, or to seek out Jenny. She was on duty until ten in any case. I was emotionally exhausted by the day's events and needed to sleep, perhaps curl up with the cat and reflect on the events of the day.

Debbie Redmond's story had got to me. It had made me more determined to succeed in frustrating Sheckler and his plans. His past was starting to be revealed, and yet I still didn't have the smoking gun I needed to protect my own position.

I opened the door and the cat came out to meet me. I put some food down for him and went upstairs to change into something more comfortable. As I reached the stairs, the front door opened. It was Alec, and he looked angry.

Chapter Fourteen

Things had not gone well in London. Alec's mobster friends were getting impatient and had wanted to know what he was doing to stop Sheckler frustrating their power plant project.

In the USA these decisions may well be taken by the mayor, and that had contributed to their confusion. Somehow, they had not been able to come to terms with our system of government.

Here, it is the Welsh Government who make planning decisions on major energy projects, but Alec didn't have the depth of knowledge to correct their misapprehension. Like them he thought things were going to hell in a handcart and he was taking it out on me.

I glared at him as he came through the door. His behaviour on the phone had been unacceptable and I wanted him to know it. He didn't look very repentant, so I carried on up the stairs and started to get changed.

I'd stripped down to my knickers and was hunting out some sweat pants and a baggy top, when I became aware that he was standing at the door watching me. Instinctively, I covered myself up.

'What do you want?' I snapped. 'Can't you see I'm changing. You no longer have the right to come into my bedroom whenever you feel like it.'

'I just wanted to apologise for my behaviour the other day. You caught me at a bad time and I shouldn't have taken it out on you.'

Alec never apologised for anything. He wanted something off me, I could sense it. I walked over and without saying a word, closed the door on him. I pulled on some clothes and headed back downstairs. He was still standing in the hallway.

'You could have brought some flowers,' I said as I walked past him. He followed me into the kitchen and poured two glasses of red wine, trying to use my booze to placate me.

We sat in the living room, me on the armchair, he on the couch. Myrddin jumped onto my lap and made himself comfortable.

'What is it you want from me?' I asked. I was scratching the cat's ears in the hope of appearing nonchalant. His apology had made me even more angry. It wasn't just what he had said to me, but the way he had said it. It was as if he had been talking to a stranger, not somebody whose bed he had shared for nearly a year.

'I'd like you to accept my apology,' he replied softly. 'I was out of order.'

'Yes, well you had no right to go all Jekyll and Hyde on me. I've put my job on the line in the last few weeks for you and your fucking power plant. I've walked a tightrope at work, watched valued colleagues effectively lose their jobs, had to put up with Mayor Gropey and been humiliated in front of my own staff, just so that you can get your way. I've had it with this whole affair.'

'He made a pass at you?' he asked incredulously, ignoring the rest of my rant.

'Fucking, sexually harassed me more like, but yes, he made a pass at me. I'm irresistible. Didn't you know?'

He laughed, a deep infectious laugh that didn't seem to end. I threw a cushion at him, but it just made him laugh more. Despite myself, I was laughing now, too. The cat must have decided that we had lost our minds. He scuttled upstairs looking for a safer harbour.

'That is one seriously desperate man,' Alec said eventually.

'Oi, don't push your luck,' I warned him. 'It turns out he's a serial abuser. There've been other women who have suffered at his hands. I met one only this lunchtime.'

He perked up at this until I explained why we would not be able to use it against him. Debbie was not going to lodge a complaint, she was too fragile for that. And I certainly wasn't going to go to an industrial tribunal the way things currently were.

'You didn't tell me you had a history with him.' Alec's attempt at finding out more was as subtle as his phone manner.

'I still haven't told you any such thing,' I retorted sharply and then relaxed a bit. 'It was over fifteen years ago. No big deal. Though, obviously, I made a bigger impression on him than I thought.'

He smirked. I thought that he was enjoying this rather too much. Nevertheless, I hadn't given him chapter and verse on my extensive sexual history before and I wasn't going to start now.

'I don't know why you think this is funny. The sort of predatory behaviour practised by Mayor fucking Harasser is unacceptable in any context. Using a position of power to abuse a colleague is a sackable offence. This man has seriously blighted the life of at least one young woman.'

Alec looked slightly shame-faced and apologised, with a bit more sincerity.

'I'm sorry, I was laughing at your reaction rather than the actions of that creep.' With that behind us I returned to my original gripe.

'Oh, and you're still in the dog house for that phone call. A little distraction like this isn't going to get you off the hook.' He gave a weary nod of the head.

'I know, I've apologised. I don't really know what else to do. But I'm here on business as well. I need you to get dressed again. I want you to come and meet with Don Watkins and some of his colleagues. I need you to brief them properly. Understanding obscure Welsh planning processes is not my forte. If there really is nothing to worry about then you need to explain that to them.'

Now I really was pissed. Dealing with Alec was one thing, but doing his job for him was above and beyond the call of duty.

'This isn't my problem, Alec. It's yours. I've done everything you've asked of me. I've put my career on the line to get this power plant underway. I'm fighting to keep it alive, but that's as far as I go. You're not dragging me into your murky world of organised crime.'

'As ever you exaggerate, Dawn. These are business people. You've met Don before, so why not now?'

'Because, this counts as an extra-curricular activity, something I've never signed up to.'

'I think we've moved beyond that point, Dawn. What you signed up to is in the past. We're not where we started. Byron Harris has gone, and he's been replaced by somebody who's determined to sabotage everything we've worked for. New circumstances demand a new approach.'

'And that's what I'm worried about, Alec. This isn't America, things move at a more leisurely pace here. Those ruthless bastards you work for need to understand that, they must acquire some patience.' He leaned forward, suddenly more insistent.

'And that's why you need to come with me to talk to them. Listen, Dawn, I need this. I feel as if I'm losing them. I need to reassure them, I need *you* to reassure them.'

He was very persistent. I could feel myself weakening. It was true, I'd met Watkins on many occasions... maybe if I calmed him down a bit Alec would get off my back and let me get on with my life.

'I'll do it. But this is the last time.'

An hour later I was on the back of Alec's bike, driving blind through the night. We swept through several unfamiliar side streets, in what appeared to be an unnecessarily circuitous route. It was impossible to quiz him from the back of the bike, so I had to grimace and bear it.

Eventually, we pulled up alongside a terrace of shops and

grimy-looking flats. It was not an area of Cardiff I was familiar with. I wasn't even sure we were still in Cardiff.

The whole area looked shabby. Several of the shops were takeaways, kebabs or curry houses, interspersed with Turkish barber shops, a halal supermarket and what looked like a sex shop. There was a row of rundown terraced houses opposite, with overgrown front gardens, some with abandoned sofas or black rubbish sacks nestling among the long grass and nettles. It was not the sort of place I would venture to alone after dark.

We dismounted, locked our helmets in the box fixed to the back of the bike and walked towards the far end of the row of shops.

Besides the last shop, a takeaway curry house, was a wooden door, above which were two CCTV cameras fixed to each side of the frame, pointing directly at us. Alec pressed a bell and waited. A disconnected voice responded, inviting us to enter. There was no attempt to identify who we were. We had been expected.

The door opened remotely, and we stepped through into a narrow space overlooked on the first floor by two windows. There was a further, metal door in front of us. It remained shut. A loud click behind us caused me to jump. We were now enclosed within a four foot by six-foot passageway.

Alec pressed another bell and a peep hole opened in the second door. A minute later we were inside. A burly man in a dark suit and a black T-shirt stood to one side to allow us to pass and then closed the door. He stood watching as we made our way down a dingy, badly-lit corridor.

I could just make out a staircase in front of us. The place had a distinct smell that I was struggling to place. It could have been cannabis, but there was a faint whiff of urine and shit mixed in with it. My nose wrinkled in protest.

As we reached the staircase, I noticed an open door to my right. My eyes had become accustomed to the lower light levels, so the full-on glare of the well-lit room blinded me temporarily.

As my vision adjusted, I saw two comatose women spread-eagled across several bean bags, a couple of needles and other paraphernalia were scattered on the floor alongside them. A man sat nearby puffing on a joint.

We ascended the stairs to the next level and into an ante-room occupied by four women. Three nearby doors opened-up into bedrooms. Another door was closed. It was a bloody knocking-shop. Alec had started to move towards another staircase, which presumably led into an attic room. I grabbed his arm.

'Where the fuck have you brought me?' I hissed.

'The meeting place,' he responded matter-of-factly.

'Oh. Really? Couldn't we have met at the Cardiff and County Club? They've been letting women in for some time now, just not this type.'

'Why, are you a member?'

I shrugged my shoulders and followed him into the small room that occupied the roof space. Don Watkins was standing at the door waiting for us, tieless in his trademark dark suit, McCoy was behind him. They were flanked by two heavies, looking like they had escaped from an episode of The Sopranos.

I was surprised that Pat Marshall was not present. Perhaps he wanted deniability, or maybe he had refused to come because of the venue. I certainly would have done the same if I'd known where Alec was bringing me. Pat was more of a Cardiff and County Club kind of guy.

I was surprised that Watkins was clearly familiar with his surroundings, as if he often had meetings in this place. He had always struck me as one of those expensive lawyers, who didn't get out of bed for a client unless they had mortgaged their house to pay him. He must be well paid indeed to have come to a place like this for a meeting. McCoy was looking as appalled as me.

Watkins shook Alec's hand and went to embrace me. I stepped back and took his hand instead. McCoy followed suit and then gestured for us all to take our places at a small table. The gorillas remained standing.

A woman, much older than the girls in the ante room, and with her 'working' years well behind her, entered and asked us if we would like to have anything to drink. We requested tea for four, the heavies wouldn't be joining us ... probably something to do with bulls and china shops, I suspected.

'It's good to see you again, Dawn.' Watkins was much too smooth for his own good. 'Thank you for agreeing to this meeting.'

'Lovely place you've got here.' He let the sarcasm slide.

'We borrowed it from some of our business associates.'

The reply was deadpan. I decided it was best not to inquire further into the nature of their business relationship. However, it did seem curious that a major crime syndicate, masquerading as a legitimate business to deliver a billion-dollar power plant should be doing business with a back-street brothel owner, unless there was more to these premises and their relationship to Watkins and McCoy, a side business perhaps.

I don't know much about these places of course, but it also struck me as odd that a stink-hole like this should be so strongly secured with cameras, double-entry doors and ... heavies. I was sure that these precautions had not been put in place especially for Watkins and McCoy. The only answer it seemed to me was that the place was being used to bring drugs into the city.

Watkins and McCoy were anxious to get on with the meeting. A small vein was visibly pulsing in McCoy's forehead, as he vainly tried to curb his frustration and hide his annoyance.

'My associates and I are very concerned, Dawn, at what we've been hearing about the stance of the mayor's office on this project. As I understand the situation, Mr Sheckler has ordered you to stop work on processing the supporting documentation needed to get the planning application passed. Alec tells me you have been instructed to no longer co-operate with us.'

Alec looked at me and nodded his assent to this interpretation. I let McCoy continue with his summing up without seeking to correct him or offer any further explanation.

'I've now been told that key officials, who had been working closely with us on this project have been suspended, including the mayor's head of legal and head of economic development.

'Alec also informs me that the mayor was accompanied by several Assembly Members at a recent protest rally. That is a huge problem as you know, as it will be the Welsh Government who will be determining our planning application. We cannot have the process compromised.

'Finally, I'm worried that if the mayor starts to dig in his own backyard, he will unearth your actions, Dawn, in securing the land for us in the first place, enabling us to go ahead with this project. Is that a fair summary?'

I didn't know where to start in responding to this statement. Watkins and McCoy did not fully understand our processes. They saw a very real threat in Sheckler's actions. They could not see that he was hitting out randomly to shore up his support and to give the impression of progress to the many people who were opposed to the development.

I agreed that it was not going the way that we wanted but I was nowhere near as alarmed as they were. I tried to reassure them.

'Look Rob, all of this is just voices-off. The planning process is on-track. Sheckler can't put together his objection to the scheme until all the reports have been submitted and the Welsh Government have a complete application in front of them. At that point, they will go out to consultation.

'None of the Assembly Members who took to that platform alongside him have any say in the final decision. They can lobby, but the minister will have to decide based on solid planning grounds, and as you know there is nothing in the region's development plan that stands in the way of approval. There are clear planning and economic grounds for approving it.

'Sheckler's flailing around without making any difference to the inevitable outcome. This scheme is going ahead whether he likes it or not.'

Watkins jumped in; he didn't sound mollified.

'It's good to hear you being so positive, Dawn, but you must understand that we cannot take that risk. I don't mind telling you that we're all spooked. We feel that we are losing control of this situation and given what is at stake here, that is not acceptable.

'We believe that there is a need for a back-up plan in case things get out of hand. I will be expecting you and Alec to come back to us with some ideas as to how we can achieve a more satisfactory outcome.'

I didn't work for these people; I wasn't going to take orders from them. I decided to take the path of least resistance. I nodded my assent There was no point in arguing further. Watkins turned towards my companion. 'In the meantime, Alec I have the item you requested for our other business.'

He gestured to one of the gorillas behind him, who pulled a package out of his jacket and placed it on the table. I looked closely at the cloth-covered object trying to work out what it was. Watkins moved it to the centre of the table and slowly uncovered the wrapping to reveal a gun, which he was careful not to touch.

He could see the shock, bewilderment and horror on my face, but did nothing to reassure me. This was now the big boys' league. I took it that he wanted me to know that he meant business. If these were scare tactics to get my cooperation, then he had made a big mistake.

'This gun is untraceable, it's taped so it won't retain any fingerprints, and all distinguishing marks have been filed off.' He looked directly at me as he spoke. 'Have you ever fired one of these, Dawn?'

I'd lived in the country, in an environment where guns are commonly used to control vermin. I'd spent some time on a firing range using pistols just like this one, in fact I had visited a local range with Jenny a few weeks ago in an effort to blow off some steam. This though, was a completely different kettle of fish.

'What, you're going to shoot him?' I was almost speechless. 'What the fuck, this isn't Chicago. You can't go around shooting people if you don't get your own way. I don't want any part of this. I'm out.'

I stood up and tried to leave but Alec restrained me. I tried to pull myself free, but he insisted.

'Just wait a minute, will you? Nobody is suggesting you or anybody else is going to use a gun on Sheckler. The weapon is for me and is for self-defence on an entirely different job.'

I was certain he was lying, but I decided to let it ride because I needed to get out of there, and storming out of a secure drug den full of locked doors and armed guards was not an option.

I looked to Watkins for confirmation. He grinned.

'Of course, I was just teasing you, Dawn. The gun is for Alec, as he says. I'm more than happy to accept your assurances. But you'll understand that we will be monitoring progress very closely. We cannot have any delays. Things need to go according to our timetable. The mayor can't be allowed to get in our way.'

He was looking at Alec as he spoke that last sentence. I thought his meaning was very clear, but I chose not to react. Alec carefully wrapped the gun up again and stuffed it inside his leather jacket. We started to walk towards the door, but Watkins called us back.

'This isn't a very pleasant place, is it, Dawn? But sometimes things must be baldly stated – and the fact is that our, er… organisation, makes many millions of pounds working with some of the shadier members of society.

'The profits that are earned in places like this fund our bid for the power plant and some of our other enterprises. This is the world we live in, Dawn, and when you agreed to help us in our endeavour, you walked into this world, too.

'I wasn't lying when I said that the gun is not intended to be used in dealing with the Mayor, but I wanted you to see it anyway so that you'd know the sort of people you are dealing with. We still have the evidence of your father's wrongdoing, but it doesn't hurt to have an additional incentive, now does it?'

I could feel my blood run cold as Watkins delivered these threats to my face. I was starting to feel trapped, but I was also angry, angry at Alec, angry at my father for the stupidity that had allowed them to drag me into this mess in the first place, and angry at myself for being so naïve.

'We've all seen news reports of what happens to those who fall foul of people in this world,' Watkins continued. 'You need to be fully aware that those risks are there for you, too – and for your loved ones. Having meeting in boardrooms and hotel suites is all very well, but this is the reality behind those genteel surroundings. As I said, this isn't a nice environment for someone of your sensibilities, but we felt it important that you see it none the less.'

I could still smell the peculiar stink of joints, piss and shit as we walked down the street. It had permeated my clothes. There was something else too … a sour taste in my mouth, a forewarning perhaps of what was to come.

Chapter Fifteen

We rode back to my house in silence. I was scared and furious at the same time. I clung tightly to Alec on the pillion as he weaved through Cardiff's back streets, plotting what I was going to say and do when we got to my house.

As he pulled up outside, I dismounted quickly and watched as he wheeled the bike around the back. I let myself in and for once, ignored the felicitous attentions of the cat. I was not in the mood.

I loosened the zip on my leather one-piece to breathe better and put the helmet on the sofa. then went straight to the drinks cabinet and poured myself a large straight vodka, knocking it back in one before turning to face Alec.

'What the fuck?' I shouted out the words as the anger swelled up inside me. My face was flushed, my body tense. I was struggling to retain control. 'What do you think you're fucking doing? Are you an assassin now? A hitman? Is that how we're going to proceed?'

He walked towards me intent on calming me down. He placed an arm on my shoulder and attempted to hold me. I pushed him away. He persisted so I pushed him away again. Suddenly I felt a sting on my left cheek and lost my balance, falling back against the armchair. He had slapped me hard, without holding anything back.

I picked myself up and stared at him, shocked. Nobody had ever struck me in that way before. I struggled to find the words I needed. In the end, I raised my arm and pointed at the door.

'Get the fuck out of here,' I ordered him in as calm a voice as I could muster. The tone was closer to that of somebody considering murder. He didn't budge an inch. Instead he loosened the zip on his leather one-piece and sat down on the sofa.

'I'm going nowhere until we've talked this through,' he said.

I considered running into the kitchen and grabbing a knife or leaving him there and summoning Jenny and her officers. But wielding a knife would have brought me down to his level and things were far too complicated to even think about involving Jenny.

I was starting to become a bit more rational. I reasoned that if I was going to get Alec out of there then I needed to cooperate or at least give the impression of cooperation. Once he was gone, I could take stock and decide on a way forward.

I wanted to go to the police, but it was difficult to judge how deeply I would be implicated. I could just imagine the headlines: 'Plot to assassinate mayor', 'Disaffected employee planned to kill former lover.' My imagination was going into overdrive.

I realised that I wasn't thinking clearly and looking back I still don't understand why I didn't extricate myself then and there. Maybe it was because of some residual loyalty to Alec, or perhaps I was worried that after a nine-month relationship with him and surreptitious meetings with his employers, I would be seen as part of the problem.

Ultimately though, I was afraid of losing Jenny. She was a serving police officer, she couldn't afford to be associated with anybody who had a criminal past or criminal connections. What would she think of me? She would be forced to dump me and I couldn't bear to go through that. Was it a risk I had to take?

If Alec went down, then I was convinced he would take me with him. But I couldn't let him and his mobster friends flood Cardiff's streets with drugs either.

Maybe Jenny and her colleagues were already aware and monitoring what they were up to. I needed to speak to her, to alert her to what I knew, but first I had to get Alec out of my life.

He sat there waiting for me to react. Perhaps he expected me to try something. Or maybe he thought that he had succeeded in placating me. If looks could kill, he would have dropped dead on the spot.

'You're not staying here,' I said. 'And you can take that weapon, that gun, with you. This is Cardiff. It's not the United States of Fucking America. It's not a fucking gangster movie. This is real life.'

'Yes, it's real life, Dawn. It's a world where people don't like to be messed with. A world where some people like to get their own way and will bend the rules accordingly. What do you think we're doing here? We're not playing a game. We're fighting to protect an important investment.'

I was appalled.

'But a gun, Alec? You can't shoot people to get what you want.'

'I've no intention of doing so. The gun is for self-defence.'

'Don't treat me like a fucking idiot. There aren't armed gangs roaming around Cardiff trying to take your fucking power station off you. Nor is Sheckler going to come storming in here brandishing a sawn-off shot-gun.

'We both know that your untraceable gun is a weapon of last resort, that if it looks like you're not going to get your way you'll use it to finally rid yourselves of Morgan Sheckler.'

'Don't be ludicrous. I'm not an assassin. And believe it or not I do have other business in South Wales apart from this fucking power plant. And yes, there are armed gangs around here, determined to protect their very illegal business. A trade that some of our business associates are heavily involved in.'

This took me aback. I'd not even contemplated that Watkin's story, that there was another reason for the gun, could be true. But could I believe him? Was anything he said credible anymore?

'Do you mean drugs?' He refused to answer. 'You do.

For fuck's sake, Alec what have you dragged me into?'

'I'm not involving you in anything, Dawn. As far as I'm concerned, our business relationship is solely to do with the power plant. I'm just sorry that Don and Rob mixed things up while you were there. They had no right. They should have kept that meeting strictly about the mayor. There was no need to introduce a controversial element at the end.'

Whatever the gun was for I had no desire to be caught up in it. On this I agreed with my mother, people who sold or dealt drugs were vermin. Prison was too good for them.

'A *controversial element* … is that how you describe it? I want nothing to do with sleazy drug deals, nor with anybody who has any association with them. I'm not sharing my life with a drug dealer, least of all a violent one.'

'Fucking hell, Dawn, I'm not a drug dealer. I can't stand the stuff anymore than you can. But this is business. My job is to make connections, get things moving and to watch out for the principals when they're in the UK. They asked me to work with some new partners, give them some back-up. I need to protect myself as well, Dawn.'

My feelings towards him at that time were a mixture of contempt, hate and fear. I was physically afraid of him. He had to go. I didn't want him in my house ever again, but what did I need to do to get him out of there?

I rubbed my cheek. It was still smarting from the slap. Thank God, I'd ended the relationship when I did, but we were still tied together by the power plant business. Did I really need to work through him, even with all he knew about me?

I had to sort out the planning issue by myself. I couldn't be having Alec and his mobster friends getting in my way anymore. I wasn't going to be intimidated by the gun, the heavies, or whatever they might think they have on me. I was confident that if I was left to my own devices, I could get the job done.

'You need to leave,' I told him. 'Get out of this house,

out of my life and don't come back.'

He stood up and approached, grabbing my chin with his hand, half-lifting me off the ground. The anger was painted on his face. He snarled the words at me.

'Or you'll do what? Go to the police? Run to Sheckler?'

For the first time, I was genuinely terrified of what he might do. I struggled to free myself. He almost threw me into the armchair.

'What are planning to do?' I demanded, gasping. 'Kill me, get your mobster friends to bury my body under a motorway somewhere?'

He turned away in mock-disgust.

'You watch too many movies,' he said walking towards the living room door.

'Where are you going?' I was shouting again.

He turned back towards me.

'To pack some things, so you can have the place to yourself.'

I poured myself another drink. I could hear him moving about upstairs. I was past caring where he would go at this late hour. I looked at myself in the mirror. I was a mess. My hair was all over the place, my face was red from the blow.

I wondered once more whether I should go and get a weapon to ensure that he went but decided against it. He was fit and strong. I would have been asking for trouble.

A moment later he was back in the room, carrying a small holdall. He picked up his helmet and turned towards me. I sensed myself flinch.

'Don't worry, I'm going. I just want to say this before I do. My job isn't one I can easily resign from. It's a job for life. You could say that there is only one way out, though that isn't strictly true. But my employers expect total loyalty.

'You should also know that they expect you to be loyal and are counting on your discretion. You may not want me here now, but you won't have me out of your life until our business is concluded.

'I expect you to continue to report to me and to keep me up-to-date with any developments, good or bad. You shouldn't forget that we know what you did to win the tender for us, that we still hold compromising information on your family, and if we find things become difficult for us then we'll take you down. My colleagues expect your co-operation and for you to deliver. So, do I.'

I was in no mood for lectures. Nor was I going to allow myself to be intimidated, even if there were consequences for my family and me, if Alec went public with what he knew.

'Just fuck off, Alec. Go, and don't come back.'

He gave me a long, knowing look and walked out of the door. I rushed to close it behind him and put the chain in place to prevent him getting back in. I heard a rattling sound at the back door and panicked. I rushed to the kitchen just in time to see Myrddin reappear through the cat flap.

He rubbed himself against my leg, demanding to be fed. I watched as the cat scoffed his food. He was as selfish as ever, but his presence was reassuring.

And then the accumulated stress and worry of the last few hours started to overwhelm me. I sat down at the kitchen table and felt the sobs wrack my body. I was drained and could barely keep my eyes open.

I was shaking and kept imagining noises and shadows moving around me. It was as if the whole house was closing in on me, conspiring with Alec to imprison me in my own fear. I had to get out.

I grabbed my mobile phone and started to text Jenny. What to say? I didn't want to alarm her, but I didn't want to appear needy either. I settled for playing it cool.

'Hi gorgeous, fancy meeting up after work?'

I put the phone down on the table and waited. There was no reply. I waited a little longer. Five minutes passed, ten, twenty, half an hour, an hour and still no response. Should I ring her? Maybe she was asleep. It was past ten o'clock, surely, she was off-duty by now. Perhaps she was with somebody else. My fear of being abandoned was starting to overwhelm me.

There was no reason why she should be at home. We had not made any arrangement to meet. In fact, I may have told her that I had something else on that night. I couldn't really remember. Maybe that was some other day.

What if she'd had enough of me for that week? We'd already spent three of the last five nights together. Perhaps she needed a break. I worried that we were getting serious. What if she was a commitment-phobe?

I tried to reassure myself. She'd been held up at work, I told myself. Or out with friends. It was unreasonable to expect her to sit at the end of a phone day-in-day-out to respond to my random text messages. She had her own life. We hadn't even agreed on exclusivity. And she had never once questioned me about my relationship with Alec.

Why was that? Did she not care? Did she just want me for my body? For sex? I had never told her how I felt about her. Come to think about it, she had never told me how she felt. Fuck, this was a complete mess.

I was falling apart. I'd been abused, assaulted, threatened and abandoned all in one night. And now I didn't know where I stood with the woman I loved.

I'd always been sceptical of that word. I couldn't remember ever using it. Surely, I must have done at some stage in my life. Somebody, I couldn't remember who, had told me that he loved me, only to redefine the term later.

Apparently, loving somebody is just one stage above friendship. It would have only meant something, he said, if he had told me that he was 'in love with me'. He was such a tosser, I was well rid of him.

But to me, 'I love you' seemed so final, so binding that I'd shied away from saying it to anybody. And now it was all I wanted to say to Jenny, as if my life depended on it.

Ninety minutes had passed and still no reply. I went upstairs and pulled the leather gear off and threw it into a corner. I pulled on a pair of jeans and a T-shirt. My one-piece black leather body suit, gloves, boots and helmets were looking at me accusingly, almost as if they were passing judgement on me.

I gathered them up, rushed downstairs and out of the back door. I was going to dump them in the bin, but had second thoughts. Instead I brought them back inside and threw them into the cupboard under the stairs, along with all the other junk I hadn't had time to sort through.

There was no padlock, so it was not possible to symbolically put that episode of my life out of reach, to throw away the key as I wanted to, but it was a start.

I went to the kitchen, where the cat had curled up and gone to sleep on the table. My glass was empty. I wondered whether to refill it or to get into my car and drive down to her flat in the bay. I was sure I wasn't above the legal limit. I picked the empty glass up and took it with me into the living room and curled up on the sofa.

I drifted off. When I awoke it must have been one-o-clock in the morning. I tried to refocus my mind. Should I call it a night and go to bed, or make a further effort to contact Jenny? I still felt shaky. Perhaps it would be for the best if I went up to bed and slept properly.

I staggered to my feet and made my way up the stairs. I had just got to the top when there was a knock on the door. I froze.

There was a second knock and then the letter-box opened. A voice called my name. It was Jenny. I almost ran down the stairs to open the door. She was standing on the other side looking radiant, as only she could.

She was wearing a two-piece charcoal suit and a white blouse. Her hair was tied up in a pony-tail. She was smiling. My legs were weak just watching her step into the house.

'I got your text,' she said. 'I was held up at work, but I

thought it might be worth calling around on my way home, on the off-chance that you might still be up.'

I put my arms around her and held her as tightly as I could. I didn't want to let go. She reciprocated. I started to cry again. I couldn't stop myself. I was just so happy to see her, so pleased that she had responded to my call for help, even if she didn't know that was what it was.

She pulled back to look at me, my dishevelled hair, the mark on my cheek where Alec had hit me and my red eyes.

'What's wrong? What's happened?' she demanded.

She led me into the living room and sat me down while she went into the kitchen, returning shortly afterwards, carrying a hot mug of strong tea. By this time, I'd managed to calm down.

I took the mug and sipped from it. Jenny sat next to me drinking her own tea with one hand while resting her other arm around my waist. We curled up close to each other.

'Now, do you want to tell me what happened?' she asked quietly.

I didn't know what to say. I couldn't hide the truth from her, no matter what it cost me, but I wasn't ready to tell her everything. I hadn't reckoned on her training as a police officer.

'I'm sorry,' I said, 'I don't know what came over me. I've had a tough day. It started with a former colleague pouring out her heart to me about how she was sexually abused at work and ended with the mayor suspending two senior colleagues. The atmosphere there is poisonous. It's so stressful. I just let it get to me.'

'And which one hit you?' I looked at her askance. How much could I tell her? Could I trust her to place me ahead of her duty as a police officer if I explained my connection to Alec and the hold, he had on me? What would she do about the gun and the drug deals, and would it put me at risk of losing her?

'Oh, Jenny,' I sobbed, 'this is such a mess. I don't know

what to do for the best.' She pulled me closer and stroked my hair softly.

'Just start at the beginning,' she said. I tried to pull myself together.

'I've been seeing a man called Alec Croxley for the past nine months. I finished with him shortly after I met you,' I added hastily. 'The problem is that I can't get him out of my life.'

Jenny looked at me intently, not giving anything away as to her feelings about this rival relationship.

'Alec works for Maga Power Holdings, who are developing the power plant, at least I thought he did. It turns out that they're just a front for a bunch of gangsters in the States. Anyway, the previous regional mayor, for some reason, wanted this company to win the bid to buy the land. He put me in charge of the process and asked me to do all I could to assist.'

So far so good, now for the really difficult part.

'That's how I met Alec. He was the company's mover and shaker, charged with clinching the deal. We hit it off straight away and quickly ended up in bed together. It was a convenient arrangement, rather than a serious relationship. The sex was good but that was all there was to it, or so I thought.'

I grabbed a tissue and dabbed at my eyes. I felt that I needed a break to freshen up, but I knew that if I paused, even for a few minutes I would lose my nerve.

'It turns out that Alec knew more about me than I had thought. In particular, he was aware of the affair between my mother and Byron Harris…' Jenny gasped in surprise. '…and more seriously he told me that high-ups in Maga Power Holdings had documentary evidence of a number of corrupt deals that my father had made with councils around south Wales, to win various contracts.

'He said that he wanted to protect me and get the evidence destroyed, but the only way to do that was to help him fix the tender process, so that his firm won the bid for the land, enabling them to build the power station.'

I paused to see Jenny's reaction. She was looking very serious, and was beginning to understand the mess I was in. She was clearly thinking through what it meant for our relationship.

'Go on,' she said.

'I couldn't allow my family's name to be dragged through the mud, nor could I allow Marshall, McCoy and Watkins to finish my mother's political career. I figured that, as Byron wanted Maga Power Holdings to win the tender anyway, the risk involved was very low, so I did as I was asked. I didn't for one moment think that Sheckler would come along and take over as regional mayor.

'In my innocence I reasoned that Alec had stood by me, so I stayed with him. I trusted him. It's only recently, and especially after tonight, that I've fully realised the extent he's been manipulating me.'

I sat back, relieved to have finally shared the whole sorry story, but concerned at what Jenny would do and say next. She didn't react. Instead she pressed me for more information.

'And what happened tonight?'

'Alec and I had a massive row. He took me to meet some of his business associates so that I could convince them that the power station was still on track. I've no idea where exactly we went, but we ended up in some drug den and brothel.

'It turned out that Alec had other business to carry out. I think he's working as some sort of enforcer for drug dealers. They gave him a gun, which he brought back here. I told him to get out, that I didn't want anything more to do with him, and he hit me. He packed and left and then I texted you. That's it, the whole story.'

Jenny's tone turned serious at this last revelation.

'Do you know where this Alec Croxley is now?' she

asked.

'No, I'm sorry. He could be anywhere.' Jenny wanted to know more but she could see that I was exhausted. The events of the last few days had finally caught up with me. She decided not to press me any further.

'It's late,' she said. 'We both have to work tomorrow and you need to rest. We can leave all this for another time. Let me worry about Alec Croxley. For now, we just need to get you to bed.'

She helped me to my feet, supported me up the stairs and undressed me. I got under the covers and watched as she removed her clothes.

'I love you. You know that, don't you?' I said.

She smiled.

'Yes. I love you too, Dawn.' I fell into a deep sleep.

Chapter Sixteen

I hadn't heard from Mother for some time so the summons, when it came, was a bolt out of the blue. For once it was packed with detail, a request for me to join her and Byron Harris for Sunday lunch at her home. There was no other information, just that this was a single invitation. She must be as jittery as Alec over this power plant.

I set off in good time. My mother lives north of Llantrisant and Talbot Green in a detached house, set in its own grounds in the Ely Valley. It is not the most accessible of venues and I certainly would not be able to drink over lunch, unless Mother was prepared to have her chauffeur drive me home. There was no way I was going to stay over.

As I drove through the gates, memories flooded back. This had been my childhood home. I'd returned to live here on and off for a year after my parents split up, and had visited it on many occasions since, before Mother became too preoccupied with her work and had forgotten to invite me again.

The driveway was a long one, dominated by two oak trees. The boundary wall was supplemented by a hedge, making it difficult to see into the property from the road. Ahead of me I could see the front porch of the house. My mother was standing by the front door accompanied by Sam, her border terrier dog.

I parked the car and walked over. She pecked me on the cheek and then went into the house with Sam and me trailing behind. The dog was excited to see me, but then he was the sort of dog who would be excited to see anybody.

Byron was sitting in the conservatory at the back of the house. He stood to greet me as I entered. He was looking so much more relaxed than when I'd worked with him, as if the lifting of the cares of office had rejuvenated him.

The checked slacks and open-top blue shirt were far removed from the suited look I remembered. His hair was slicked back, as always. At sixty-eight years, he was a bit older than my mother

'Dawn, it's lovely to see you. I hope that you're well.'

He'd always been a mentor to me, somebody to look up to. He was as effusive as usual. Mother beamed; she loved reunions. Byron hugged me, and we sat down on the rattan chairs scattered around the edge of the conservatory. I helped myself to a glass of lemonade from a jug on the table.

Mother hadn't moved. I wondered if she was going to pull out three packets of sandwiches for Sunday lunch. She must have read my mind.

'Don't worry, Dawn, I have caterers in. You can't expect me to find the time to cook with all my responsibilities.'

I gave her my best pity look. Byron laughed.

'We always got by on sandwiches and crisps in the old days,' he said. 'Thank God those days are behind us. Nowadays, I prefer to eat properly.' He patted his substantial stomach. 'As you can see, I'm much better for it.'

'Yes, I've tasted some of those sandwiches,' I said without a hint of bitterness in my voice.

'Now, now dear. They were Waitrose sandwiches. You don't get better quality than that,' She was taking the joshing well. She was always so much more at ease around Byron.

We all laughed; our good cheer spurred on by the fact that for once Mother was putting her hand in her pocket to feed us properly. Thank goodness for Byron. If he hadn't been present then I'm sure we would have had to settle for a bowl of soup.

The cook appeared at the door to summon us to eat. We all trooped into the dining room. Mother had done us proud. A proper three-course Sunday roast awaited us. I might have to book extra sessions at the gym to compensate for the day's excess.

As we ate, Byron turned the conversation towards my

position with Sheckler. He was anxious for news, but he was also concerned for my welfare. Mother listened but didn't contribute in any substantive way. She'd already had her say and I'd given her my answers.

I gave him a potted history of Sheckler's rants, his sackings and his whole unpredictable nature. My tale of woe was met with pinched brows and tuts of sympathy.

'So, how is retirement?' I asked him.

'To be honest, Dawn I'm bored out of my mind. I hadn't planned on such an extended period of inactivity. As you know there was still so much to do, but alas the voters decided that somebody else should be tasked with that responsibility instead.'

'It must have been a shock?' I wasn't involved in the campaign; I wasn't allowed because of my job. 'Did you have any inkling that he was going to win?'

'No, not really. We knew that he'd latched onto several campaigns around the region and that he was well-funded, but he did so much under the radar, through direct mail, targeted adverts on social media and telephone canvassing, that it was impossible to keep track of his support. As far as we knew our vote was holding up.'

'It was that stupid electorate system,' Mother added. 'What idiot decided that we should elect a Regional Mayor by preferential voting?'

'The same idiot who decided that you should be elected Police Commissioner three times by the same method. Aileen,' Byron was not one to let my mother get away with anything.

He'd been a solid mayor, with good ideas for how the region could be improved but had got caught up in the 'we know best' mentality that afflicted many of those who've been in power for too long. He'd lost touch with his electorate and that was reflected in the election result.

Unfortunately, that misjudgement had given Sheckler his opportunity and he'd taken it with both hands. It was a fine mess that Byron had created for us all. He was not the only casualty.

I could see that Mother was slightly put-out by this slap on the wrist. She picked up the dirty plates and took them into the kitchen, leaving the hired help trailing behind her. It was the first time I'd seen her undertake a domestic task for over fifteen years. I wondered if she'd also be serving us the dessert.

As she left the room, Byron leant across the table towards me in a blatantly conspiratorial manner. He seemed anxious to impart some news while Mother was absent.

'Listen Dawn,' he started, 'I just wanted to warn you about Sheckler. He's been asking a lot of questions about you recently, and your links with me. Fortunately, some of the people he's been interrogating are friends of mine and they reported back to me. Naturally, they didn't give him anything, but it's only a matter of time before somebody does.'

I reassured him that there was nothing to tell. As far as Morgan Sheckler was concerned all his remaining staff were signed up to his agenda and were loyal to a fault. Even as the words left my mouth, I could see that Byron wasn't buying it.

'Good, then there is nothing to worry about. But tell me, this Alec Croxley bloke you've been courting, wasn't he the same one who I met with Pat Marshall at the beginning of the power plant affair?'

I was completely taken aback by this question. Not just because of Byron's good memory, but also that he knew I'd been seeing Alec, a fact that even Mother was unaware of to my knowledge. I must have looked startled as Byron gave my hand a reassuring pat.

I struggled to answer him, not least as I was trying hard to forget Alec had ever been in my life. In the end, I settled for a cautious non-answer.

'I was seeing him for a short while, why?'

'Because Sheckler has been specifically asking people about him and his relationship with you. Don't worry, I don't think he's connected Croxley with the power plant. Apparently, he bumped into the two of you at his little rally behind City Hall.

'When my friend told me that Sheckler was asking after an Alec Croxley. I put two and two together and got four. It took me a while to remember who he was, but when I did alarm bells started ringing.'

'Well, you don't have to worry about me Byron. Alec's out of my life and that's where he's going to stay.'

'Oh, don't get me wrong, I've no problem with who you see in your private life. It's none of my business. I just thought I should warn you that Sheckler was sniffing around and that if he made the connection it could get tricky for you.'

I thanked him. Byron had always looked after my best interests. He had been loyal and faithful to my family. I knew him as somebody who stands by his friends for life, or until they give him a reason not to. And yet there was a nagging doubt at the back of my mind that perhaps, this time, he had other motives for his concern. I could hear Mother returning.

'For God's sake, don't mention Alec to Mother,' I hissed.

Byron laughed.

'You're as bad as my daughter. Why is it that children always keep secrets like these from their parents?'

'It's to stop you interfering,' I half-joked.

Mother reappeared followed by one of the caterers carrying desserts. She seemed pleased with herself, as if she had cooked the apple tart herself. I knew that was not an option. Not only did she not do domestic but I recalled from my childhood that she was an appalling cook. Fortunately, the dishes being served to us had been professionally prepared.

The hired help poured us some more lemonade. Mother

doesn't drink and both Byron and I were driving. He looked at the glass longingly. I could see that he would have preferred a pint of beer.

'Now then,' Mother said, 'are we going to discuss what we can do about that bloody stupid man in the regional mayor's office?'

Neither Byron nor I were in any mood to have such a conversation, not with her anyway. We both knew that it would end in one of her rants, and that we would be no further forward than when we started. Instead, Byron moved the conversation to a more interesting angle.

'Do you know what, Aileen, I was speaking to Bill Franklin the other day. He's an officer in Rhondda Cynon Taf, Dawn. His sister Liz worked on Sheckler's campaign as a volunteer. Turned out she only lasted a month - won't speak about it. But she hates that man with a passion now. Don't you think that's strange?'

'I'm sure I was at university with an Elizabeth Franklin from the Rhondda,' I told Byron, 'Would it have been the same one?'

'Yes, Bill said his sister knew you in college. It's a small world, isn't it?'

It became clearer now. Elizabeth Franklin had been a pretty girl, very religious, but also a bit of a commitment-phobe. I recalled that she'd dumped boyfriend after boyfriend as soon as they showed any sign of getting serious.

'So, do you know what happened between this girl and Sheckler?' my mother asked. She almost spat out Sheckler's name and couldn't bring herself to acknowledge his current office. She had met him a few times in her Police Commissioner role, and thought him an arrogant ass.

I thought that I might be able to guess at the sequence of events. Had this Liz Franklin been a victim of his groping in the same way as Debbie Redmond or had there been a more fundamental disagreement? Byron cut short my thoughts.

'It seems that our new regional mayor has wandering

hands,' he said. Mother was open-mouthed. Byron was as perceptive as ever.

'I see you'd guessed already, Dawn.'

'I've heard a few things,' I confirmed, being careful not to give too much away. I liked a good gossip as much as Mother but not if it was going to involve my friends and me. It was best if some things remained unsaid. Mother though, had already climbed onto her high horse and was halfway around the racetrack.

'Can we get this girl to go public?' she asked. 'Surely she'll help us bring this scum to his knees.'

Byron shrugged. I think he was beginning to regret moving the conversation in this direction. Whatever else he was, he had never been the vindictive type. And he'd always prided himself on fighting his campaign on the issues, never on the personalities. If only his opponents had been so honourable.

'Well, I was going to suggest that Dawn meet up with her to see if she could get the full story,' he said. 'But you know me, Aileen. I've never been one to fight dirty and I'm not going to start now. I only raised the matter because I was concerned for Dawn. She has to work with the man, so she needs to be aware of what to expect.'

It had apparently escaped them both that I'd worked with Sheckler before and I well-knew what he was like. However, a pattern had emerged, that might prove useful in the future. All I had to do was work out how to use it.

I was more worried by what Byron had told me about Sheckler's inquiries into Alec and my relationship with him. I didn't like the idea of him sniffing around my private life, no matter that I had been doing the same to him. Nor did I want him to stumble across my connection to Pat Marshall through Alec. That could prove to be very awkward.

Mother directed us to her sitting room where the caterer served coffee and after-dinner mints. I could quite get used to this life. What a shame a show like this was only ever put on for Mother's old friends and lovers, never for her only daughter.

I had never told them that I was aware of their clandestine affair, and if they suspected that I knew neither of them had said anything to me. Instead, we carried on as if nothing had or was happening, comfortable in our pretend ignorance. There was no denying though, that my already conflicted relationship with Mother had become still cooler, once I did know the truth

I wondered about Byron's motives in raising Sheckler's history. He was not someone who did things on a whim. Was he just enjoying a good chat with old friends or did he have another agenda? Maybe he was hoping I had information that might be of use, or perhaps he genuinely did want to look out for me.

Of course, his concern for my welfare might also be self-interest. Like me, Byron had a lot invested in this power plant, including his own standing in the community. He must have known or suspected that some short-cuts had been taken in getting the plant off the ground, not least in the tendering process. He had after all encouraged me to get the right result and left me to my own devices.

Byron had been at arms-length for much of this process, but I believed that he knew what was going on. It was all about deniability. And I hoped now that he was trying to protect me as best as he could by briefing me on what he knew about Sheckler's latest manoeuvres.

I was conscious that I'd not given much in return. Mother was still chomping at the bit to do Sheckler down. But I had decided to stick to my original instinct of keeping her out of it. This was my fight. I didn't need her taking up cudgels on my behalf. I wondered, if she had engaged, would she have done so for me, or would it have been for her own selfish interests?

As the Sunday afternoon eased into early evening, we started to wrap up our little get-together. Byron had promised his daughter that he would call in to see his grandkids and I was anxious to get back to Cardiff to prepare for a conference I was attending later in the week.

Mother went into the kitchen to see off the caterers. Byron took advantage of the opportunity to pass me a piece of paper. It contained Liz Franklin's contact details. I gave him a quizzical look.

'Does Liz know that you're giving me this?' I asked.

'No, her brother gave it to me, but only on condition that it was you that spoke to her, not me.'

'I don't know, Byron. It feels intrusive. What if she doesn't want to speak to me? Worse, what if my contacting her brings back bad memories?'

'That's something you've got to judge for yourself, Dawn. Speak to her if you think it will help you, otherwise leave her alone.'

I took the paper and put it into my jeans pocket just as Mother re-entered the room. She gave me a look as if to question what we were up to and then proceeded to show us out.

She embraced me as I got into my car. Sam had been released from whatever room she had locked him in during dinner and was jumping up and down, wanting me to play with him. I petted him and handed him back to Mother.

On the drive back I reflected on what Byron had told me. I was debating with myself whether I should contact Liz or not. It must have been ten years since we had last spoke. We hadn't even kept in contact through Facebook, though we were connected there.

Did I have the right to dredge up bad memories, to upset her all over again? Would it not be selfish of me to do so? By the time I reached my house I'd made up my mind to let it go. A few hours later I'd changed my mind three times. Not for the first time, I didn't know what to do.

Chapter Seventeen

If I was going to contact Liz Franklin at all then it would have to wait. There was another commitment that I couldn't get out of, as much as I tried - two days and a night in a soulless hotel in Birmingham city centre discussing regeneration.

I considered sending my apologies but that wasn't an option. I was giving a presentation on the work of the Cardiff Capital Region, much of which I'd led alongside Byron, and it was already over-subscribed.

I was due to catch an unnaturally early train on Tuesday morning to register at 10am. I'd thought about travelling up the day before but that would have precluded my night of passion with Jenny. She had to be at work in the city centre at an equally ungodly hour on the Tuesday, so a lift to the train station the following day would be guaranteed.

When she let me into her flat, she was wearing a short, patterned silk robe and was holding a large glass of wine. She placed her free hand behind my neck and drew my face towards hers. As we kissed, I slipped my hand inside her robe onto the small of her back and then down to her arse.

She pulled me closer to her and kicked the door shut. I dropped my small overnight bag on the floor as we almost fell into her living room. She put her wine glass down on a small coffee table and pulled my blouse loose, undoing each button methodically. Her robe was now wide open, revealing her perky breasts and neatly trimmed blonde pubis.

She undid my bra and pulled it off, kissing my nipples until I felt them stiffen. At the same time wrestling with the catch on my trousers. I placed my hand between her legs and started to stroke her. She gasped at my touch, before yanking my trousers and pants down to my knees.

As we entered her bedroom, we rid ourselves of our

remaining clothes and dived onto the bed. I fell into her arms and we kissed passionately. For over an hour we made love before collapsing into a sweaty, breathless, fleshy mess alongside each other. She was smiling. I grinned back.

'So, am I going to get any of that wine?' I asked.

'That depends. Have you eaten?' I demurred. She picked up her mobile phone from the night stand and tapped out a few instructions on it. 'There, I've ordered pizza for us.'

I kissed her on the mouth, my hand exploring her soft warm skin, sliding surreptitiously towards her more intimate areas.

'How long do we have?' I asked. She kissed me back, pulled me closer to her and slid her fingers inside me.

'Oh, thirty minutes at least.'

'Perfect,' I said, kissing her slender neck.

Afterwards we sat, curled up together in her living room in robes, drinking wine and eating pizza. I was feeling exhausted, not through the love-making but the constant pressure of work, the tension and the uncertainty.

The row with Alec had drained me, as had Sunday lunch with my mother. I just wanted to bury myself under a duvet and pretend that the world didn't exist. Jenny sensed my mood. She was good at that, part of her training as a police officer, I guess. But unlike my mother, she didn't try to interrogate me. Instead, she pulled herself closer to me and stroked my hair with her free hand.

'I hope you're not getting grease from that pizza in my hair,' I joked. She laughed.

'If you're good I'll let you use my shower.'

'I may have to anyway,' I said smirking, 'I'm covered in your bodily fluids.'

'And me yours,' she grinned, paused and then adopted a stern, mother-hen-type look.

'Listen Dawn, about the other night. You know that you just need to call me if you need anything,' don't you?'

'Yes, of course.'

'I've been doing some digging into Alec Croxley. He doesn't exist.' I pulled away from her open-mouthed. 'He's must be using a false name - however some surveillance photos of known drug dealers have found somebody who looks remarkably like him, or so I'm told, because I haven't really had a good look at his face.'

She grabbed her phone and opened the photo album to show me a picture of two men talking. One of them was clearly Alec. I had no idea about the identity of the second man. I nodded to acknowledge that it was him.

'Good, at least we have something to work on,' Jenny had become very serious and matter-of-fact all of a sudden. 'These are very dangerous men, Dawn. They're also proving to be elusive. We're doing all we can to find Croxley again, but for now he's disappeared. Perhaps he knows we're onto him, more likely he's just out-of-town.'

I wasn't sure how to respond. It was nice to have a strong policewoman looking out for me, but I didn't want to come across as helpless, either. I pulled her close to me, and bathed for a minute in the comfort of her embrace. When Jenny next spoke, her voice was softer.

'When I said I loved you, I meant it,' she said. 'You're special to me and I'll move heaven and earth to protect you. But you've got to be open and honest with me, no more secrets.'

I struggled to avoid crying. She kissed me on each eye and then properly on the mouth.

'I feel the same about you, too, Jenny. Thank you for everything you've done. I'm sorry if I've been evasive. Everything has been getting on top of me. I still don't know what to do about Sheckler, and to top it all I was summoned to Sunday lunch with my mother yesterday.'

She chuckled loudly.

'Do you know, I'm sure your mother isn't as bad as you make out.'

'Seriously?' I almost shouted the words. 'She's a fucking monster. Have you ever met her?' I was only half-joking, but it was enough to startle her.

'No, but she's your mother.'

'Yes, when it suits her.' Jenny decided to leave well-alone. I told her about Byron and Liz Franklin. She didn't seem impressed.

'You know, I'm not sure this digging into Sheckler's past helps us,' she said. 'The sort of insurance policy you're looking for won't protect you if he pulls up those documents and finds that you've been fiddling with them. That's a criminal matter, and by rights I should put you in irons and march you down to the police station right now.'

There were times when it was difficult to know whether Jenny was joking or not. I decided to play along by holding out both hands towards her.

'Now's your chance,' I said, 'but there are more creative uses for handcuffs.'

She smiled.

'If I was going to arrest you, I would've done so already. No, what I meant is that we need a more decisive solution, one that takes Sheckler out of the game altogether.'

'What are you suggesting,' I asked cautiously. 'You do remember that you're a police officer, don't you?'

'Of course.' She smiled. 'But I have a low tolerance level for anybody who messes with me and mine, and I wouldn't hesitate to take the opportunity, if one presented itself, to act to protect you.'

This was an entirely new side to Jenny, one that I hadn't seen before. She was telling me that her commitment to our relationship was absolute, possibly extending beyond her oath as a police officer to uphold the law. I wanted to examine this further, but it was getting late and we both had an early start.

I could feel my eyelids getting heavy, and I couldn't stop

myself yawning. I placed my head on her shoulder, as she helped me to my feet and led me back into the bedroom, where we slept like two overfed cats.

I woke first the next morning and lay staring at her naked body for the few minutes before the alarms went off. She was gorgeous. With her long blonde hair, her smooth, sculpted back, her firm bottom and toned legs she could have been an elite athlete. She was the rock I was clinging to as the storm blew around me.

I ran my hand along her prone figure, allowing it to explore every contour, every crevice. She stirred as I gently kissed her neck just below her ear, and turned towards me. I put my lips to hers. She responded and then, as the alarms sounded on our respective mobile phones, opened her eyes to look at me.

We showered together, grabbed a cup of coffee each and headed out in her car. As she pulled up in the car park at the rear of Cardiff Central station, she turned to me. I could see that she was uncertain, no, almost insecure. It was an unexpected moment.

'I don't want to lose you,' she said. I started to respond but she placed a finger on my lips to stop me. 'Remember, I love you. Just look after yourself, and don't do anything I wouldn't.'

'I'm only going away for one night, Jenny.'

'I know,' she responded kissing me. 'But even that absence is too long.'

I was concerned. I'd never seen her like this before. I wondered if she was alright. She assured me that she was and that it was my state of mind that was worrying her.

I got out of the car and pulled my overnight bag after me. Jenny turned off the engine and followed. She put both her hands on my waist and kissed me, ignoring the stares of the commuters and taxi drivers nearby. And then she was gone.

I bounded up the stairs to my platform and onto my train. Our night of passion had lifted my spirits. I was with somebody at last who loved and cared for me, somebody who would put her career on the line for me. I forced myself to drag my laptop out of my bag to review my conference presentation.

The conference was every bit as mind-numbingly tedious as I'd anticipated. The hotel though was unexpectedly comfortable, complete with a combined TV/computer on the wall, king-size bed and jacuzzi-style bath.

I gave my presentation on regeneration in South Wales, including an exposition on how the power plant would act as a catalyst for new investment in the area. Thank goodness Sheckler wasn't there, he would likely have sacked me on the spot.

Afterwards, I answered questions on the difficulty of delivering the project now that the political weather had changed. To be honest I was a bit stymied on that one and stonewalled by falling back on the impartiality of the planning process and the role of the Welsh Government in considering major applications.

It was then my turn to listen to presentations on attracting funding and working with the private sector. By the end of the day, I was glad to get back to my room and to slip into the bath. I turned the whirlpool function on and lay back, sipping a glass of wine. This was the best way to endure conferences. Perhaps I would stay here for the next morning's sessions as well.

There was nothing on the television and I'd had enough of work for one day, so I abandoned my emails, put on a dress and headed down to the bar. There were several delegates there already, many of them were known to me from previous conferences. This was an exclusive group of people, well-used to each other's company.

I grabbed some food in the restaurant and then joined a group of delegates from West Midlands and Merseyside. We drank lager, with the occasional round of neat vodka shots. They seemed intent on getting blind drunk quickly, I was more cautious, but as the night drew in could feel myself getting more and more light-headed.

As we chatted and drank, I noticed a man watching me. He must have been about thirty years old and was dressed in a trendy grey suit and a dark tie. He had a large languid mop of brown hair and was quite handsome in his own way. Perhaps, I was looking at him more favourably because I was drunk.

In any other circumstances, I would have been interested but I was in a relationship. He smiled at me, I returned the gesture. He walked over and offered his hand. I shook it as he introduced himself.

'Mark Icken. I'm with West Sussex Council. I very much enjoyed your talk. Can I buy you a drink?'

'Thank you,' I was conscious that I was slurring my words. He went to the bar and returned with a large vodka.

He sat down next to me and started to talk about my presentation. By this time, I was so far gone I could barely remember anything I'd said, so I suggested he might like to talk about the work he was doing in West Sussex. Mark grinned.

'Why don't we talk about you instead?'

I looked to my companions for assistance. They were engrossed in their own conversation. I drank some vodka and looked him straight in the eye. What was the harm in talking?

We stayed in the bar for another hour at least, chatting and drinking. When it came time to retire for the night, I stepped off my stool and almost fell over. Mark caught me just in time. I leant on him and giggled.

We made our way up to my room with Mark supporting me at each step. As we got to the door I fumbled for my key card and struggled to fit it into the slot. He took it off me and opened the door at his first attempt, then helped me inside and lay me on the bed.

I stretched out my arms and yawned loudly. He didn't

take the hint, so I sat up and tried to ask him to leave. Instead he closed the door and sat down next to me. Then he leaned over and kissed me. I pulled away.

I could feel him unzipping my dress behind my back. It was now hanging loose on my shoulders. His other hand pressed on my breast through the fabric. Now he was kissing my neck and fiddling with my bra strap.

He pulled his jacket off and dragged his half-unbuttoned shirt and tie over his head. My dress was now around my waist and my bra lay on the bed next to me. This was going too far, it wasn't what I wanted. I was starting to sober up and realised that I needed to extricate myself from this situation quickly, before it was too late.

I dragged myself away from him and slid backwards onto the floor, pulling myself upright so that we were standing on opposite sides of the bed.

'I think you need to leave,' I said, trying to cover my own nakedness. He looked confused and started towards me. I grabbed the phone off the bedside table and brandished it at him. 'I mean it, don't make me call for help.'

Fortunately, he saw sense, gathered his clothes together and left. It was a narrow escape, and entirely my own doing. What the fuck had I been doing drinking so much? I wasn't twenty-five and single anymore. I started to feel guilty for having so nearly betrayed Jenny.

Thank goodness I'd pulled myself together in time. Who knows what would have happened otherwise? I yawned and fell onto the bed. The booze was still working its evil in my system.

When I awoke, it was daylight. I dragged myself to the bathroom and then pulled a bottle of still water from the mini bar. My mouth felt like it was inhabited by a colony of moths. I looked in the mirror, I'd gone to sleep without removing my make-up. It was not a pretty sight.

It was eight o'clock in the morning, I was due to sit on a panel in two hours to debate regional policy. Could I risk eating something. I decided I should and ordered some orange juice, coffee and muesli through room service. There was not a chance in hell of me making an appearance in the restaurant in my present condition.

After I'd eaten and showered, I felt a little better. I put my business suit on and restored my make-up. With just five minutes to spare I finally felt able to face the world by taking my place with the other panellists on the stage.

As I entered the hall, I saw Mark sitting in the front row. He nodded to me, sheepishly. Had he been wearing that wedding ring last night? I had no idea. I was surprised he could even show his face.

Somehow, I got through the event without any major cock up. Not being able to face sitting through any more sessions with Mark Icken sitting in the same room as me, I packed, checked out of my hotel and walked to the train station. It was only a short walk and the fresh air helped me to focus.

While I waited on the platform, I fiddled with my smartphone. I resisted the temptation to check the conference hashtag on Twitter. Instead I caught up with local Cardiff news, and there was a text from Jenny. It was short and sweet:

'Missing you tonight. Ring me when you're home xx'

This had been a salutary lesson. The world was full of predators like Sheckler and Mark Icken, ready to take advantage of any drunken lapses of judgement. Instant gratification was there if you wanted it, but it always came with a price. There was no substitute for the stability of a loving relationship.

The train journey back to Cardiff seemed to take an age. I watched in a daze as the countryside flew past. Should I tell Jenny what had so nearly happened? I wasn't sure. We'd agreed no secrets, but this was one misadventure that had come to nought, other than to reaffirm the strength of my feelings for her.

I was still pondering on the events of the night before as I walked back to my home from the station. It was a fine sunny day without a cloud in the sky. My spirits lifted as I wound my way through the city centre towards Roath. There's no better medicine than returning to one's home city after a difficult time away.

I opened my door and was greeted by Myrddin at the entrance to the living room. I was pleased to see that my neighbour had been feeding him as requested. The mail had been placed on a side table. I took my bag upstairs, placed it on my bed and changed into something more comfortable. As I walked back towards the stairs, I noticed that the door to the spare room was ajar. I could have sworn it was closed a few minutes earlier.

At that moment, I heard a noise downstairs – the distinctive sound of the back door closing. I rushed into the spare room and looked out of the window, just in time to see Alec making a getaway on his motorbike. My returning home in the middle of the day must have caught him unawares, possibly disturbed him before he had finished whatever he was doing here. I wondered why I had not seen him and concluded that he must have got past me while I was changing.

I went into the spare room, except for a bed and a wardrobe, it was empty. I opened the wardrobe door; most of Alec's clothes had been removed. The bed had been stripped and some other items that had been stored on the floor were missing, though others had been left behind in his haste.

I breathed a sigh of relief and sat down on the unmade bed for a minute while I composed myself. This could not go on.

Chapter Eighteen

I went and locked the back door and then returned to survey the near-bare room. I didn't know whether to be relieved that Alec had cleared out his stuff or annoyed that he had done so behind my back and without my permission. I was certainly pleased that I had missed him, even if it was a close call. I needed to get the locks changed at the next opportunity.

He hadn't done a very good job of clearing the room. The carpet was a mess and it needed vacuuming. I decided to get that job out of the way then and there, and set to work with a vacuum cleaner. What items Alec had left behind I placed in a black bin bag and stored in the empty wardrobe.

I pulled the bed away from the wall to clean beneath it. It must have been the first time I'd moved it since it had been put there five years previously. There was a lot of dust, an odd sock, a stray pair of knickers and a pound coin. It was always a mystery to me how items like this ended up in these places.

There was one more item…it was a small metal box, no more than eighteen inches square. I'd not seen it before. I stood and stared at it for a few minutes, trying to recall how it might have got there. The only conclusion I could reach was that it belonged to Alec. So why hadn't he taken it with him?

I picked it up and placed it on the bed. It was not unduly heavy. It was though, locked. I shook it. There was at least one heavy object in there. I went to my utilities cupboard and found an old screwdriver and a hammer.

It took a couple of minutes, but eventually I was able to break the lock. Inside was the gun, still wrapped in the cloth that I'd seen it delivered in. I put it to one side and inspected the paperwork that accompanied it.

There was an envelope containing several hundred pounds in crisp new twenty-pound notes, Alec's passport and a file of papers. I pulled it out and flicked through the documents. It was the blackmail material they had gathered on my dad, detailing all the dodgy deals he had made when he was living in South Wales. I had no idea how they might have got hold of this stuff, but it was as damning as I'd been told.

I sat back in shock. Why would Alec leave material like this lying around in my home? Was he trying to send me a message? Were these the only copies? I thought that was unlikely. Perhaps it was a warning, a message that I should do his bidding or else.

And what about the gun? Didn't Alec need that for his own protection? Or for his enforcement activities? Was this a message that he hadn't finished with me? Was he trying to tell me that he would be back? Perhaps he hadn't expected me to find the box at all.

I decided straight away that I was going to destroy any incriminating evidence that might compromise my parents. But what about the gun, the money and the other papers? I needed to consult with Jenny. We had agreed no secrets and that was how I would proceed.

I put the blackmail papers to one side, placed the gun and the other contents back into the box and closed the lid. I carried the box into my bedroom and placed it at the rear of my fitted closet behind a pile of shoe boxes.

Myrddin had come upstairs to see what I was up to and was now sunning himself on my bed. He followed me downstairs. It was almost time for his tea and he wasn't going to let me forget it. I emptied a pouch of cat food into a bowl and presented it to him. He gobbled it up gratefully.

I keep a small shredder in the kitchen, which I used to dispose of unwanted personal paperwork. With so much identity theft about, you can't be too careful. I fed all the evidence against my father into that machine. There may have been copies, but I was determined to make sure that none of them were in my house.

I made myself a cup of green tea and sat down at the kitchen table to think. I looked at my mobile phone, wondering if I should text Alec and ask him to remove his box of stuff from my house. I didn't really want to see him again. Maybe it was better if I looked after it for a while. The contents of that box were safer in my hands than his.

I remembered Jenny's text and contemplated phoning her. Would she be on duty? I needed her advice on what to do about Alec. Perhaps she could use the box as bait to draw him out. I needed to think this through. I was no legal expert but it seemed to me that she might need a bit more evidence if she was to charge him with anything.

So far, it was mostly my word against his, and him being photographed chatting to known criminals, who he might have just met in the pub for all the police knew.

There was the assault on me of course, but that would involve me testifying and God-only knows what would come out in court if Alec got into a witness box. And if I did take that course of action, would his mobster-friends come after me. They could hardly keep Alec in prison right up to the trial. Maybe he'd try and seek his revenge on me.

I realised that I was worrying myself unnecessarily. Jenny would know what to do. I reached for my phone, as I did so the cat jumped up on my lap and nuzzled at my hand. I smoothed him gently. It was a strangely satisfying and comforting experience.

Just then there was a loud knock on the door. I started, causing the cat to jump up and onto the floor. I stood up to answer but then hesitated, wondering who it might be.

Maybe it was Jenny, having developed some sort of sixth sense, turning up when she was needed, a bit like Superman always rescuing Lois Lane?

There was a second knock. I walked into the hall and checked myself in the mirror. I looked a mess, but then

Jenny had seen me in a much worse state. I took a deep breath and opened the door.

It wasn't Jenny. Instead I was confronted by a vaguely familiar face, a woman in her late thirties, with shoulder-length frizzy hair and a slim figure, poured into skin-tight black leather bike gear. She was carrying a black helmet. Behind her I could just make out a motorbike pulled up against the kerb.

I couldn't quite place who she was or where I'd met her before. She grinned at me. It was one of those grins people give you when they're nervous. She obviously knew who I was.

'Dawn, I hope that this is a convenient time.' I looked at her blankly. 'Oh, I'm so sorry, it's been quite a while. Elizabeth Franklin.'

She held out her hand. I took it but still failed to invite her in. I guess I was too shaken by my discovery in the spare room. I was distracted, rather than being deliberately rude.

'I hope you don't mind me calling. My brother, Bill, suggested that I come and see you. I had your address off Byron Harris.'

I shook myself out of my stupor. It felt forced even to me. I really didn't feel up to another episode of the amorous adventures of Morgan Sheckler.

'Of course, how nice to see you Liz. Please come in. I'm so sorry for leaving you standing out there.'

She followed me into the kitchen, put her helmet on the table and sat down while I made some coffee for us both. She watched in silence as I prepared our drinks, only opening-up as I joined her at the table.

'It's been a long time, Dawn. Please forgive me for imposing on you out of the blue like this. I was led to believe that you might want to talk to me about our beloved regional mayor.'

She paused dramatically, before slowly enunciating the last three words. Byron was right, there was no love lost there. Even so I decided to play it cautiously. I'd had enough shocks and betrayals in the last few months to have learnt not to trust anybody, even an obvious ally like Liz.

'I think Byron's been match-making,' I said. 'He knows that Sheckler and I don't see eye to eye on some things.'

'Such as politics?'

'Yes, politics is one. I understand you were on his campaign team?'

'I was. I'd already been working for his company for a couple of months, so I volunteered out of a sense of duty, and because he appeared to be making a lot of sense, but the man can't help himself.'

'The groping?' A pained expression flashed across her face.

'Yes, the groping. But there's more. For somebody who was supposedly ranged against the establishment, his relationship with that businessman, Jack Chaffont, was always a matter of concern to me. The more I saw, the more I realised he was just like the others.'

I sipped my coffee. 'What happened?'

'I challenged him on it, naturally. And then things really started to get nasty.'

I was fascinated. This woman had more nerve than any of us. She had confronted Sheckler and delivered some home truths to him. That was a conversation I would have given good money to watch.

I tried to size her up. She looked utterly focussed, determined to make her point. But what else did she want? Was she just out to make trouble for Sheckler? If so, then I was more than happy to assist.

And why involve me? Was she trying to find common cause, or did she want something? Had she been plotting with Byron or was it him putting us together to see what happened? I urged her to give me the full story.

'He threw me off the campaign team, sacked me and

then, somehow, he turned my boyfriend against me. I still don't understand it. He told Dave that I was seeing somebody else behind his back. The idiot believed him. It didn't matter what I said, he couldn't get past the lies.

'I would have taken him to a tribunal, but the changes to the rules, put in place to help employers, made it impossible. I hadn't been working for him long enough, and in any case, I didn't have the money to pay the tribunal access fee.' She paused, as if trying to summon up some inner strength.

'Sheckler seems to have this power over some people. It just takes a few sentences and they're putty in his hands. He went out of his way to undermine me with my boyfriend; he made things up about me and he convinced people that he was telling the truth.

'He started rumours to destroy my credibility, so that nobody would listen when I tried to expose him. He got some of his influential friends to back up his lies and I ended up unemployed, alone and nearly homeless. I'll never forgive him. I wanted to destroy him - I still do, but it is proving a lot more difficult than I hoped.'

I sat back and looked at her. Somehow, I couldn't see this once self-confident, purposeful woman allowing her life to be wrecked in this way. I wondered how she had allowed Sheckler to get under her skin.

And yet here she was, in my kitchen, looking for affirmation of some sort. She didn't need my approval. Did she need my help? Was I just somebody she could tell her story to, or was I to be recruited as her instrument of revenge?

I tried to recall what she'd been like at college. I knew that she'd been bought up in deepest Powys. She was a country girl, self-reliant and ambitious. That inner-steel was still evident and yet, she was another of Sheckler's victims.

I remembered an incident in our final year. Liz had broken up with her then boyfriend and in doing so had humiliated him in public. She had walked away, apparently unaffected by the rift and had gone on to get a first. He struggled to get a third-class degree.

I'd decided then not to have any more to do with her. I had a lot more time for her brother, Bill. Despite being two years older, he had spent a summer with us in France and Italy, as we worked our way around that part of Europe. I'd even tried to seduce him one drunken evening, only to discover that I was the wrong gender.

I'd not given a second thought to trying it on with Liz. She never struck me as being remotely interested in women. Indeed, despite her brother's obvious sexual preferences I had detected a hint of homophobia in her manner.

What I knew for certain was that Liz was totally self-centred and self-interested. For someone like Sheckler to come along and force her to re-evaluate her outlook must have been very disconcerting. No wonder she was angry. I needed to know more.

'How can I help you, Liz?' My tone was deliberately dispassionate, I was starting to tire of being the crutch for Sheckler's victims. I was frustrated, too, that none of them had been able to provide me with the smoking gun that would overcome my own difficulties, even if Jenny thought that such a thing didn't exist.

She looked taken aback by my directness. I could see her evaluating my usefulness, just as I'd assessed hers. She paused as if searching for the right words.

'I think we need to make common cause, Dawn. We must do whatever we can to bring this man down, because if he continues to get in my face on all the television, radio and social media channels, so help me God, I'm going to get a shotgun and blast his head off.'

I laughed nervously. She was stressed and upset, and her language reflected that. The Liz I knew, was not the type to resort to violence as a means to solve problems, but then we had not seen each other for years.

She hesitated, sensing my disbelief.

'I'm deadly serious, Dawn, really I am. That man has ruined one life too many. Somebody has to stop him.'

'Have you told Byron this?' I asked. 'I'm not sure that when he suggested we meet up he envisioned us turning into Thelma and Louise, and embarking on a quest to assassinate Morgan Sheckler.'

She grimaced and then repeated her mantra in a more studied and deliberate way.

'Somebody has to stop him; the man is a menace Maybe you're right, violence isn't the answer, but we have to do something.' There was a hint of desperation in her voice.

There were times when I felt like this as well. My issues were not dissimilar to the ones Liz had faced. Sheckler represented a threat to my job, my way of life and to many of my friends. It would be so much easier if he wasn't standing in the way, unravelling everything I'd built over the last four years.

I put my hand onto Liz's, it was soft and warm. She'd taken off one of her leather gloves to drink her tea. It was her only concession to being indoors. I realised at that moment that my hate for this man was also overwhelmingly strong, that I, too, would be happier if he were dead. I just wasn't prepared to admit it openly. It was not a feeling I would act on, certainly not at this stage in my battle against him. I tried to reassure her.

'We will stop him, Liz. But not by killing him. There are better ways of dealing with this problem, ones that don't end with us facing life imprisonment. Thank you for telling me your story. But we both need to be patient. Our time will come.'

She pulled her hand away. I could sense the disappointment, not at my refusal to join her in her rather tenuous act of premeditated murder, but at our failure to move any closer to dealing with her issues.

'Thanks Dawn, it's been good to see you again. Talking about this has helped a little bit, even if I do still want to kill the bastard.'

She pulled her gloves back on and stood. We hugged, and I walked her to the door. Just before she left, I handed her my business card.

'I've got your number already,' I said. 'But if you want to talk, all my details are here. Maybe we can meet for a proper catch-up.'

'I'd like that.'

She put her helmet back on and mounted the bike. I watched as she drove off. She was trouble; there was no way that I was going anywhere near Liz Franklin and her obsession ever again. I just hoped that she could find her own personal resolution. If that involved her killing the mayor in one last desperate act, then I wouldn't mourn for either of them.

It was dark already. How late was it? I panicked. I hadn't rung Jenny as I'd promised. She must think that I'd abandoned her, or that something had happened to me. I needed to speak to her about Alec.

I walked back into the house and picked up my mobile phone. I found Jenny's number and sat staring at the screen for a few minutes as I collected my thoughts and purged Liz's visit from my mind.

Jenny answered straight away. She seemed relieved to hear my voice. We agreed that I would drive to her place. I hadn't got around to changing the locks and didn't feel safe in my own home anymore. Alec may have just called in to collect his stuff, but after all that had happened his action felt like an intrusion, and a threat.

When I got there, she was waiting for me in a pair of tartan flannel pyjamas. There was a half-drunk glass of wine on the coffee table and the remains of a pizza. The TV was paused on some current affairs programme.

'I'm sorry,' she said. 'I started without you. I didn't know when you would call. Have you eaten?' I realised that I hadn't. 'Good, I've got a vegetarian pizza for you in the oven.'

I hugged her. I was starving. I felt that I didn't deserve this attention, but I submerged myself in it anyway. I wanted to bury myself in her love and affection to try and forget all my troubles for an evening. But I knew that I couldn't put off telling her about Alec's latest transgression.

We sat and ate, as I told her of my discovery on returning home. She took it all in, a mixture of seriousness and concern written all over her face. When I had finished, she hugged me.

'You've done the right thing telling me,' she said. 'You're right of course, we don't have enough to arrest and hold him. But at least he's not actually carrying this gun around Cardiff, himself and threatening people with it.

'We need to locate him urgently and put some surveillance in place. We're having no luck finding him through his mobile phone, he appears to have it switched off most of the time.

'At least once we have found him, I'll be happier about your safety. In the meantime, I think you should stay here.'

I said I would think about it.

Chapter Nineteen

When I awoke the next morning, our bodies were still intertwined from making love a few hours earlier. I remained physically and emotionally exhausted from the events of the previous day. It was as if my encounter with Liz had sucked all the energy from my body.

I pulled myself closer to Jenny and kissed her neck. She stirred, smiled and opened her eyes. She didn't have to be in work until that afternoon, I, however, needed to be in City Hall in two hours. It was the last place I wanted to be.

Jenny stroked my hair, her lips touched mine, her hand slipped down to the small of my back. We kissed passionately. I held her tightly, enjoying the warmth and softness of her skin. Why couldn't I stay here in her arms for the rest of time?

'Poor baby,' she whispered, 'You look drained. Why don't you ring in and take the morning off?'

It was tempting. A few hours extra sleep and more making love was just what the doctor ordered. I reached over to my phone and tapped out a text to Tim Finch. I thought that two strenuous days at a conference entitled me to some personal time. He responded with his consent almost immediately.

Sensing my tiredness, Jenny didn't press her earlier advances. My self-confidence had taken a knock as a result of Alec's actions and the persistence of Mark Icken. I was vulnerable and confused, and yet when I was with her, I felt safe.

A few hours later we were sitting together drinking coffee. I was wearing Jenny's robe, she had pulled her pyjamas on. We sat side by side at the breakfast bar enjoying a comfortable silence. Jenny looked like she had just won the lottery but was afraid to celebrate too much in case she attracted begging letters. I'd reached maximum contentment, the worries of the past few weeks behind me.

By the time it came for us to leave for our respective work places, I'd managed to put things into perspective. I was calm and ready for anything. I felt as if I had the chance of a fresh start.

I walked into my office, put my bag down on my desk and pulled out my work laptop. There was something different about the place, but I couldn't put my finger on it. I looked again. Had I really left all those papers in such a neat pile on the corner of my desk? Had somebody been rifling through my desk drawers and my filing cabinets?

Tim appeared at my door. I gave him a puzzled look. He grimaced. I could see that he was out of his comfort zone once more.

'Sheckler would like to see us,' he said. I nodded and continued to sort out my stuff. 'Immediately, I'm afraid.' I took the hint and followed him down the corridor towards the regional mayor's office.

'What's happening, Tim?' He didn't answer. He increased his pace so that he established a clear gap between us. Once he reached Sheckler's door, he knocked and entered without waiting for an answer. I followed him.

Sheckler was standing with his back to us, looking out of the window. He was wearing yet another of those double-breasted pin-striped suits. I remember clearly the way he seemed to merge with the drab office décor. He turned to meet us, his face was deadly serious, almost volcanic. He didn't say a word but indicated for us to both sit. He remained standing.

'Dawn, I hope that the conference was useful. I'm told that your presentation went well, that you did a good job in selling our region to the delegates.' My confusion must have been evident as he felt it necessary to caveat his remarks. 'Oh, I had some friends there, people I worked with previously. They were very impressed. Well done.'

'Now, perhaps you can tell me how far you've got in implementing my instruction to stop this power plant. I'm getting a lot of people contacting me to say that we're not making enough progress.'

I was getting a bit tired of this. The man may be obsessed but he was coming across as stupid. Maybe he was testing me, trying to gauge my commitment to the project.

I explained yet again how the process works, and that until the application was completed by the submission of several studies, the Welsh Government would not be able to start the consultation period. Nevertheless, I had staff working full time on our objection and had withdrawn co-operation with the applicants as requested. This though had delayed the studies still further.

Nothing I said seemed to surprise him. It was as if he was just going through the motions, before getting down to the real business.

'Good,' he said, 'I'm sure that it will all come together in time. Now about your boyfriend...'

'Excuse me.'

'The man I saw you with at the rally', he picked a piece of paper off his desk and studied it closely. 'An Alec Croxley, I believe. How long have you been seeing him?'

This flummoxed me completely, so much so that I was unsure how to respond. He was watching me intently, and noted my hesitation. I decided to go on the offensive.

'I'm sorry, what has my private life got to do with you or with the mayor's office? This is not a police state. I'm entitled to choose my friends as I please and the nature of my relationship with them is none of your business.'

'Yes,' he responded in the most patronising voice possible. 'Under normal circumstances that would be the case, but I do have to question your judgement, when it transpires that this man works for the very company that is seeking to impose this dreadful power station on my community. Did you not think that pursuing a relationship with him would create a conflict of interest?'

I looked across at Tim, but he didn't respond. I could see that I was not going to get any support from that quarter. I was struggling to contain my temper. How dare this man poke his nose into my affairs. What right did he have? I pinched my hand hard to calm myself. And then I tried to bluff it out.

'I think you're jumping to conclusions Mister Mayor. You have no knowledge of any relationship between Alec and me. Of course, I know him. As you say I met him through the negotiations on the power plant. But there is no relationship. We just both happened to be at your rally and were chatting when you came upon us. It's as simple as that.'

He gave me a disbelieving look. He clearly knew more than I was prepared to admit. I wondered if he'd had me followed, or had he been talking to my friends and colleagues? I doubted if he would have got anything from them. I'd always been careful not to say too much to anybody about my affairs.

'Oh, come now, Dawn. You can do better than that.' I stood up.

'If that is all you wanted me for, Mister Mayor, I have work to do.' Tim stood, too, and moved to block my exit. I looked at him and then at Sheckler.

'I'm sorry was there something else?'

'Oh, yes,' he said, grimly. 'Please sit down again.'

I didn't have much choice, so I complied. Tim was looking very uncomfortable. He had never been happy with those aspects of his job that were unpleasant or confrontational. Sheckler stood directly over me.

'Can you tell me,' he asked, 'who oversaw the tender process for the land on which the power plant is to be built?'

I immediately knew that something was wrong, but I had no choice but to admit that the responsibility was mine. It was one of those questions that would not be asked unless the inquisitor already knew the answer. I imagined a sly smile briefly crossed his face, like a cat about to pounce on its prey.

'While you were away, Dawn, we took the opportunity to review all the paperwork associated with the power plant, including the tender documentation. Tim, and one of our lawyers went through it in great detail.

'I have to tell you that I was shocked, when I discovered clear evidence that the bids were tampered with. It appears that the successful tender was altered to ensure it would be chosen.'

I tried to look shocked, outraged even, but it didn't appear to convince him. Tim seemed more willing to give me the benefit of the doubt. I denied knowing anything about any alterations to the tender documents.

'Mister Mayor, you must know that the system is designed to prevent this sort of tampering. There are very clear guidelines as to how bids must be presented, and they are opened in the presence of at least two members of staff. You are mistaken. There were no changes made to the documentation after it was opened.'

'Oh, I don't know how you did it, Dawn. Maybe you had an accomplice. But I can assure you that illegal changes were made to ensure that your boyfriend's company won the bid for the land.'

I didn't know which to be the more outraged at, the continuing but unproven assumption that Alec and I were an item or the allegation that I'd committed an illegal act. I stood up and sought to apply everything I'd learnt from amateur dramatics at college in my response.

'This is outrageous. You're throwing around accusations without any proof to back them up. I've already denied having any relationship with Alec Croxley and as for the contemptible claim that I personally altered the documents to favour his company, I find that insulting and slanderous. I suggest that you withdraw the claim immediately or I will be seeking legal advice.'

I could see that Sheckler was taken aback. He had clearly not expected such a firm and vehement denial. Nevertheless, he was not going to be thrown off-course in his pursuit of my scalp.

It was obvious, too, he had realised that if he were able to invalidate the agreement on the land by showing it to be illegal, he would win his battle to kill off the power plant once and for all. This was now a high-stakes game for him and he was not going to back down easily.

'Oh no, you don't get off that easily. By all means, get your lawyers to crawl all over this, but you can't win. The tampering is clever, but it's there for all to see, and I have other witnesses who can testify to your relationship with that man. In my view, there is a clear case for you to answer and once this interview is out of the way I shall be referring the matter to the police.'

We were now standing toe-to-toe, like two professional boxers sizing each other up. Neither of us was prepared to give ground. He wanted his quick win, I was determined to foil him. Tim tried to calm things down, but the situation was well past any attempt at mediation.

'Fine, go to the police,' I challenged. 'And I will fight your charges all the way. They're false and you know it, it's just an attempt to get the power plant killed off quickly, and without the hassle of having to fight it in planning law. In fact, I wouldn't be surprised if you altered those tender documents yourself.'

By this stage I was past caring. It was obvious how this meeting was going to end. He was trying to force me out and do so on the cheap by using my wrongdoing against me. The fact that he was right was immaterial, the fact that I had committed the offence under duress, irrelevant. But he had to prove it and I didn't believe he had the evidence to make a case in law. The problem, of course, was that it might be enough to dismiss me.

It might also be enough to foil the building of the power

plant. That could cost the regional mayor's office dear. He might win out in the end, but I suspected that Marshall and Watkins would then initiate a law suit that could well derail the rest of his term. That was a matter for him.

Sheckler had gone bright red and was struggling to get his words out to reply to my accusation. When they did eventually come, they were a mixture of indignation and bile.

'How dare you. You evil bitch. Don't you try and pin your corruption on me! I'll have you strung up in front of City Hall for your insolence.'

I smiled. I'd briefly got the upper hand by throwing his accusations back at him. Tim was standing next to me open-mouthed. I kept up the pressure.

'What's wrong Morgan, can't you take the heat? You can't go throwing accusations around without proof. You have more of a motive than I ever did to alter those documents, even if you had to do it retrospectively. Perhaps the police should be looking into *your* affairs not mine.'

I wondered whether I should say more, or keep my powder dry for the time being. I had enough rumour and innuendo to damage Sheckler in the media. I might even be able to provoke an investigation, but I'd been around South Wales long enough to know that once somebody starts to sound off, people clam up and inquiries fizzle out.

He knew this, too. He looked at me with undisguised contempt as he recovered his composure.

'You know something, Dawn, I trusted you, even when others said I shouldn't. I gave you the benefit of the doubt when friends were telling me that you were undermining my position. I thought that our past relationship meant we could work together for the best interests of our region. Instead you've let me down, betrayed my confidence, undermined my authority. You're poison, and as far as I'm concerned… you and your fucking imperious mother should be thrown into a dark pit and left to rot.'

Now we were getting somewhere. All his insecurities

were rising to the surface. He had even name-checked my mother. I laughed out loud at his preposterous rhetoric.

'You've really lost it, haven't you Morgan? You're sitting here in your little world, making all your plans for global domination, like some cartoon villain from Danger Mouse, and yet you can't get past your own inadequacies.

'You really think that everything revolves around you and your insignificant obsessions. Well let me tell you something, it doesn't. And if you really cared for the future of this region and the people who live here you would be championing this power plant and the regeneration and jobs that come with it, instead of losing your way because of your fucking myopia.'

Tim had had enough. He had tried to intervene on several occasions with no success. Now, in a move completely out of character, he banged a large book onto the desk to get our attention.

'Colleagues, please. This meeting is getting out of hand. We're here to try and resolve how the tender documents came to be altered, not to tear strips off each other.'

For once, Sheckler and I were in agreement. 'Shut up,' we shouted in unison. He then turned towards me.

'Dawn, I'm going to suspend you with immediate effect pending a disciplinary hearing around the charges I have laid down this afternoon, namely that you deliberately altered tender documents relating to the power station for your own personal reward or interest.

'As I've already said, I will be asking the police to investigate this matter and you should expect to be interviewed by them in due course. I will also be initiating legal proceedings to cancel the agreement I have with your boyfriend's company on the basis that it was fraudulently obtained.

'Tim will arrange for you to be escorted from this building and for your corporate laptop to be confiscated and retained for examination. Your personal effects will be packed up and sent onto you. Now get out of my fucking sight.'

I didn't move. I wasn't going to let him get away with this without warning him that he was playing a dangerous game that might wreck his life as well. Tim was now standing over me, waiting to walk me out of City Hall. He looked confused at my non-compliance.

Eventually, I stood up, slowly and deliberately. Tim looked relieved. He had obviously not relished having to summon security guards to remove me by force. However, instead of following him I turned on Sheckler, who was now seated at his desk pretending to work.

'Don't worry Tim, I'm going, but first I have one more thing to say to our regional mayor.'

Sheckler put his pen down on the desk and swivelled his head in my direction. His smug face fuelled my anger, but I was careful to channel it into a deliberate and calculated final broadside, rather than to just lash out.

'Don't think that you are going to get away with this,' I said calmly. 'You have your own skeletons in the closet and they are going to come out to haunt you if you pursue this vendetta against me. And Tim, it's important that you're a witness to this.

'I've spoken to a number of people you've worked with over the years, all of whom you have sexually assaulted. I am going to line every one of them up behind me as I take you to an industrial tribunal and the standards board for the assault you perpetrated on me only a few weeks ago in this very office.

'By the time I'm finished you will be exposed as the sexual predator and abuser you really are. A man who drove one female employee to a nervous breakdown and another to abandon your campaign. Somebody who has consistently used his power and position to get his own way and who, when denied, will go so far as to crush the livelihood of those who resist him.'

Sheckler's face was impassive. He didn't flinch either when I paused. Tim, however, looked shocked. The poor bloke had no idea of how monstrous the man he served could be. It was clearly a turning point for him. But true professional as he is, he would carry on regardless.

'I haven't finished,' I said turning to Tim. I fixed my gaze again directly into Sheckler's eyes. 'But it isn't just your libido we have to worry about, is it Sheckler? Because essentially, for all your pontificating about how you are an anti-establishment politician, you're just as bad as all the rest.'

This did produce a reaction, albeit a raised eyebrow. Tim, however, was entranced. I suspected he was enjoying my rant. He could not say so, of course, and had to remain impassive, but I had nothing to lose, even though it was doubtful if I could ever back up my claims of corruption.

'I know that you've taken campaign donations in return for favours, you fucking hypocrite. I know, too, that you financed your campaign for Mayor from those donations. The truth is Sheckler, you wouldn't be sitting in that chair if you weren't a corrupt, self-serving politician who worked the system for his own selfish ends.'

He raised himself from the chair and leant across the desk towards me. I could see that I'd got to him. Although he feigned anger, his eyes showed fear. He was worried. He was wondering what evidence I had from the various meetings that I knew he had been monitoring through his group of friends.

He may not be aware that I'd met Liz Franklin, but he had almost certainly been told that I'd spoken to Debbie Redmond. I was in no doubt either that Maria and Gwilym had reported back to him, and that somehow, he would have been told about my lunch with Jack Chaffont.

It was all a sick game being played out by competing parties, using information about meetings and interactions to gain leverage, to impose pressure. His network may well have been feeding him stories about my activities, but people were also briefing me and I'd use every scrap of information as leverage.

I doubted whether my mother would have been involved in this wheeling and dealing. She hated Sheckler passionately because of what he had done to Byron, and because of what he stood for, and for all her distance and indifference, she wouldn't have done anything to hurt me. But Byron would have been up to his neck in it. I knew that whatever his connection to my family, he could not be relied on. He was out for himself, he always had been.

It was a sobering moment...one with which I'd been happy to play along, even when it was clear that I was being used. In my heart, I knew that, while I had been fighting for survival, others had been plotting around me, and that I had ultimately been dispensable. But I had clung to the belief that, even in the face of outright blackmail, the threat to expose my father's crooked dealings, my actions were in the best interests of the region.

At the end of the day, though, none of them gave a damn about me, least of all Alec. It was about money and power. That was the game, no matter what else they told me.

In retrospect, I wonder to what extent Sheckler was out of his depth in this environment. He had stood up against vested interests all his life, but it seemed that when it suited him, he was hand-in-glove with those very people. They took advantage of each other as much as they took advantage of me.

My willingness to help Byron and Alec and my naivety had backed me into a corner, and now Sheckler was going to use my vulnerability to extract his pound of flesh. My libido had been my undoing as much as Sheckler's would eventually finish him. But what about Jenny?

She had never been part of this morass of deceit and deception and yet, there was a danger that she might suffer from it. I loved her, and she loved me, but could I realistically ask her to continue supporting me if I was disgraced and facing possible criminal charges? The thought of losing her hurt me more than anything Sheckler could do.

His response when it came was succinct. His eyes were flashing anger as he positioned his face just inches from mine.

'Get out of my office,' he said, 'and never come back.' He gestured towards Tim to remove me. Tim opened the door and I followed. I was drained, but I had enough of my wits about me to insist on collecting my bag from my office on the way out. He was decent enough to allow me that.

I eyed up my laptop on the desk and went to pick it up. Tim took it from me. It was the property of the regional mayor's office and might contain evidence that could be used against me. I tried to remember what was on there… nothing incriminating. I'd always been careful not to put stuff on work computers that I didn't want others to see.

As we walked down the corridor and stairs towards the impressive reception area, I felt the eyes of other employees upon me. They knew that Sheckler had secured another scalp and, no doubt, they feared for their own jobs. This was meant to be the walk of shame, but I held my head high.

I may have broken the rules but at the time I'd been given little choice. I'd been trying to protect my family, but I was also fighting for my home region, to bring jobs and prosperity to South East Wales. Morgan Sheckler was as much a villain as me, or Alec, or any of his pals. It was not much of a defence, but it was all I had.

Chapter Twenty

As I left City Hall, I was at my lowest ebb for some time. I didn't know how to react to my suspension, while the prospect of a possible police investigation gnawed away at me.

I pulled out the spare key to Jenny's flat. She hadn't thought I would be safe while Alec was still on the loose, and had wanted me to stay with her, at least until I'd arranged for somebody to change all the locks at my home. I thought of heading down to Cardiff Bay, but changed my mind and, still in a defiant mood, and not really thinking clearly, headed to Roath instead.

I agonised over whether to call Jenny or not. I needed her to hold me, to tell me that everything was going to be alright. I longed to feel the warmth of her skin on mine, to taste the softness of her lips, to lose myself in her embrace. In her arms, everything was right with the world. Without her it was chaos and darkness.

Above all I needed to hear her voice. She could be reciting the council's parking code for all I cared. That soft Devon brogue never failed to calm me and seduce me in equal measure.

But Jenny was at work and although we had talked about the possibility of my tampering being discovered, the reality made me nervous. Jenny had not flinched when I told her what I had been forced to do, but would she react the same way now the police were being called in to investigate me?

Would she stand by me, irrespective of the consequences for her career, or would she distance herself from possible culpability? It was impossible for me to know and I didn't really want to test her. But I couldn't face this crisis alone.

Even the soft, warm body and purring of Myrddin on my lap failed to raise my spirits as they had done in the past.

I sat in my living room pouring glass after glass of wine down my throat. I kept telling myself: 'I am a self-reliant, professional woman. This is just a setback. I will not let that bastard win.' It didn't sound very convincing.

Outside, the sky remained clear and unsullied by my fate. I'd half expected huge black clouds to form and follow me home. I felt as if I should be in the eye of a great storm, that ripped off roofs, felled trees, and pulled down power lines. The calm stillness of this August summer day unnerved me. Even the weather had abandoned me.

Eventually, the combined effect of the wine and my dark mood caused me to drift off to sleep. With the empty wine glass hung perilously between my fingers, my gentle snoring and dribbling and the smudged make-up from an earlier bout of tears, Myrddin and I must have looked a real sight as we dozed together in my armchair.

I awoke suddenly. I don't know why. For a second, I was disorientated. The sky outside was darkening as dusk sought to embrace and deepen my depression. The cat had perched himself on the opposite sofa from where it observed me keenly, waiting to be fed. A chill had penetrated the room, I shivered involuntarily and rubbed my arms.

There was a buzzing sound coming from my bag on the coffee table. It took me a moment to realise it was my mobile phone. I struggled to stand up to get at it before the caller rang off, but it was too late.

I scrolled through the record; it was Jenny. I rang her back.

'Thank goodness you rang me,' she gasped. 'I'm sorry if I sound out of breath, I've been running. Just got back to the station and was about to head home, when I heard what had happened. Are you okay?'

'Yes, of course. What have you heard?' She seemed reluctant to discuss it over the phone.

'Are you at home? I thought we agreed you would go to my place. I'll call around now. I won't be more than five minutes.'

And then she was gone. I had no time to argue, no time to express any doubts or put her off until the morning. I inspected myself in front of a mirror. I looked dreadful. There was no time to put things right. Instead I fed an insistent cat and made myself a cup of instant decaf coffee. I prepared one for Jenny, too. When she said five minutes, she meant it. I'd never met anybody before who took time so literally.

Sure enough, there was a knock on the door as I poured hot water over the coffee granules. I let her in and handed her the drink, no milk or sugar as she took it, and sat down at the kitchen table, inviting her to sit opposite me.

'Christ Dawn, you look dreadful.' She took my hand in hers. Her beautiful blue eyes radiated concern, her oh-so-kissable lips were pouting slightly as she thought what to say.

'I'm sorry, I couldn't talk properly on the phone. There were too many colleagues around. I was told at work that Sheckler lodged an official complaint against you.'

She was blunt as usual, going straight to the point without any attempt at softening the blow. I could sense an air of expectancy about her, as if she wanted me to spill the beans before she could tell me. Instead, I played dumb and waited for her to continue.

'Do you want to tell me what happened?' she asked. I shook my head, fighting back tears. 'He found the altered tender documents then? He wants us to investigate you for fraud.'

Still I couldn't find any words to respond to her, my face was about to melt under an avalanche of salty water. I struggled to hold back the torrent once more. I was still unsure if she would feel differently about me now that it had all come out into the open, as we had feared it would.

Jenny was the most tolerant person I knew. She'd never judged me, never sought to have me change my lifestyle, instead, she accepted me for what I was, warts and all.

She'd waited patiently for me to commit to her, allowed me to divest myself of former relationships like Alec, without once challenging me or showing any hint of jealousy or possessiveness, and now she was here for me again.

'Dawn, this is serious. You need to talk to me.' Her voice had softened, her hand was stroking mine tenderly. She leaned across the table towards me, trying to establish eye contact. I reluctantly turned towards her.

'I've been suspended from work,' I sobbed eventually. 'That bastard took advantage of my absence at the development conference to rifle through my stuff, and pull up the tender documents. We had a stand-up row in his office. I told him a few home-truths.

'The fact is though Jenny, he hasn't actually got any concrete proof that I carried out the alterations. It's all circumstantial. I was in charge of the tender process, I was seeing Alec Croxley, and that's it. But I guess I let it get to me. I'm sorry.'

Jenny got up and moved to stand next to me so that she could hold me. She kissed me on the cheek, and the tears really flowed. It was awkward with me sitting and her standing, but for some reason I felt rooted to the chair.

She stroked my hair and made soothing noises. I started to feel a bit better, as if I'd jumped a major hurdle without falling off my horse.

'Don't you worry, we'll make this alright somehow. After everything you've told me about Sheckler, he's the one who should be standing trial. He's a complete bastard, and a sex-pest to boot. If I had my way, I'd string him up by the balls.'

I smiled. This was the sort of fighting talk that I needed to hear. Her voice softened.

'I've been on the receiving end of sexual harassment myself. I know how it degrades you, makes you doubt your own self-worth. Men who treat women in this way, should be hung, drawn and quartered.'

This was news to me. I could see that even mentioning

this episode in her life, was painful. I pulled myself to my feet and held her. Now it was my turn to comfort her. When we sat down again, she had composed herself and had a serious expression on her face.

'I had to tell my Super I was in a relationship with you,' she said. 'It was the only way to recuse myself from the investigation. He warned me off, told me to steer clear of you until it was all sorted. I shouldn't really be here, but I couldn't abandon you. I'm not going to leave you to face this alone. I had to be here for you.'

'Won't you get in trouble,' I asked.

'What he doesn't know won't hurt him,' she said matter-of-factly. 'But we need to find a way to resolve this once and for all. I've been doing a lot of thinking over the last few days. We need to take Alec Croxley, or whatever his real name is, out of the picture. I doubt if he'll talk, but if he does that could incriminate you more.

'But we still don't have anything concrete to pin on him. As we discussed last night, the gun is here, he's not actually dealing the drugs himself and all we've got is a couple photos of him with some known criminals. He could have been selling them life insurance for all we know.'

'Shredding those blackmail documents wasn't such a smart move. Unless we can get the originals or some copies, then it's just your word against his, that he forced you to change those tender documents.

'If you can't prove that you were blackmailed, then it comes down to your denial, pitched against the evidence in court that changes were made. As far as a jury knows, you had motive, through your relationship with Croxley, and you had opportunity. The balance of probability as far as they are concerned is that you did it, and the chances are that they will convict.'

I started to feel uneasy again.

'Haven't you been able to use the photos to link him to any crimes?' I asked. 'I thought there was state-of-the-art equipment that can do that sort of thing nowadays?'

'If only. He needs to have a criminal record to be on our files in the first place, and from what the drug squad have established, so far, he's clean. For now, they've just tagged him as a person of interest and are waiting to see if he shows up again.'

'And what about Marshall, McCoy and Watkins? Surely they must have come up on your radar?'

'No, nothing at all. I did a bit of freelance digging, spoke to some contacts in the States. Any mob connection they may have, is hidden from us. You told me Croxley was working for another group, who were financing the power plant. He seems to have fingers in a lot of pies.

'This group, Croxley and the company who you've been working with may well all be interconnected, but at this stage I don't know how. Remember that I've been working unofficially on this. I need my bosses to sign off on any in-depth work, and they won't do that unless I give them the full story.'

I took her hand.

'I'm sorry I dragged you into all this,' I said. 'It's a complete mess. I feel as if I've let you down, and put your career in jeopardy.'

'Don't be silly. I wouldn't be doing this if I didn't want to. I love you and I want to help.' She put on her serious face again. 'Look, Dawn, it seems to me that we have two problems. The first one is Alec Croxley, the second, Morgan Sheckler.

'If we can deal with Sheckler, I believe we can make Croxley go away. He'll get his power plant, and that'll make his bosses happy. If he continues to do work on the side with some of the other dodgy people, we've seen him with, the drugs squad will have him anyway.'

'But how can we deal with Sheckler?' I asked. 'The man seems untouchable. Even if I can get all his victims together, and that's a big if, it will hardly cause a ripple, a day's headlines and then it's tomorrow's chip paper.

'I've been around politicians all my life, Sheckler has got a dedicated group of followers, a popular cause and a hide like an elephant. It may make it more difficult for him to be re-elected, but it won't shift him out of City Hall anytime soon, and that means that my problem is not going to go away either.'

'Then we're going to have to find another way to remove him,' said Jenny

'Like what? You're a serving police officer, Jenny. You can't be involved in anything dodgy.'

'I don't know, Dawn. But I have no intention of losing what we have here. Maybe we just have to wait for an opportunity. Perhaps some of his other enemies will do it for us. Maybe Alec Croxley will. I'm just clear in my own head, that drastic action is needed, and that if necessary, I will act in any way I can to protect you and all his other victims.'

I hadn't realised the depth of Jenny's feelings for me. She'd always been so professional when talking about her duties as a police officer, now she was putting herself on the line to resolve my problems.

'You know I wouldn't ask you to compromise your career for me,' I said finally. 'But I feel so much better now that you've said it.' She grinned.

'Shall we take this somewhere more comfortable?'

'I thought you'd never ask,' I responded.

We walked into the living room, hand in hand. The remains of the bottle of wine were sitting on the table. I had some in my glass already, which I topped up. I finished off the bottle by filling a glass for Jenny.

'How much of this have you drunk?' she asked disapprovingly.

'I've had a few glasses. I thought I was entitled. Why, have you turned into the wine-police now?'

'Not at all. I'm just sorry there isn't more for me to share with you.'

'Don't worry, there's another bottle in the fridge.' I cwtched up to her on the sofa.

Jenny put her glass down.

'If I drink this, then I'm staying the night. I can't drive if I've drunk alcohol.'

'That's fine with me,' I said relishing the distraction. 'I would much rather spend the night making love to you than drowning my sorrows in a glass of pinot grigio, even if it is Waitrose's finest.'

She grabbed her glass, drank deeply from it and then kissed me passionately on the lips. Her hands were pulling at my clothes. Her skin was warm and soft. Her long slender fingers slid down my spine. We held each other close.

'Tell me about your experience with sexual harassment,' I urged. She seemed reluctant, but relented after I pressed her further.

'It was a long time ago, when I was just starting as a police officer in Devon. My sergeant was a complete creep, old school, he just didn't understand how to relate to women.

'We were stationed in a small town in what some of my South Wales colleagues would term 'the-middle-of nowhere'. I was one of only two female police officers amongst a group of sexist, self-entitled men. The skipper was the worst of them, constantly making inappropriate remarks, brushing up against us and, at one Christmas-do pushing me into a corner and groping me.

'Of course, if you report this behaviour then you are ostracised. Police officers close ranks behind colleagues, even when they are in the wrong. It's like the cosa nostra, there's a code, you don't rat on other officers. And in those days, if somebody was caught with their hand up a female officer's skirt, well let's just say the consequences are not very severe… a slap on the wrist or in extremis, early retirement with full pension.'

I could see that just telling this story was upsetting her. It may have been many years ago but the recollection of being groped, and the feeling of helplessness to do anything about it had caused Jenny to well up.

'You don't have to go on,' I said. 'you can tell me this story again.'

I went out into the kitchen to get the other bottle of wine and topped up both our glasses. Jenny drank a huge mouthful from her glass, pulled herself together and adopted a look of fierce determination.

'I need to get this off my chest,' she said. 'I need you to understand why I am so angry with Sheckler, why this is not just about what he is doing to you but also what he and his kind have done to me and countless other women.'

I nodded my agreement. I found myself envying her fervour. Jenny's emotions may well have been raw, but she wore them proudly for all to see.

'This last Christmas party was the final straw. The other female PC and I decided we needed to teach him a lesson. So, we bided our time and waited for an opportunity. It came sooner than we thought.

'The skipper had a habit of finishing his shifts with a hot chocolate laced with a stiffener. He kept a bottle of dark rum in his locker especially for this purpose. One night as he was preparing this concoction, one of us managed to distract him, while the other slipped a small measure of chloral hydrate into the drink, that stuff is strong enough to put a tiny elephant to sleep.'

I sat in awe as I listened to this tale of revenge. I just wished I had the courage to do something similar to Sheckler.

'So, what happened next?' She grimaced at my impatience.

'Don't rush me. It was the early hours of the morning so we had the town to ourselves. Our big problem was the size of this bloke. Somehow, we managed to manhandle him into the back of a car, where we stripped him naked. Just so we could add to his confusion the next morning, we took care to properly fold his clothes and store them in his locker.

'The rest was pretty straightforward. We took him to the town hall and handcuffed him to a nearby lamp post with his own handcuffs. The local newspaper office was opposite and we knew they ran an early morning shift, so his embarrassment would not go unnoticed the next day. And we left him there.'

If anybody else had told me that story they would have done so as an amusing anecdote with a moral twist, and embellished it with an air of triumph, but Jenny's eyes were full of a palpable hurt and anger, as if every word was painful to her. I tried to lighten the mood.

'He could have caught pneumonia,' I protested, half laughing.

'Summer nights in Devon are pretty warm - besides he had plenty of blubber to keep him cosy.' I laughed, and she couldn't help but smile at my amusement.

'That must have been quite a sight. What happened? Did he ever find out who did it?'

'He had his suspicions, of course, but he could never prove it. Needless to say, when I applied for a transfer to Plymouth, he didn't stand in my way. And as far as I know he didn't molest anybody again. He certainly didn't come near me or my colleague.

'That move was the best thing I ever did. My only regret was that I could no longer borrow my brother's motorbike to explore the countryside. Indirectly, that incident was also why I ended up in South Wales. The evil bastard had friends throughout the force and some of them tried to make life difficult for me. It became clear that I could only go so far, so I transferred to here.'

'God, you police really are badass, aren't you?'

'Don't you believe it, chick.' She leaned over and kissed me. 'Now, do you understand that when I say we're going to get our revenge on Sheckler, I mean it? I don't know what that will involve yet or when it will happen, but just give me the opportunity and I will take it. Nobody messes with me and mine, and gets away with it.'

I was a bit nervous at this declaration, not just because of its vehemence but also because I worried that if Jenny did anything illegal then I would lose her.

'Surely, you have to keep within the law,' I protested. 'Isn't that what being a police officer is all about.'

'Not everything is black and white in the police force,' Jenny said trying to reassure me. 'The fact I am here in defiance of my Super should tell you that. There are grey areas.

'Do you think that other officers haven't faced similar dilemmas, taken matters into their own hands before? All I'm asking is that you think about it and that when the time comes, we'll decide what to do together.'

I wasn't so sure I would get a say in it, but she was so sure of herself and so protective of me that I let it go. If she could sort this out for me without any consequences for the two of us then why not allow her to have a go? She picked up her glass and finished her wine. I did likewise.

'There's no way that I can drive home now is there? So why don't we start by sleeping on what we've just discussed?'

I laughed, a happy nervous laugh. She stood up, took my hand and started to lead me up the stairs. I paused.

'There's one condition,' I said. 'We're not going to do much sleeping.'

Chapter Twenty-one

When I awoke the following morning, I was alone in bed. I tried to focus my thoughts, to remember what had happened to make Jenny leave. I switched on my bedside lamp. The room was empty. Her clothes were gone from the floor where they had been thrown during our initial moments of passion.

I found my phone and started to search for her number. I was interrupted by the sound of the toilet flushing. I was overcome with relief. She was still here.

Throwing the duvet to one side I grabbed my robe and rushed towards the bedroom door, only to run into her coming the other way. She caught me in her arms. She was fully dressed.

'Woah, Miss, I was just on my way in to wake you up. I need to get to work. Didn't want to disturb you too early.'

'Because I have no work to go to?'

'No,' she said slowly. 'Because you've had a very stressful couple of days and I thought it would do you good to have a few hours extra, especially as we didn't sleep much last night.'

I kissed her and put my arms around her waist.

'I de-stressed quite well last night actually. And what makes you think I'm going to let you leave now.'

She was smiling.

'It's within my powers to make an arrest for obstructing a police officer from assuming her duties you know.'

I held out my hands.

'Cuff me then, Inspector.'

'You wish. I really do need to get going. I left a pot of coffee downstairs for you. You may want to have some while it's still warm.'

I kissed her again.

'I really don't deserve you, Jenny. You're willing to compromise your career for me, and now you're making me coffee.'

'Too right, lover.'

She paused and turned back towards me. She looked deadly serious.

'Listen, Dawn, I've taken the gun. I put it underneath the spare wheel in the boot of my car, while you were sleeping. I'll work out what to do with it later. Perhaps I'll use it to shoot Sheckler for you. It might solve a lot of problems'

I stood open-mouthed at this suggestion. She laughed.

'I was joking, Dawn. But in all seriousness, I can't leave it here. It just isn't secure, and what if that scumbag ex-boyfriend of yours comes back for it. You haven't changed the locks yet, have you?'

I shook my head.

'Promise me you'll do it today, if you can. I don't like the thought of you here, vulnerable and alone, while he's running around. In fact, even then I want you to move in with me as soon as you can, at least until we can resolve the situation. Do you promise me?'

I said that I would. I still hadn't fully sorted myself out for the day, but I was sure that I could manage to organise a locksmith.

I walked her to the front door. She slipped her hands inside my robe, loosening it as she did so. Her warm hands felt so good on my naked body. We kissed one more time. I watched her walk to her car and then pulled my robe together and headed to the kitchen to sample the coffee.

As I drank, I picked up my phone to see if there were any developments on my news feeds. There was a missed call and a text. It was from Alec, but not on his usual number.

'*We need to talk. 12 noon Friday at the Owain Glyndwr.*'

I thought about what Jenny had said. Should I ring her to

say that Alec had been in touch? But, then what could she do? She had already said she didn't have enough to arrest him. Maybe, if I met him and warned him off, then we could all move on. At least he had asked to meet in a public place.

I looked at the time. I had three hours to kill. Maybe he had heard about my suspension and wanted some reassurance. He wasn't going to get any from me. I'd had enough of Alec Croxley to last a lifetime.

Perhaps losing my job was the opportunity I needed to put him behind me once and for all. I was no longer any use to him. Surely, he would have to find some other patsy to do his dirty work. I'd taken him and his mobster friends as far as I could. From now on they were on their own. It was worth going just to pass on that message.

The Owain Glyndwr is a pub on St. John's Street, near Cardiff Castle. The main bar is cavernous, furnished traditionally and dominated by a huge television screen affixed to a pillar in the centre of the room, which showed all manner of sports events. Today was no exception.

I saw Alec straight away, standing by the bar ordering drinks. He turned and gestured to a table in the corner of the room. I followed his direction and sat down on an upholstered bench with my back against the wall. He joined me soon afterwards and placed a large glass of white wine in front of me. I took a sip and watched as he took a long swallow of the beer, he had bought for himself.

He looked me up and down as if he were inspecting goods at a street market.

'So, you've got yourself a police officer girlfriend?' I tried not to take the bait.

'What's up Alec, you got nothing better to do than follow me around?' He shrugged.

'Thank you for coming,' he said. 'I wasn't sure if you would.'

'I nearly didn't. Still, you were sure enough to order my wine in advance.'

'You know me, I've always been a gambler.'

'I thought I knew you - unfortunately events proved me wrong. By the way, if you had wanted to collect your stuff you could have just texted me and arranged a convenient time.'

'I didn't want to disturb you. Besides I wasn't that keen on running into your girlfriend, if you know what I mean.' I nodded, that must have been why he was in such a rush to get away. I took a mouthful of wine for Dutch courage and got to the point.

'So, what is it that you want?'

'I heard on the grapevine that you had a run-in with Sheckler and that he suspended you. Is that true?'

'Yes, that's about the nub of it. What else do you know?'

'Not a great deal really.' He looked concerned. This was obviously a problem he had not anticipated. Why that should be so, puzzled me, after all I'd briefed him and his colleagues on many occasions on what they might expect with Sheckler in the saddle. I continued:

'Well, for a start I'm no longer any use to you. You've lost your inside woman. I'm afraid you're going to have to do what every other developer does from now on and work blind.'

'Yes, I'd figured that one out for myself. Is there nothing you can tell me that will help?'

'Oh, I think everything is going to be much the same as I described to you before. Sheckler is preparing an objection, it will go before Welsh ministers and they'll decide on the merits of the case. As you know, there's some momentum behind the objections and that will play a part.

'But why do I have to keep repeating it to you over and over again? Do you people not understand the system you're working within?'

He looked blankly at me, maybe he had an inkling of the really bad news. I pondered whether to give him a clue or not, and decided to let him suffer a bit more; after all, I didn't owe him anything after the way he had treated me, not least his culpability in blackmailing me.

I was going to enjoy telling him that his little project was holed beneath the water. I wondered how he would take it. It wouldn't sit well with his pals. They stood to lose a lot of money simply because they couldn't let things take their natural course; because they had to control every stage and every person involved in the process; because they believed they could buy anything and anybody.

'What I want to know, Dawn is what happened with Sheckler and how it impacts on us,' he said eventually.

I gave him the basic details of the conversation I'd had in Sheckler's office. He looked troubled when I told him that the alterations to the tender documents had been discovered.

'For fuck's sake Dawn, you told me that nobody would notice the changes.'

'And if Byron had stayed as mayor no one would have looked. Listen, Alec, I'm not a master forger, I did what I could in the narrow slot available to me.

'Our real problem is that the bastard has now referred it to the police, and he knows about us, or rather what used to be 'us'. That means that not only did I have the opportunity, but as far as they are concerned, I also had a motive. We could go to jail.'

He snorted in a very disconcerting manner.

'You mean *you* could go to jail. I'll be well gone before they get anywhere near me.'

I was flabbergasted. I suppose I had expected him to cut me loose and run, but did he have to be so blatant about it? Jenny was right about him. What a complete bastard.

'Fuck you,' I said standing up to go. 'If that's your attitude you can go fuck yourself because I'm washing my hands of you.'

He grabbed my arm and forced me back onto the bench.

His grip was strong and painful. I looked around to see if there was anybody who could assist but he had chosen the spot well. The only people who might have observed had their backs to us and were watching the big screen.

'If you don't let go of me, and allow me to leave I will scream,' I said quietly through gritted teeth. He released my arm but kept his hand nearby. He looked a bit panicked.

'I'm sorry,' he said in a contrite, hushed tone. 'I didn't intend you to become a scapegoat. We'll do what we can to protect you, of course we will. I just needed to understand where things lay with the project.'

I wasn't inclined to forgive him nor to believe him when he made promises he couldn't keep about my future. He'd lied to me and abused me enough for one lifetime, I could never trust him again. It was vaguely satisfying to be able to rub in how desperate his position had become.

I finished my wine and shuffled away from him along the bench. The repositioning of my body was not going to make my escape any easier. I still had to navigate myself past the table, not to mention, Alec. However, I could now clearly see the bar, so could summon help if needed.

'The long and short of it, Alec, is that if he can prove the tender is corrupted then he can cancel your option and abandon the process altogether without having to go through any planning process at all.

'In other words, the power plant is dead and buried. He'll kill it and he'll do something else with the land. There will be no regeneration, no energy security to attract businesses to the area, and no opportunity for your mobster friends to launder their money.

'Furthermore, all the money you, Marshall and Watkins have put up to take this development to its current stage will be lost.' I was enjoying myself, stating the obvious in this way. 'They'll have no recourse to law to recover it. In fact, the only person they'll be able to sue for their lost millions will be those who altered the tender documents in the first place.

'And then, only if they can prove that they themselves, knew nothing about the act, and that they didn't participate in any attempt to defraud the Regional Mayor's office and the good people of the Cardiff Capital Region. Good luck with that, because if I'm going down, I'm taking you all with me.'

He looked stunned. I could almost see the cogs whirring away in his head. What was he going to tell his bosses? How would they react to losing all that money because of his carelessness (and mine)? Would he end up sleeping with the fishes? I'd seen too many of *The Godfather* films.

He held my elbow in a firm grip. He intended only to detain me a minute, so he could have his say. It was the best he was going to get in such a public place.

'They won't let you do any of that,' he said grimly. 'And they're not going to be very happy having their investment go south either.'

'That really isn't my problem, Alec.' I pulled my elbow free. 'I'm not frightened by your threats.'

'I'm not threatening you Dawn, just telling it like it is.'

I stood up and eased my way past the table. He stayed seated and didn't attempt to intercept me.

'Dawn, one more thing,' he called after me. 'Thanks for coming today. I know that you didn't have to after the way we left things the other night. It's just that in my rush to clear out my things, I left something in your house. I would like to arrange to come around and collect it, please?'

I had been right, that was the reason Alec had left the box there... if anything, he said could ever be believed. After all, you don't easily leave an illegal firearm and incriminating documents lying around when you walk out of your girlfriend's home. Nevertheless, I wondered whether he been trying to make a point. He could not genuinely have thought that the box would be safe with me and I wouldn't find it.

'I don't know what you're talking about,' I lied. 'I

checked, and the spare room was empty.'

He looked sceptical. He knew that I was lying but he wasn't in a position to challenge me. I turned to walk away. As I did so, he called after me again:

'I have copies of all the documents you know.'

I pretended not to hear him, walked out of the pub and closed the door behind me. As I wandered aimlessly around the City centre, my phone buzzed, it was Mother. She never rang me. She must have been briefed about the allegations against me.

I couldn't face speaking to her. I could just see it now, once I was pulled in for questioning, she would be standing metaphorically, on the other side of a one-way mirror supervising and taking notes. Once more, my fuck-up would be turned into her political crisis. I could imagine the pleading now:

'How could you embarrass me like this? I'm in charge of the police, I need to be re-elected, I can't afford to have a criminal for a daughter.'

It was always about her and her fucking career. Everything in my life revolves around Aileen Highcliffe nee Jenkins and her golden future in the party. Even when her only daughter stands accused of fraud and malfeasance in public office, she is ringing to berate me about how it's going to fuck up her life.

I pressed the reject button on my phone and carried on walking. It buzzed again. This time it was a text.

'Dawn, we have to talk. Ring me urgently.'

I smiled inwardly. It wasn't good that I was becoming more and more fatalistic. It was as if I'd already accepted that there was no way out of this mess. I'd got into this to protect her and her fucking career, to keep my family out of the scandal sheets, and yet that was where we were all heading.

I had to pull myself together and fight this. I now knew there was a future with Jenny, I couldn't lose sight of that happy ending. There were many hours ahead before we would see each other again. I needed to find something to fill that time.

There was no work to focus on, which would help me avoid thinking about my fate. Did I even have any friends to turn to in my hour of need? All my social life had been centred around my work, so the answer to that question had to be 'no'.

My phone buzzed again with another text. I was suddenly very popular. It was Liz Franklin. Somehow, she had heard about my suspension, possibly from Byron via my mother, and wanted to talk. She seemed more determined than ever to take Sheckler down, even suggesting that we meet to plan the deed together. She added that she would deal with him without me if she needed to, always being careful not to specify exactly how.

I was shocked but also a tiny bit tempted. Maybe I would get in touch. Perhaps she was serious about killing the bastard. She certainly seemed angry enough. Was my suspension, him ruining yet another life, the catalyst she needed to finally carry out her threat? How much easier things would be without our maverick regional mayor to fuck up our lives.

As I was contemplating this course of action, my phone rang yet again. I looked at the screen, it said number withheld. I pondered for a minute whether to ignore it or not. Perhaps my mother was trying another way to reach me. Then, fuck it, I pressed answer and placed the phone to my ear.

'What?' I barked. 'Who is this?' I was taken aback when my bad-tempered question was met with the familiar drawl of Jack Chaffont.

'Is that any way to talk to a potential benefactor?' His voice was calm, almost soothing, the fake Southern drawl was a welcome change to the threatening tone of my previous conversation with Alec.

'Jack?' I said, surprised at his timing. 'I wasn't expecting to hear from you again?'

'Now, didn't I tell you that I would be there for you if you got into trouble?'

'Well, yes, but a lot of people have told me a lot of things over the last few months and it's difficult to know what or who to believe.'

'I am a man of my word Ms Highcliffe. When I say I will help then I will step up and help.'

By this time, I had reached St John the Baptist City Church. I sat myself down on a low wall opposite the entrance to Cardiff Indoor Market and leaned back against the railings.

This was a pedestrianised area and was already thronging with locals going about their business. Just up the road was an Italian Coffee Bar advertising espresso. I could really have done with a strong coffee about now.

'What is it you can do for me, Jack?'

'Well, ultimately I am happy to find you alternative employment. A little bird told me that our friend had dispensed with your services,' he paused for effect, 'with extreme prejudice.' I confirmed the accuracy of his statement, marvelling at how bloody small a place Cardiff can be…first Franklin, now Chaffont.

'Our problem, of course is this rather inconvenient allegation that you somehow doctored the tender documentation. It is not an insurmountable problem, but it is nevertheless one more obstacle to overcome.'

'Who tells you this stuff, Jack? How do you know so much about what is going on?' He chuckled.

'Information is power, it wasn't just good fortune that got me where I am. But we are digressing. It occurs to me that a bit more information on Mr Sheckler might assist you with discrediting him, and possibly causing him to drop those charges against you.'

'I am all ears, Jack.'

'Well, a few years ago a good friend of mine was walking through one of the sleazier parts of Cardiff, when he saw Morgan Sheckler coming out of a rather disreputable establishment. My friend had some interests he was looking for help with in East Gwent, and so he made it his business to find out more.

'It turns out that this particular establishment specialises in supplying underage girls, if the price is right, and that Mr. Sheckler is a frequent visitor. Of course, I mentioned it to our American friends as soon as they started putting pressure on me, but it seems that the Mayor must have found other...er...outlets, for his perversions and they are having difficulty pinning anything on him.

'I don't expect that you will have any more luck, but you of all people will know how damaging rumours can be in politics, and I am sure that with your connections, you can get something out there.'

'So, if you knew this, why did you back him to become regional mayor?'

'Unfortunately, I only became aware of this behaviour a few weeks ago, well after the election. If I had known beforehand, I would have taken a very different decision.'

I had difficulty hiding my disappointment. I had been hoping for something a little more solid, something that I could prove. I thanked Jack for taking the trouble to ring me, and we parted with him promising to speak to me again, once the air had cleared over the tenders for the land.

I carried on walking, still fuming over Alec, frustrated and angry at the mess I had got myself in. I could feel the muscles tensing in my body as I thought through everything that happened over and over. I needed to get it out of my system somehow.

At home, I picked up my gear and headed to the gym for an hour of vigorous exercise, pushing myself to the absolute limit. It didn't make me feel any better.

I got to Jenny's place just as she was returning from

work. She seemed relieved to see me and greeted me with a kiss and a long hug.

'Have you been here long?' she asked.

'No, I've just arrived. I figured you might be home about now. I thought we might go out and get something to eat.'

She looked doubtful. I picked up on the vibe straight away.

'I'm sorry, did you have other plans?'

'No, not at all. How has your day been?'

'To be honest, I've been bored out of my mind. I hadn't realised how difficult it was to fill a working day when you haven't got a worthwhile job to do. And I've been craving your company.'

She kissed me on the cheek.

'I'm quite tired, to be honest, Dawn. It's been a long and difficult day. Can we order in some food and chill out?'

That sounded a much better idea. Even though I'd suggested it, I wasn't in a sociable mood either. We settled on Chinese. I ordered while she changed and showered. The food arrived just as she emerged from her bedroom wearing only a robe and a towel around her head. We chatted as we ate.

'I have to be honest, Dawn, things are a bit difficult at work because of our relationship and these allegations against you. The Super had me in again today, to lay down the law about me seeing you.'

'Oh, I thought we'd talked that one through?'

'Yes, we did, and I haven't changed my mind. If I must choose between my job and you then you win every time. It's just that for the time being, and until things settle down, we shouldn't be seen together in public too much.'

I understood, or I thought I did. It wasn't as if we did much together outside of each other's homes anyway, except for the gym. What I wasn't sure about was how long this restriction was going to apply for.

Did I need to clear my name before we could acknowledge our relationship publicly? Would she be able to visit me in prison if it came to that and still hold down her job? Would she wait for me if I did go to prison? All my fears and doubts flooded to the surface yet again. She seemed to read my mind.

'Don't worry, this is just until the investigation is over. I'm not going to abandon you. Once you're cleared it'll be all good.'

'And if the worst comes to the worst…'

'Then I will quit my job, go into the private sector somewhere in Gloucestershire and spend my spare time visiting you at Eastwood Park Prison until you're released, and we can be together.'

I hugged her as tight as I could. I felt that I didn't deserve this level of support, not after the mess I'd made of my life. I told her about my encounter with Alec. We'd agreed that we would have no secrets, and I was happy to honour that. She was annoyed.

'For fuck's sake, Dawn, what did I tell you about that man? He's dangerous. You know he's dangerous. He's already hit you once. Do you think you have a charmed life? Do you think you're immune from the sort of damage he and his mates can inflict on you?

'When I said to stay away from him, I wasn't joking. I wasn't being an over-possessive girlfriend. I was genuinely worried for your safety.'

I tried to protest that we had met in a public place, and that I had taken precautions to protect myself, but she was having none of it. I think she was more irked at the fact that I had acted wilfully, and gone behind her back to meet Alec, than at the fact that I had put myself in danger.

'I really don't know what to say, Dawn. You know I care for you. I love you and I don't like to see you taking risks like this. I feel as if I should be there protecting you all the time.'

I told her how sorry I was and asked for forgiveness in an attempt to placate her. She held me tightly.

'I'm so sorry,' she said, 'I don't mean to come across as controlling. You can do what you like, of course you can. But I deal with people like Alec Croxley all the time. I know how dangerous they are. I can't help but worry.'

I cwtched up and described the phone conversation I'd had with Jack Chaffont. When I finished, Jenny said she thought she might know the establishment that Sheckler had been seen at. She was outraged.

'Underage girls!? What a complete and utter bastard. I've seen those kids, Dawn...most of them have been trafficked from abroad – they barely speak English, half of them, and they're terrified to break free from their pimps.

'Drugged-up, beaten, most of the money they earn taken from them so that they've barely enough cash to live on, and certainly not enough to get out from the hell-hole they find themselves in...and its fuckers like Sheckler who take advantage of them. That bastard doesn't deserve to be in City Hall. Somebody should chop his balls off, and hang him stark naked by his feet from Cardiff Castle.'

I smiled. This was becoming a recurring image from Jenny and one I could relate to, even if I was slightly disturbed, and just a bit turned on, by the passion with which she embraced it.

I pulled myself up to kiss her, undid her robe and gazed upon her naked body. I touched her perfect breasts, rolled my hand over her firm stomach and let it rest on her crotch. She placed her hand on my cheek, pulled my face towards her and kissed me.

I shed my clothes, one by one as we spiralled towards the bedroom still locked in our embrace. Plastic cartons and metal trays from the takeaway were scattered in our wake. We fell panting on the bed, stark naked and made love. When we had exhausted ourselves, we slept for a few hours and then did it again. It was the best takeaway I'd ever had.

Chapter Twenty-two

It should be compulsory that Saturday mornings are earmarked for sleeping and making love. That's how it used to be when I was a student, less so once I became a working adult with responsibilities. Nevertheless, I still like to start the weekend curled up under the warm sheets and duvet for as long as Myrddin lets me.

I would have done so again at Jenny's on this particular Saturday, but she needed to get to work and I was keen to show off my domestic skills by making her breakfast. It had taken me a long time to master poached eggs on toast washed down by coffee and orange juice, but I now had it sorted to near-perfection.

I grumbled of course, in a good-natured way. Jenny took it in the spirit it was intended. She too, would have preferred to spend the morning in my arms, however she had no choice but to go into the station.

It was Cardiff's first game back in the Premiership and all leave had been cancelled. Jenny had been given a list of all the most senior dignitaries who would be attending and their estimated time of arrival to ensure security was in place. Those who had not been rostered to work had been called-up, and officers were being shipped in from all over South Wales.

I knew that it was an important day for Sheckler, too. I'd been privy to his diary before I was suspended and was aware that not only would he be attending the game against Manchester City, but he was excited at the prospect. His family's long association with the Bluebirds had helped him in winning the mayoralty. He wasn't going to miss the opportunity to steal some of their glory at getting back into the top flight.

And his presence at the match had added to Jenny's

workload. After all the threats against him, the police had been told to monitor his schedule and be on hand to respond to any danger. It was a light-touch approach, but a necessary one, nevertheless.

When she had told me about this new duty, she had been apoplectic. The last thing Jenny wanted was to protect a serial abuser of women, who was seeking to put her partner behind bars.

It was a beautiful sunny day, so we had opened the French windows in front of the Juliet balcony in Jenny's flat and moved the table and chairs to enable us to enjoy the view while eating in near silence. We had reached that stage where we were comfortable just being with each other.

In the distance we could just make out the Wales Millennium Centre and the St. David's Hotel. Beyond that, out of sight, was the Cardiff Bay Barrage. At the end of the dual carriageway, the tower of the Pierhead building was just about visible. At one stage, it had been envisaged as the seat of the Welsh Government. Instead, it had been turned into a visitor centre and a venue for conferences and meetings.

The Welsh Assembly had spent hundreds of thousands of pounds repointing the brickwork and installing a new roof. Like the rest of Cardiff Bay, it was a magnificent example of tone-deaf regeneration, investing in the heritage of the area, and in yuppie flats, like Jenny's, next to one of the poorest communities in Wales, the people of which reaped no benefit from the expenditure.

It was why I was so passionate about the power station. At least that would create employment, and offer hope to communities such as this one. We had to do better. It was not something that Sheckler understood, with his monied background and narrow obsessions.

I wanted to talk more to Jenny about my indiscretion in meeting Alec, but the traffic noise below was starting to build up and could be heard clearly even above the line of trees that masked the flats from the road. Time was getting on, she was due in work, so we had to leave.

My car was parked next to Jenny's, in her visitor's parking space, but as I was planning to return to the flat that evening, we decided to leave it there. Instead she offered to drive me, reasoning that it would enable me to spend more time with her.

As we pulled up outside my house, I leaned across to kiss her. I tried to prolong the contact as much as I could. I wanted to shout out our love from the rooftops, and never leave her side again. She, though, was in a hurry to get to work.

Despite this, I didn't want to get out of the car. I had a terrible sense of foreboding. I clung to her until she insisted that she had to go and reassured me that it would not be that long before we could spend the night together. I stood and watched her drive off.

I would have waited for her in her flat in the Bay, but I had made arrangements for a locksmith to come around later in the afternoon to change all the locks, and I wanted to tidy up the house.

Myrddin was on the garden wall waiting for me to feed him when I neared my front door. I walked over and smoothed his fur. He seemed happy to see me. I tried to encourage him to come into the house with me for breakfast, but instead he stayed put, watching me. He was obviously enjoying the sun, and maybe one of the neighbours had already fed him. They had a habit of doing that.

'Suit yourself,' I thought, and opened the door. He would come in when he was ready. I picked up some mail and a free newspaper from the door-mat and looked around. Everything was quiet and yet the house didn't feel quite right.

I closed the door gently behind me and placed my bag on the floor. The small telephone table in the hallway, appeared to be slightly out of place. And did I really leave the understairs cupboard door open?

Slowly, I checked out the living room and the kitchen. They were empty. I edged up the stairs and pushed the door of the spare room open. I could see that the bed had been moved. Carefully, I stepped into the room. Suddenly, I felt an arm around my neck. I was pulled back violently. It was Alec. He held me there so that I could barely move.

'Where the fuck is it?' he snarled into my left ear. I struggled to free myself. I could barely breathe let alone talk. 'What have you done with the box?' he persisted. I gasped, trying to force out some words, pointing at his arm around my neck. He was strangling me.

He got the message and lowered his arm so that it was now around my chest. His other hand held mine in a tight, very painful grip.

'You're hurting me,' I complained.

'I'm going to be doing a lot more than that if you don't tell me what you've done with that box.'

'I told you, I don't know anything about your fucking box. You cleared the place out when you left.'

He spun me around and struck me hard across the face, sending me flying onto the bed. I lay there in a daze as he advanced, pulled me up by my collar and struck me again with the back of his hand.

He grabbed my arm and hauled me down the stairs, almost throwing me into the living room, before dragging me onto a chair and standing over me. I tasted blood in my mouth. My head was throbbing.

Alec's face was flushed red with the effort. He was wearing his one-piece leather biker gear, so he must have parked the machine out-of-sight around the corner. Now I understood why Myrddin had been so reluctant to come into the house.

'If I have to tear this house apart piece by piece, I'm going to find that box,' he said. 'However, you can save me that trouble and yourself a lot of pain by telling me where you've put it.'

I was puzzled. Had he expected to find me here and if not, where did he think I would be? I surmised that the intention had been to surprise and intimidate me into giving up the gun and documents. When he found the house empty, he had been forced to start the search himself.

I watched, stunned, as he ransacked the living room. He pulled books off shelves, emptied drawers onto the floor, upturned my settee and ripped off the covers. When he was done with that, he flung me off my chair and set about ripping it apart. I could only look at him from the floor as he worked.

'Seriously Alec, do you think I would store your stuff in the lining of my furniture? You're deluded. Your mobster pals must have scrambled your brain.'

His response was to drag me into the kitchen. He started to pull out the drawers and empty their contents onto the floor. He was completely absorbed in this task, so much so that he didn't see me grab the meat tenderiser where he had dropped it with the other utensils, and hide it behind my back.

He was frustrated and I could see that he had become tired of ripping my house to pieces. Suddenly, he grabbed me by the hair and pulled me to my feet. I screamed out of shock and pain, then gasped as he punched me in the stomach. I fell to the floor bent double, grasping for breath.

'Scream like that once more,' he said, 'and I'll silence you for good.' I struggled to regain my composure. I decided to go on the offensive.

'So, this is the real you is it? A thug who beats women for kicks? To think that I once shared my bed with you. What's happened to you, Alec? When did you turn into this monster?'

He turned and grabbed me by the throat. I thought he was going to throttle me.

'Shut the fuck up,' he snarled, 'don't think you're going to sweet talk me with all your psycho-babble. I'm not hanging around, so you can grass me up to your police officer lover. Just give me what I want, and you can be rid of me.'

I was tempted, but as the gun was no longer in the house, I doubted whether he would be satisfied with what was left in the box. He dropped me back on to the floor, grunted and then resumed his search.

The tenderiser had fallen on the floor next to me. Alec was oblivious to its presence, either that or he was over-confident. He turned his back on me to pull out contents from one of the cupboards.

I calculated quickly. The blow would not incapacitate him for long. I needed to strike and then sprint for the front door. If I could get out into the street, I would stand a chance. I just needed some members of the public to be around what, in normal times, is a quiet residential street. It was a long shot, but I felt that if I didn't try it, he would kill me.

It was now or never. I summoned all my remaining strength and energy, grabbed the mallet and pulled myself upright. He started to turn towards me, alerted by my movement. I swung the mallet as hard as I could against his head.

It only took a few seconds, but it seemed like an hour. Alec, already off-balance, staggered backwards from the blow and fell, striking his head on the edge of the marble work surface. He hit the floor just as I entered the hallway.

I stopped briefly to inspect the scene, ready to seek out the front door if he started to get to his feet. Instead, he lay there, motionless, blood oozing from his head where he had come into contact with the marble top. He spasmed and then was still. I waited another minute, still no movement.

I edged backwards towards the front door, my gaze locked on his prone body. On reaching the entrance, I felt for the latch and slowly turned it. The door opened a few inches. There was still no movement from Alec. I felt ill.

What if I'd killed him?

Carefully, I pushed the door towards its frame, leaving it slightly ajar, and edged my way back up the hall. Grabbing the tenderiser once more, I approached his body. I shook his shoulder and then jumped back ready to strike him again if he stirred. There was no reaction.

I couldn't tell if he was breathing or not. I sat down on a chair and surveyed the scene. The drawers were upended on the floor, their contents scattered all around. Cupboard doors were open, pots and pans, foodstuffs and crockery pulled out onto the floor. Some of it was broken. And that was before I took account of the mess in the living room. I couldn't just walk away from the house and abandon a supposedly dead body.

I started to panic. Had I really killed him? I was certain by now that he was dead. I pulled myself upright and walked over to where I had dropped my bag earlier. As I passed, I caught sight of myself in the hall mirror. I was a mess, my hair was dishevelled, bruises were starting to form where Alec had hit me, my lip was cut and bleeding, and my eyes were red from crying.

I felt my knees wobble, as the enormity of the events of the past few minutes sunk in. I had to sit down, or I would fall. I managed to reach the bag and pulled out my phone. Who was I going to ring? Should I contact the police and suffer hours of having to explain myself in some featureless interview room. I knew that was where this would end up, but I couldn't face it without support.

I scrolled down the contact list until I found Jenny's number. It rang a few times before she answered. I tried to speak but all I could do was to sob out loud. She sounded panicked.

'Dawn, what is it? What's happened? Are you okay?' I tried to control my breathing to enable me to speak.

'It's Alec…I…think…I've killed him.' There was silence on the other end of the phone as if Jenny was waiting for me to say more.

'Where are you? Are you at home?' I made some guttural noise that she took to be a 'yes'. 'Stay there, don't do anything, don't speak to anybody else, I'll be there as soon as I can.' And the line went dead.

It seemed like hours before Jenny got to me. In fact, it was only ten minutes. She told me later that she had just left City Hall after finalising the arrangements for Sheckler's attendance at the football with his staff. I could imagine her distaste at the task.

I closed my eyes and tried to regain some composure. When I opened them again, Alec's body was still were I left it. If he wasn't dead then he was giving a good impression of a corpse.

The front door opened slowly, and Jenny's head appeared. She quickly took in the scene and rushed forward to hold me. I felt some sort of safety valve switch off, and collapsed into a flood of tears. She was stroking my hair, trying to calm me down, and then placed me gently back onto the floor. She put on those blue latex gloves you see police officers wear at crime scenes on television and went to inspect the body.

'Yes, he's definitely dead,' she confirmed. And then adopted a serious, determined look. 'Go and get a bin liner, will you, Dawn.'

I nodded numbly and did what I was told. When I returned, Jenny was bent over Alec's body. 'What are you doing?'

She looked at me with an expression I'd never seen before. It was calculated...cunning, and then she told me what she had in mind.

Chapter Twenty-three

What happened next is still a blur. I dialled 999 and told the police dispatcher that I'd been attacked in my home and that the attacker was dead, and then I waited. All I can remember after that is that there were lots of blue lights, police officers and forensic people in white hooded overalls taking photographs and examining the body.

I had Alec's box with his money and passport inside and I gave that to the police. They put it in an evidence bag, as they did the meat tenderiser. Then they took swabs from the marble surface, where Alec had hit his head. They were still taking my house apart room by room as I was put into a police car to be taken to Cardiff Bay police station for further questioning.

At the police station they photographed my cuts and bruises, and a doctor arrived to treat them. I was told to strip all my off clothes, so they could bag them for further examination. The doctor found a few more bruises on my body, which were duly photographed, and then I was given one of those sexless forensic suits to put on.

They sat me down in an interview room and a uniformed officer brought in a strong cup of tea and watched while I drank it. I was still in shock and trying to come to terms with an overwhelming sense of loss.

I hadn't seen a dead body before, least of all caused somebody's death. Alec may have been a monster, but we'd been lovers and had shared some good moments.

The door opened and a funny little man in an expensive blue pinstriped three-piece suit was ushered in. He must have been in his early sixties with a tightly groomed head of grey hair. He wore a deeply unfashionable pair of gold-coloured, metal-rimmed glasses. As if to complete the picture of a man out-of-time, he had a gold watch chain running from a buttonhole to his waistcoat pocket.

Despite appearances, I detected a sharp intelligence lurking behind his brown eyes, and a sense of entitlement, that came from success in his chosen field. This was a man, who was used to getting his own way, I just hoped that he was on my side. The new arrival advanced towards me and stuck out his hand.

'Miss Highcliffe, it's pleasure to meet you. My name is David Delano-Dollis. I am your solicitor.'

I marvelled at the alliteration in his name, as if some vengeful parent had decided to subject their child to a lifetime of hurt. But this was not the time for whimsy, and although the name and the man were vaguely familiar, I had no idea why he was there.

'I'm sorry, I haven't asked for a solicitor.'

'Ah, yes, well I have been asked to protect your interests by your mother. I think that, given the circumstances, you should have a legal representative present for any questioning.'

'But I haven't done anything wrong, in fact I was the victim.'

Delano-Dollis looked at the police officer standing by the door, who had been witness to this encounter, and waved him away.

'You can leave us alone now, officer. My client and I need to have a private consultation.' The officer acknowledged the instruction and left the room. Delano-Dollis checked the door was shut and then sat down opposite me.

'There has been no suggestion of wrongdoing on your part, Miss Highcliffe, in fact, as you say, you appear to have been the victim of a vicious assault. However, your mother thought, and I agree, that as a man has died, it is important that your account of events is consistent and that whatever happens you do not say anything, however unlikely, that might incriminate you. That is my job.'

229

For once I was grateful to Mother for her interfering ways. It had never occurred to me to ask for a solicitor, but whether I needed his legal expertise or not, it would be good to have somebody else in the room with me when I was questioned. I indicated my acceptance of the role he had been assigned. Mr Delano-Dollis was keen to get down to business.

'Now then, your mother tells me that the late mayor had made a complaint to the police that you had illegally altered tender documents?' I confirmed that this was correct. 'And the man who was found dead in your home, an Alec... er... Croxley, was associated with the company which won that tender?' I nodded again.

'Your mother also tells me that the police believe that prior to his invading your home and assaulting you, the late Mr Croxley is suspected of shooting the mayor and killing him. The police believe he then sought to recover some travel documents and money he had stored in your spare bedroom. You argued and he fell, suffering a fatal blow whilst you were in the process of defending yourself against a violent attack upon your person.'

'Yes, I think that about sums it up,' I responded impatiently.

'Good, well before we invite the police in, I have two pieces of advice for you. Firstly, tell the truth. Set out the facts clearly and without equivocation. Secondly, and this is very important, you are being interviewed about the death of Alec Croxley. The charges that the late mayor sought to level against you are irrelevant to that incident.

'My advice is to refuse to answer any question on that matter. I will intervene on the issue of relevance if they persist of course, but it is important that this interview remains focussed on the matter at hand.'

I thanked him for his advice. It had never occurred to me that the interview might be widened out to include Sheckler's accusations against me, nor did I know what would happen to those charges now that he was dead. I suppose it depends on who succeeded him. There was one last query, however.

'Could I ask you, Mr Delano-Dollis, would it be possible to see Inspector Jennifer Thorne?'

'My dear, why would you want to do that?'

'We're a couple, and I could do with some reassurance. Her superiors do know about our relationship.'

'Ah, I perfectly understand, but no I would advise against you even asking for such a thing. You concentrate on getting through this interview. I'm sure she will be waiting for you on the other side.'

'In the meantime, we will have to get you some normal clothes. That may have to wait until after the interview.' And with that he rose sharply to his feet, opened the door and invited the two officers who would be conducting the interview into the room.

The police officers were both detectives, one male and one female. She must have been in her late twenties, smartly dressed in a beige skirt, blouse and jacket combo and had mousey brown hair, expensively organised into a bob. The man was over six-foot tall, but slightly built and wearing a dark suit, straight off the peg at Marks and Spencer's.

They settled down in front of me, while Delano-Dollis repositioned himself at my side. The male detective poured out three glasses of water, neglecting to offer one to my solicitor. There was no love lost there, or maybe he wasn't expecting Delano-Dollis to contribute to the interview.

They switched on the tape and introduced themselves. Detective Sergeant Simon Gunnersbury was overseeing the interview. His colleague, Detective Constable Jane Kenton, was assisting. A wry smile came over Kenton's face when Delano-Dollis stated his name for the record. She was an alliteration geek, too.

As expected, they focused on the reasons why Alec had come to the house. I told them about the box containing his passport – that he must have needed it to get out of the country after the murder. I explained that I had hidden the box and was reluctant to hand it over to him because of the way he had treated me when I had thrown him out of my house.

'He was in such a hurry, tearing my house apart to find it and shouting and hitting me. He said that he'd already killed Sheckler and he'd kill me, too.' I clutched at my hands, trying to quell my rising panic as the scene replayed itself in my mind.

'Must have made quite a racket... I mean the state the place was in... you two fighting. It's a wonder the neighbours didn't come in or ring us,' Gunnersbury said.

'Well, the match was on, wasn't it? Half the city was either at it or in a pub watching it. I wish there had of been somebody there... they might have stopped it before things ended the way they did,' I sniffed.

They moved on to my relationship with Alec. Gunnersbury didn't seem to know about my relationship with Jenny and looked surprised when I revealed it in the interview.

They asked if I had ever gone motorcycling with Alec. I had to say yes, in case the neighbours were questioned – I'm sure they'd seen us heading off for a ride in the country from time to time. They wanted my biker gear, but I told them that I'd thrown it away after Alec and I had split up.

They seemed satisfied that, even though I had a clear motive for killing Sheckler, there was no opportunity for me to actually do so. Kenton tried to explore the possibility of me conspiring to commit the murder with Alec, falling out with him and accidentally killing him.

'With respect, Detective, we cannot agree to pursue that line of inquiry,' interrupted Delano-Dollis, 'this is mere speculation... there is no evidence to suggest any such thing.'

'I ended my relationship with Alec because of his violent, controlling ways. I would never consider involving myself with him again, and certainly not to murder anybody. He was like a lunatic, spouting all manner of things. I'm lucky I wasn't murdered myself,' I added for good measure.

Gunnersbury then tried to link the deaths of Alec and Sheckler to the accusations of fraud levelled against me. Delano-Dollis cut him short straight away. He wasn't going to allow any crossover between two unrelated inquiries, even if it did give me a motive for conspiracy to murder.

I pointed out that I had fallen out with Alec some time ago and thrown him out of my house. The last time we'd met was in a pub, which was likely to have CCTV, and that we had argued. I was sure that anybody watching that meeting would have been able to see that I wanted nothing to do with him.

By the end of the interview, they seemed to have accepted that Alec's death was an accident, following a violent struggle. The evidence for that struggle was documented by the bruises that were beginning to emerge on my face. They also appeared to be satisfied that I could not have been involved in Sheckler's murder. I sensed they were still unhappy, but it was obvious that their bosses thought it was an open-and-shut case and wanted to close the whole thing down.

I was exhausted. Emotionally and physically. It was all I could do not to break down in tears during the interview. There were moments when I had to stop and take a deep draught of water just to calm myself. On two occasions, Delano-Dollis asked for a short break so that I could compose myself.

When they finally switched off the tape and informed me that I would be allowed to leave the station, but not to leave the country without first informing them, I put my head in my arms and disintegrated into a flood of tears. Kenton was sympathetic and placed her hand on my shoulder. Gunnersbury found a box of tissues in the desk drawer, which he handed to me.

'I'm sorry, Miss Highcliffe, this must be very distressing for you, he said. 'I think that we have a good picture of what happened now. We found the gun that killed the mayor, in Croxley's bike. It's no wonder that he was in a hurry to escape. I'm sorry that you got in the way.'

I wasn't sure if he was meant to give me that information. No doubt, having the Police Commissioner as my mother and a police inspector as girlfriend, put me in a more privileged position than others who might find themselves in a similar situation.

Delano-Dollis helped me to my feet and supported me into the corridor. The two police officers led the way to another room, where my mother and Jenny were waiting. Jenny had some clothes for me to put on. My mother was looking grim, but relieved that I was safe, and, I speculated, had not done too much damage to her political career.

The two detectives left us, while Delano-Dollis and my mother also made a tactical retreat, ostensibly so that he could brief her on what had occurred, while forewarning her about the enormous bill coming her way for his services.

Jenny embraced me and kissed me on the lips. I responded, pulling her body closer to mine. She felt warm and comforting. We held each other like that for what must have been five minutes or more, me sobbing onto her shoulder. She gently moved my head so that she could look directly at me and wiped away my tears with her hand.

'Hey, it's all over" she said gently. 'Nobody can hurt you now. You're safe.'

I managed a half-smile and kissed her again. She stroked a stray strand of hair back from my cheek and used a tissue to try and restore some semblance of order to my face.

'Why don't we get you out of here. I think your mother might want to see you as well.'

She helped me to dress, and then called my mother back into the room. Delano-Dollis had left, so it was just the three of us. Mother walked over and hugged me. Her spontaneity was not a sensation I was used to. I had a bone to pick with her, however:

'Seriously, Mother, what sort of name is David Delano-Dollis?'

She smiled. It was a rare moment. 'Apparently, his mother is half-American, something to do with being related to Roosevelt. He wears it as a badge of honour.' Jenny looked confused, but let it go.

Mother was keen to get out of the police station. 'We've got a lot of things to talk about,' she said. 'Why don't the three of us go back to my place.'

And with that she ushered us out of the building and into Jenny's car, with me trying to work out what exactly Mother knew about our relationship, and why she was being so nice.

Chapter Twenty-four

A few days had passed since Sheckler had been killed, and the furore had not yet died down. Jenny and I had agreed with Mother that we should lie low at her place until things were more settled. At her house we would be away from the hubbub, and protected from prying journalistic eyes behind a boundary wall and hedge.

Jenny had arranged some leave, while Mother spent the time working from home. I was just grateful for the peace and quiet. My nerves were still on edge, and my body ached from the battering it had received at Alec's hands. It was only now, three days later, that I felt able to address what had happened.

As we sat with cups of tea in Mother's plush living room, I tried to sort through the hundreds of questions that were going through my mind. Mother was occupied in her study, no doubt phoning around all her various cronies to catch up on the latest news. I suspected that Byron would be top of the list.

Jenny was playing with Sam, the dog. One moment Sam was on his back, having his stomach rubbed, the next, he was playing tug of war with a squeaky toy. This was just going to cement the favourable impression that Jenny had already made on my mother. I didn't know what to ask her first.

She threw the squeaky toy across the room for the dog to chase after and turned to look at me. She was grinning. I was puzzled as to how she could be so unaffected by all that had happened. I was still traumatised by the incident with Alec. I would be having nightmares about it for months afterwards.

This was not the place to discuss it, but it was time we talked, if she was willing to do so. I suppose people react in different ways to these experiences, and that Jenny was made of much sterner stuff than me.

'Okay, then, and this is the sixty-four-million-dollar question, what exactly did you tell my mother about us? She seems to have accepted us as a couple without even interrogating me once. It just isn't like her.

Jenny flashed a sly, almost bashful grin at me. Now she was looking really pleased with herself. I wondered if I should be worried.

'I told her the truth, that we were in a relationship and had been for some time.' She winked at me. 'Apparently, you've been mixing with unsavoury company recently, so she was relieved that you're going steady with a respectable, upstanding member of the community. Your mother's really sweet, you know.'

I grimaced. I had never tried to hide my bisexuality from Mother, so her learning about me and Jenny wouldn't have been such a huge revelation. And it seemed that Mother was just as susceptible to the subtle charms of a west country accent as I was. Jenny was beaming now. She stood, leaned over me and kissed my lips. I pulled her in towards me and responded in kind. Her body was warm and comforting.

I reflected on how safe I felt in her company, how she always had my back. She'd become an indispensable part of my life, had dragged me out of a hole and even won over my mother. Whatever happened next, whatever fate had in store for me after Sheckler's death and the charges that still hung over me, I couldn't see how I could face the future without her.

'Will you marry me?' I asked.

She looked taken aback. 'You're asking me to marry you?'

'Do you want me to get on one knee?' I said squatting down in the traditional position.

She laughed and pulled me upright. 'Of course, I'll marry you, you daft girl.' She pulled me closer and we kissed. We held each other for some time, enjoying the feel of each other's body, taking comfort in our mutual warmth. We were still holding each other when my mother walked in.

'I'm glad to see you two getting on so well together,' she said cheerfully. She obviously had things to tell us, but I wanted to get in first.

'We're getting married, Mother.'

'That's fantastic news, dear. Congratulations to both of you.' She embraced each of us in turn. 'I was beginning to despair of you ever settling down, Dawn. I'm so happy for you.'

This had gone better than expected. I was suddenly in my mother's good books again. Perhaps, it had been the shock at hearing about Alec's violent assault on me that had driven home to her what she might have lost. Maybe, I had misjudged her.

'I'm sure I have a bottle of prosecco in the fridge with which we can celebrate,' she said. 'Don't worry about driving, Jenny dear, you can stay here for another night, if you wish. You're not working tomorrow, are you?'

Jenny confirmed that she was not expected in work the following day and Mother went to get the bottle. Jenny was beaming.

'I've no idea why you've been so defensive about her, Dawn. She's lovely.' I mock-punched her on the arm. She seemed ecstatically happy.

Mother reappeared with the prosecco and three glasses. The dog, who was sitting quietly in a corner, looked up as she placed the glasses on the table, and then went back to chewing his toy. Mother popped out the cork, poured us each a drink and then proposed a toast.

'To my lovely daughter, and her future wife. May you have a long and happy life together.'

Mother refilled the glasses and sat us down. She had information to impart.

'Naturally, I can't get involved in this mess you've got yourself into, Dawn, but they have given me the heads-up that you're likely to be in the clear.'

This was a huge relief to both of us. We were seated next to each other on the sofa, and Jenny gave me a little hug.

'There will have to be an inquest into both the death of Sheckler and your gangster-friend, but they seem pretty convinced that he was the one who shot and killed the mayor.

The theory is that faced with the collapse of his power station project, he decided to remove the main obstacle to it by killing Sheckler. Then he drove to your house to pick up his passport and money, only to find you were home.' She paused to give me a sympathetic pat on the back of my hand.

'I'm told that they found the gun, some evidence that he had fired it and some of Sheckler's blood on his biker gear. He was also known to them as consorting with local drug dealers.

'They accept that Croxley's death was an unfortunate accident as you sought to defend yourself. They tell me that they think there was no intention on your part to do anything but get away from him and that it's unlikely any charges will be laid against you.'

She looked pleased. No doubt this would help avert a crisis for her career as well, but perhaps I was being uncharitable.

'I also spoke to Byron,' she said. 'In time, there will be a by-election for a new regional mayor. He tells me that he'll stand again. I expect he'll win, and if he does this nonsense Sheckler conjured up against you, Dawn, to kill off the power plant, will go away.'

I started to cry. It was as if a huge weight had been lifted from my shoulders. Jenny put her arms around me and kissed me on the cheek. I felt both overwhelmed and exhausted. I realised that I hadn't eaten since breakfast. Mother saw that I was struggling.

'Jenny, why don't you take Dawn up to your room,' she said. 'I'll sort out something for us to eat. It shouldn't be long.'

'It's alright, I can go by myself. It's a lot to take in and I'm worn out. I just need to get my head down for a while.' Jenny made to help me up the stairs. 'Thanks, but I'm fine. Why don't you stay here and give Mam a hand; I'm sure she's dying to grill you on how policing could be improved in the district, or some such thing.'

I turned and made my way up the stairs to my childhood room. It had been completely refurbished since I'd last stayed there, and now boasted a double bed and fitted wardrobe. Jenny and I had made it our own for the few days we had been staying with Mother.

The news was so much to take in. I sat on the edge of the bed trying to fathom what had happened. The power plant deal, Sheckler's killing, Alec and his cronies… could it all really be swept away so easily. Could somebody, really… get away with murder. I suddenly felt the need to confirm what I knew beyond a doubt.

I took out my phone and searched for articles on Sheckler; there were plenty to choose from. Instead of reading, I found myself scrolling through footage of the killing itself – TV news reports, mobile phone video, CCTV from the scene… it was all there for posterity.

The black-clad motorbike rider pulling up and shooting him down. Sheckler lying dead on the red tarmac forecourt in front of City Hall, his white suit standing out like a sheet covering a corpse. The motorcyclist zooming away on the high-powered bike, the people beginning to finally react to what had happened, I played it over and over again. How long I sat there I don't know. I only stopped when Jenny came in to the room.

'Just thought I'd check-up… see how you are,' she said, sitting on the bed beside me.

I turned the phone towards her so she could see what was on the screen. She took it from me, turned it off and put it on the bedside table, then we sat there together and held each other in silence for what seemed like an hour but was in fact just a few minutes.

'It'll be alright, you'll see,' she said, her soft soothing voice like a balm to my strained nerves.

'I thought I was going to prison,' I said, burying my face into her shoulder.

'Pity you didn't in a way… '

I looked up, surprised.

'Well, you know, you looked fucking sexy in that boiler suit they had you wearing down in the police station,' she said, smiling.

'Not as sexy as you looked wearing my biker gear when you were on Alec's motorcycle. Black leather suits you.'

'Shame I had to get rid of it after I returned the bike to your house, once I had put Sheckler out of our misery.'

'It was smart using Alec's gloves and helmet,' I said, nuzzling her neck.

'Gunshot residue and blood spatter… never fails to convince,' she replied.

'And even smarter turning up the thermostat on the radiator to confuse time of death.'

'Well, we couldn't have a pathologist saying Alec had died before Sheckler, could we?'

I held her tighter, still stunned by what she had done… what *we* had done. Fooling the police into blaming Alec for the murder.

'So,' I said, slowly, 'no consequences?' It was not a question asked out of a feeling of triumphalism, or even relief. I was genuinely worried about the future. I didn't know if I could face any more shocks and I was looking for reassurance.

Jenny's face was deadly serious. For the first time, I saw concern and anxiety in her eyes. The last few days had taken its toll on her too, and she seemed tired and a little out-of-sorts. It wasn't a surprise after everything she and I had been through, and the huge burden she had taken upon herself in dealing with Sheckler, that it was now showing itself in the strained expression that had invaded her face in the days following his death. When she finally spoke, her voice was brittle.

'There are always consequences' she said, and we held each other tight.